A Method
of Reaching
Extreme
Altitudes

Lynn and Lynda Miller Southwest Fiction Series
LYNN C. MILLER and LYNDA MILLER, Series Editors

This series showcases novels, novellas, and story collections that focus on the Southwestern experience. Often underrepresented in American literature, Southwestern voices provide unique and diverse perspectives to readers exploring the region's varied landscapes and communities. Works in the series range from traditional to experimental, with an emphasis on how the landscapes and cultures of this distinct region shape stories and situations and influence the ways in which they are told.

Also available in the Lynn and Lynda Miller Southwest Fiction Series:

The Llano County Mermaid Club: A Novel by Kathleen M. Rodgers
The Problem You Have: Stories by Robert Garner McBrearty
The Last Hanging of Ángel Martinez by Kate Niles
Nopalito, Texas: Stories by David Meischen
Hungry Shoes: A Novel by Sue Boggio and Mare Pearl
The Half-White Album by Cynthia J. Sylvester
Girl Flees Circus: A Novel by C. W. Smith

A Method
of Reaching
Extreme
Altitudes

and Other Stories

Nancy J. Allen

University of New Mexico Press

Albuquerque

ISBN 978-0-8263-6927-7 (paper)
ISBN 978-0-8263-6928-4 (ePub)

Library of Congress Control Number: 2025944343

Founded in 1889, the University of New Mexico sits on the traditional homelands of the Pueblo of Sandia. The original peoples of New Mexico—Pueblo, Navajo, and Apache—since time immemorial have deep connections to the land and have made significant contributions to the broader community statewide. We honor the land itself and those who remain stewards of this land throughout the generations and also acknowledge our committed relationship to Indigenous peoples. We gratefully recognize our history.

Cover illustration by Isaac Morris, adapted from photographs by
    Rusty Clark and Adrian Scottow via Flickr and Raquel Moss,
    SpaceX, and Cindy Williams Moore via Unsplash.
Designed by Isaac Morris
Composed in Athelas, and Freight

This book is for my girls, Lacy and Jamie
—and, as always, for Roger

Contents

Stolen Boy — 1

Gospel of New Eyes — 16

A Method of Reaching Extreme Altitudes — 30

Impulse — 45

Mehrangarh — 59

Running — 74

Camouflage — 88

Eat You Up — 104

Real Life — 117

ADVENTURES OF CORN MAIDEN: A TRIPTYCH

Alvarado — 140

Mezzanine — 155

Galisteo — 169

Acknowledgments — 189

Stolen Boy

FRAN AND ROLLO LEFT BEHIND THE SUN-GLINT SEA AND THE SAILBOAT WITH its languorous days of lazy swells and sunsets mixed with cocktails and crawled into the dim interior of a tiny car. A stone-faced driver carried them high into the dry, cracked mountains of the island. Rollo punched at numbers on his cell phone, but curves of treacherous switchbacks slung Fran time and again against him, ruining his sequences. Fran's attempts at conversation, disrupted by Rollo's defensive elbow jabs, failed to breach the fortress of the driver's silence. Their destination was only forty miles from a sea that had been tamed by the Minoans three thousand years before, but it took the car a very long time to get there.

The excursion to the village had been arranged the previous night to satisfy Fran's desire to see its fourteenth-century fresco. The guide was a surprise. "My name's Lucky!" he shouted as he opened the door so Fran could crawl out of the car. Small exploding stars of pain traveled the length of her curved spine, blurring her eyesight.

Her pain, the switchbacks, the guide's fantastical appearance—all combined to make her unsteady. She stood, trying to find her balance, in the middle of a highway that was also the village's main street. Fran's clothes had been chosen for their purposeful blocks of solid color, then altered to hide her scoliosis. Her bluegreen silk blouse hung loose and long to cover her hiked-up hip; the left leg of her aqua pants was triple-hemmed to create the illusion that her legs were the same length. When her unsteadiness subsided and her eyes cleared, Fran saw that, indeed, she'd not been mistaken: their guide *was* wearing a hairnet, black nylon like the one her grandmother had worn to sleep in. He held a biblical-looking staff with a shepherd's crook rising high above his head. She stood, mesmerized, then movement behind him caught her attention. Stepping daintily out the front door of the single, deserted café: a white goat with a piebald eye, its dinking bell the only sound in the place.

Rollo advanced on the guide, jabbing a finger at his wristwatch, "No mucho time-o. Famous fresco pronto. Esta noché—"

"He's Greek," Fran said. "Not Spanish."

"Not Greek," Lucky said in perfect English. "Cretan. There is big differences."

By the time Lucky had finished explaining about the Greeks and their untrustworthiness, he had led the Henleys away from the café's narrow strip of macadam and onto a wide dirt track. When he politely suggested that cell phone service was spotty, Rollo shoved his phone into the pocket of his khakis. He shot Fran a look, then retreated into a stony silence that matched the landscape. She refused to let Rollo's mood penetrate her: he could sulk if he wanted. Fran concentrated on the feel of the sun on the back of her neck, smelled the clean dirt, and felt something within her release. Because it was their thirty-fifth wedding anniversary, Rollo had acquiesced to her desire to see ancient ruins. He liked Vegas jaunts that involved drinking, gambling, and golf. "I like ruins *and* bars," Fran had said reasonably, and when Rollo continued to balk, she invented a reasonable statistic. She told Rollo that 65.8 percent of couples who get married in college—it didn't matter why; it didn't *have* to be a pregnancy—divorce when older. She told him she could imagine it. She didn't tell him how very often she did imagine it: Rollo would never be able to push a wheelchair with grace.

There'd been few bars on their holiday to the Aegean, and no gambling or golf. For ten days, while she'd limped with her guidebooks through places she'd dreamed of—Lindos, Knossos, Akrotiri—Rollo had talked on his cell phone. To his lawyer, his sisters—the three siblings supported by the same third-generation hardware store, their

2

community standing dependent on it. Rollo had no interest in ancient excavations. It was the new foundation dug and poured by Walmart within the Roswell City Limits that occupied his mind—imperiling, as it did, HENLEY'S, estab. 1921.

It was mid-afternoon, hot even in October, rich in silence and ruin: abandoned buildings covered with trumpet vines and apricot-colored bougainvillea; fragments of walls. These soon yielded to hills covered with olive trees. New Mexico had no olive trees, was not surrounded by water, but its adobe dwellings resembled these, and the colors of the Cretan landscape, sagey greens and soft shades of ocher, not to mention the third-world quality of it, mirrored home. Not Roswell, but the landscapes Fran drove through when recruiting art students.

"At least a thousand years old, this tree!" Lucky said, tapping a massive gray trunk with his shepherd's staff. The ground around the tree lay covered with black nets that resembled his hairnet, but it was Lucky's staff that caught Fran's attention: its foot had been sharp-planed into a miniature goat's hoof.

"This tree," Lucky said, reaching out to tap another stumpy trunk. "Nine hundred years!"

Fran laughed. She didn't believe him, but his enthusiasm fizzed in her body. Rollo used to make her feel this way—lighter, physically buoyant. But, then, Rollo's self-delight had always been infectious, his hazel eyes cutting sideways, full of teasing laughter. Did this boy have that same quality? Was it the wildness of Lucky's exaggerations or the pain pill that was making her feel floaty?

She examined the guide. He looked as though he might be in his mid-thirties, but it was hard to tell because his thick mustache with its curlicued tips made him look both old and young. Also, the hairnet distracted her. He'd tied it so that a single long fringe hung down against his right cheekbone. Fran fought a motherly urge to push the fringe behind his ear.

"Eight hundred years, that one!"

Even Rollo barked at this outrageousness.

"Why do you laugh?" Lucky demanded, his brown eyes merry. "Do you think I lie?"

"Absolutely," Fran said. "I love it!"

Lucky walked on and Fran followed. His staff left cloven oval imprints in the dirt that pleased her. Studying the impressions, she thought they could pass for symbols in some ancient script: Egyptian hieroglyphics, Hittite pictographs, Assyrian cuneiform. So many places and civilizations she longed to see! Her back spasmed. She lowered her head and devoted herself to putting one foot in front of the other. Ten days on a boat, no matter how luxurious, was too long for a body that required physical therapy and chiropractic adjustments—not to mention massages—to keep the pain manageable. She smiled to herself at the irony: she was the one who'd planned the trip, picked the luxurious sailboat, but she'd never once thought about the cost to her body.

They climbed steadily. Roosters crowed now and then; goat bells rang amid the sere grasses. They passed a tumbled grist mill, a defunct olive press, sites that Lucky pointed to with his staff, announcing, "Grist mill!" "Olive press!"—as though these slumped ruins in the middle of nowhere equaled the glory of Athens or Ephesus. Soon the silence of the afternoon had swallowed all the small sounds, and it seemed to Fran that the three of them were *alone*, the only people alive. Next to her, Rollo trudged, head down, brown hiking boots deliberately scuffing up dust. Fran felt his frustration as a slight but insistent pressure on her body. She called out for Lucky. Hastening toward him, she peppered him with words. Why did he live in this village rather than Heraklion or Chania? Did he go down to the beaches at Paleochora?

Lucky shook his shiny brown curls and expressed surprise at her knowledge of Cretan place names. Fran pulled a guidebook from her flatwoven Greek purse and rifled its pages to show him her underlinings and margin notes.

"Always the good student, our Franny," Rollo said, catching up, breathing heavily.

The muscles in Fran's back constricted, warping her hip. Inwardly she hardened, but she kept her smile in place. She'd had to study, hadn't she? Rollo wouldn't have known what he was looking at if she weren't there to tell him.

"Lucky me," Rollo said.

"No, I'm Lucky," Lucky said.

The spark of life in Rollo's face was answered by Lucky's laugh, and then the two men were laughing and slapping each other on the back. They laughed at their cleverness for a long time. Fran watched them as if from a far distance, but the hitch in her hip relaxed.

When they resumed walking, Lucky talked about himself as a "restorer of the old ways." This was a good reason, no?, to live in his ancestral village? But he'd lived in America until he was six. In Chicago. They were climbing as he talked. Bees sounded in the honeysuckle; sheep bleated, hurrying out of their way. At each turn in the path, there was a new vista to the distant sea. Fran heard herself babbling about the views, how artistic they were. So many angles created by the up-thrust land. Extraordinary, really, the beauty of rock and—

"*Frances.*"

She stopped walking and jerked silent. She was talking too much—again. Was there some over-talking virus? Had she been infected due to years of exposure to Rollo's never-silent mother and sisters? She had always been reserved, had never talked to fill empty space like she did now. But, then, there'd never been so much emptiness to fill. "You got to give yourself a jolt. Thirty-five years is too long to be married to the same person!" This was what she'd said to explain their Aegean excursion and every time she'd said it, she got the laughs she looked for. *That Fran Henley. Isn't she a card? Shame she's crippled—and it's getting worse. You can tell.*

"I'm sorry," Fran said. "I was running on. Rollo, it's a lovely afternoon, we just need—"

"Don't tell me what I need. I need a little shade and a big Scotch."

She turned to Lucky with a smile and a shrug that said, *You see how this doesn't bother me.* How many times had she done this? Acted like Rollo's rudeness was nothing? And his drinking? Why should *he* quit, just because his father had had a problem?

Eight years ago, with the girls married and moved away, Martha to Albuquerque, Lucille to Santa Fe, the silences in their house had grown, squeezing Fran until she'd felt words—prattling, haphazard words—physically forced out of her. She would've done anything, with or without pay, to escape, but she'd found a paying job where her chattiness became capacity. When you conversed with shy high school students and their parents, dead space often dominated, and the new Fran Henley could fill every silence. As a recruiter for the Albuquerque School of Art and Design, she was her own boss. She could drive the state's back roads as much as she wished. Five days out of seven? Ten straight? It didn't matter to ASAD: student art portfolios were manifold, endless. Her new ability also saved her from being labeled peculiar. *That Fran! Such a talker!* Meaningless social conversation was a known quantity. Mrs. Rollo Arthur Henley III, prominent Roswell socialite, tooling down dirt roads into God knows what pueblo or reservation, was not.

"Let's get on with it," Rollo said. "Where's this fresco?"

Lucky had led them to a whitewashed building that stood alone against massed vines. "The fresco is very famous," Lucky said. "People travel to it from all over the world. But I want you to see this first." He took Fran's elbow. "The step is high. I will help you."

She jerked away. "I do *not* need help."

Lucky pulled back. Fran cursed herself; she should take another pain pill.

"You'll forgive her, I know," Rollo said smoothly. "She has scoli—she's had a condition since childhood. She can't run, but otherwise she's perfectly capable."

How dare Rollo talk about her as if she weren't present! As if she couldn't hear him! She hid her fury and managed to modulate her tone. "Thank you, Lucky. I'm fine. Really."

Lucky climbed the stone steps, followed by Rollo. Fran limped in last, face flaming, eyes stung with tears. Now Rollo had ruined Lucky for her. Now he would treat her with the special care everyone in Roswell showed. With her odd body, she'd only wanted to be normal, to fit in. Her specialness suffocated her. Was she her body? She didn't think so. She was somewhere *in* it, but she herself wasn't odd or misshapen. She pulled down hard on the hem of her shirt, stretching the silk over her hip. How had not fitting in come to feel like home?

The building was one long dusty room, stuffy with disuse.

"This is our museum," Lucky said. "One of our main tourist attractions."

Fran slipped a pain pill with a swallow from her water bottle. Lucky leaned his staff by the front door and furtively centered his hairnet with a palm—a boyish gesture that belied his actual age. She smiled to herself and felt her furious pulse slow.

"One of your main tourist attractions," Rollo repeated in a flat tone. He cut a little smile at Fran that said, *How charmingly naive this boy is.* She understood this as an attempt to soothe her and was able to return the smile. It always amazed her how easily their mutual annoyance could mutate into camaraderie.

She studied her husband as he stood at the front door, seeing him as he'd once been—like Lucky, slim, with a full head of chestnut brown hair. But Rollo had never been naive. Early on, he'd acquired the nickname "Ropes." *Ropes Henley gets anything he wants.* She was in the ninth grade when she'd overheard a boy say this, her arms full of books, making her way through a hall packed with students. She'd had no idea what the comment meant.

When Lucky started in about village history, Fran wandered away. The "museum" was uncomfortably hot. She ambled down its length in search of a pocket of coolness, waiting for the pill to kick in, gazing distractedly at the crumbling documents, the antique weapons in the exhibit cases. Behind her, she heard Lucky say something about *village vendettas.* He began recounting *hundreds of years* of murderous activity, his voice drifting in fragments through dusty streams of sunlight as she walked. *Ambushed, like outlaws.* Black-and-white oversized portraits of mustachioed men stared down at her from the walls. Photo after photo, the same frozen face. *Pistols, like cowboys.* These old Cretans could have come from any Hispanic community in Northern New Mexico. Suspicious of outsiders, of any place other than home. Behind her, the men laughed. *An outlaw named Billy the Kid.*

She turned to look down the long room to where Rollo stood in sunlight. Wasn't it just like him to act like Billy the Kid was a personal acquaintance? As if he'd ever visited the town where the Kid was gunned down. Fort Sumner, like this village, was a dying place, trying to scrabble itself together with a scrap of fame. One of her scholarship students lived there. Eduardo Gonzalez. She'd sat in the hostility of his home, trying to damp down her Anglo forthrightness, her tinted hair, her stockings and pumps. You would've thought she was trying to kidnap their son—when all she'd wanted was to save him! Where had his big, angry talent come from? Skinny and sweet-faced, expected to join the family's Sheetrock business, Eduardo had sat, head bowed, between his parents. Let me give him a scholarship, she'd begged.

Fran thinks she's saving the world. This was what Rollo said in public, at parties, making a joke of her commitment. In private, he accused her of traveling more than she had to, of exaggerating the importance of her insignificant job. Her retort? "You might be in the color business, Rollo, but yours is Sherwin-Williams, mine is *art.*"

She had dreamed of being an archaeologist like Schliemann, discovering ancient treasures at Ilium and Mycenae—or maybe she'd decipher the Linear A script of Knossos. Magical words, unimaginable places. Her mother had repeatedly pointed out that any career involving physical exertion was closed to her—she'd already had surgery, wore a brace at night so her chest wouldn't rotate—but then Rollo found her hand in the darkest dark and all her dreams changed. But hadn't she found a way, finally, to discover treasure? In tucked away corners of New Mexico, she, Frances Henley, unearthed hidden—

What're you going to do when you're not able to travel?

On the wall, a stern-faced bandit stared down at her from behind his glass prison. Had this come from him? She glanced around. Had *she* said it? She'd never asked herself this question, hadn't allowed herself to think it. She hid her disabilities well enough from others; had she been hiding them from herself as well? She felt woozy. *This* was the trip she'd fought for? This airless room with its dried-up artifacts?

And what about you, with your dried-up spine?

She returned the bandit's glare. She was physically shorter—so what?

She walked on. Several portraits later, she realized it wasn't only her spine. The length of her recruiting trips had also shortened: her curvature's compression forcing her home more often for care. She stumbled, reached out for the wall—and glanced up. Was she seeing double? She stepped forward, then back; shook her head to clear it.

No, there were two photos: smaller than the others and ornately framed, sepia rather than black-and-white. The men held old-fashioned flintlocks, and wrapped around their heads so that fringe hung down against their faces, hairnets. *Cretan freedom fighters.* The words came into her head from nowhere. Where had she studied Cretan freedom fighters? The answer floated to her through the shafts of sunlight in the long room. In Miss Garrett's World History class.

She let the long, dusty room get vague. She saw herself in bobby socks and white suede loafers, starched petticoats and tight-cinched waist, the wide belt misshapen on the left side by her hiked-up hip. By the tenth grade, she'd run the gauntlet of high school cruelty—measured looks, whispers, exclusion—and had emerged, finally, for some reason, popular. And behind her in Garrett's World History, Ropes Henley, looking over her shoulder, teasing her, telling stupid jokes while he copied her answers. She wasn't in awe of him like the other girls were—he was too far out of reach—and she'd matched his teasing with her wit. Is that why he'd picked her? His choosing her over all the other girls had always been a mystery—and not only to her. All during high school and those first years of college, it had been made clear that even taking into account her intelligence, she was lucky—undeserving, really—to be on the receiving end of Rollo Arthur Henley III's affections.

The sepia portraits came back into focus. The hairnets were clearly tribal headgear. Handwoven of thick cotton, they looked nothing like Lucky's mass-produced nylon net. Fran turned to look at Lucky. She'd assumed he was playing the fool; he hadn't told them his costume was a gesture toward authenticity and gravitas. But what else did "restoring the old ways" mean? A purposeful life—isn't that what everyone wanted?

She turned back and studied the freedom fighters with their dangling fringe. Restoring the old ways—if only she could. Their purposeful life with children to rear, a business to grow; and even earlier, when Rollo had been *her* purpose. Wild and willful he'd been, like these fierce-looking men. So full of life it spilled over. Forcing his friends to bring him to her neighborhood of tiny flat-roofed houses, calling her name, insisting she crawl out her window or he'd wake up her mother, maybe the whole goddamn street. Urgent whispers in the early morning. And when she'd finally appear—always through the front door—Rollo would pick her up with both arms around her hips and bow his head against her body, calmed. *That Fran! What's she thinking, wearing PJs out in the yard with all those boys?*

Fran followed the cuneiform hoofprints. Her body ached and her left foot slopped out of sync. The wide dirt path became a thin trail, then a narrow alley between high stone walls. The walls pressed in. She felt she was being herded down a slot—except the men weren't behind her, but in front. She saw Lucky, then Rollo, disappear through an unexpected marble arch. Willing her legs up the high step, she walked through the arch and into an open courtyard. It fronted a whitewashed Greek church, one that seemed built on top of the world.

She limped back and forth across the marble pavement, looking out, unable to speak. She could barely take it all in: a sky striated hot pink, craggy mountains rosy with light, and far below, down and down, opening out at the end of the world, a triangle of glittering sea. For a moment, her body lightened. It had been a long day, but now there was this! Her reward for pain endured. She turned, and her joy fell away. *Rollo.* He'd dug out his cell phone. Here, in this ancient and sacred place with the world's grandeur before him, and all he could think about was the damn store. Founded by his grandfather to sell hammers and nails, it now overflowed with hair dryers, lightbulbs, mousetraps—and out back, a lumberyard and a nursery with bedding plants and fertilizer. All the material goods of modern civilization.

Derision hit her spine full force, then just as suddenly, her shoulders slumped: Walmart had poured a foundation.

Lucky stroked his mustache, one side and then other. Hadn't he told them? Hadn't he said there was nothing like his ancestral village anywhere else in the world?

A goat with a long white face and a piebald eye stepped through the arch. "Ho, Yarrow," Lucky said. "How did you find us up here?" The goat's bell dinked as it trotted daintily across the marble—straight to Rollo's leg. Rollo swiveled his body this way and that, turning smoothly from the animal's attempts at affection, all the while punching in numbers. He looked like some balding, overweight matador.

Fran laughed out loud. She identified with the goat. She'd bought new clothes and hennaed her hair a flirty new copper color for this trip, hoping that she and Rollo could resurrect their old passion. They'd had a wildness in them when they were young—and for many years after. But long years of marriage, like water dripping on stone, had worn away desire's sharp edge. Such a mysterious, never-to-be-deciphered imprint, desire . . . She stopped her thought: No, that was wrong. It wasn't only the years.

She sat down on the stone wall that fronted the gorge and watched Rollo evade the goat. Ten days in a room too small for their big American bodies, their suitcases too large to slide beneath the twin beds, no space in the bathroom, and outside the portholes, the hypnotic motion of a sea moving at eye level. Without speaking of it, the two of them had established a routine that flowed naturally and involved moving in and out of the bedroom to grant the other privacy. A gracious routine that meant they were never naked in the same space at the same time. Eleven nights they'd gone below deck, and every night Rollo had had too much to drink, or she had, or he'd fallen asleep by the time she'd finished squirming undressed—always hiding for fear Rollo would see the deterioration, the changes.

Rollo cursed, slapped his phone shut and dropped down beside her on the wall. Yarrow trotted off to interrogate Lucky, who was capering about with her camera. Fran adjusted her bra strap to ease the drag of her jutting left shoulder blade and arched her back. Rollo must have felt this effort because he kneaded the bunched muscles in her hip, all the while watching Lucky. He'd been doing this since they were fifteen—forty-one years. Fran thought how automatic the response must be for him. Why had she thought this sky, these mountains, and the plunging gorge constituted her personal reward? You didn't have to work for them or deserve them. They were here for anyone with eyes to see.

Lucky snapped photo after photo of the two of them sitting with their arms around each other's waists. How fabulous they looked against the sunset! *Smile!* Postcard-perfect! Then he wanted his picture taken with his "outlaw friend." By the time the men finished posing and Fran put the camera away, the color was drained from the sky, the gleaming water no longer visible—which meant that when the three of them entered the church, they entered darkness.

Fran waited for her eyes to adjust, but even when they did, she couldn't see anything. She was afraid to move, she might fall—and the floor was stone, she could feel that. Was there an electrical switch on the wall or a slanting rack of candles? She felt in her purse for her flashlight, a thin card imprinted with HENLEY'S HARDWARE, dozens of them hanging next to every cash register. Before she could find it, Lucky was dancing his light around. It did little to illuminate the darkness. The interior of the church was more smell than sight: mouse musk, mildew, a hint of urine—but no flavor of incense or prayer, nothing to contradict the judgment: deserted. She heard Lucky's voice. *The fresco is very famous. People travel to it from all over the world.* What a liar he was.

"The magnificent fresco of St. George killing the dragon. Right here! Fourteenth century. Imagine! Come this way, this way. Follow me!"

"I guarantee you Fran will know more about it than you do." Rollo's voice was resonant in the darkness. "Won't you, Franny?"

Fran did not respond. Blind, she held both arms out in front of her and shuffled her feet forward. From what she could make out—not much—this seemed the usual Greek Orthodox Church: hanging oil lamps, painted screens, a single choir stall. The old church in

Chimayo in the hills above Santa Fe was remarkably similar. She rode the wave of homesickness that rose up in her and landed back where she'd started: in pitch-black darkness somewhere in the mountains of Crete.

"Here it is!" Lucky said. He moved his tiny pin-light up, down, and sideways along a rough whitewashed wall. Blackened plaster bore witness to a long-ago fire—or fires. "Fourteenth century!" Lucky said, tapping his staff on the wall. "Seven hundred years of warfare and it survives!"

"Tell us what we're seeing, Franny."

In Lucky's pin-light, the fresco showed itself in fragments: long white equine face, blue armored breastplate, slender stretch of horse leg, green coil spitting flames. Fran leaned closer. Lucky continued to circle his light around the wall-sized image: St. George sticking a dragon with a spear, showing every one of its seven hundred years. Disappointment filled her. The fresco's reputation was fraudulent: it was an apricot-colored blur. But there—what? On the rump of the horse behind St. George: a small figure in blue.

Before she could ask about it, Lucky flowed into full tourist guide mode. "It is very rare, yes? To have this small boy sitting behind this great Saint George? Usually, there is no such figure. In most Byzantine frescos, it is always Saint George by himself killing the dragon. A mysterious figure, this boy. There are many stories coming down about him. He was a boy stolen from his parents and sold for his beauty to—to *outlaws*, Rollo! Outlaws, like we spoke about earlier. Perhaps Saracens, we don't know. Outlaws, anyway, keeping him for many years. But Saint George, he rescues this boy and brings him home on the back of his beautiful white horse. A miracle, no?"

For some reason, Lucky switched off his light. In the darkness, Fran could hear Rollo's heavy breathing, could feel the heat of his body, his hand fumbling for hers.

Rollo fumbling to find her hand.

She doesn't have to think about it: the memory is physical; it's in her body.

Rollo fumbling to find her hand in utter blackness.

13

Lucky was still talking about the fresco, but the closeness of the tiny church had swung wide and carried her back. An emptiness too immense to imagine—its smell too, unknown: earthy and dank. She is standing on a concrete ledge looking into an immeasurable maw, surrounded by other tenth graders, everyone subdued, their chattering silenced as they filed down and the air cooled and sunlight faded. A man in a brown uniform tells them that the bottom of the Carlsbad Caverns lies eighty stories below them. The tallest building in Roswell is three stories high; eighty stories is impossible. The enormous space with its high curved arch seems miraculous, an entrance into the infinite heart of Earth.

The man speaks about the discovery of the Caverns by cowboys who saw, night after night, millions of bats pouring out at sunset to darken the sky. He wants to show them what it had been like for those boys the first time they entered. To do this, he has to turn off the lights—Hold on! It's just for a minute. *One* minute. By the time he has twice admonished everyone to stand absolutely still, Rollo has inched his way next to her, his nearness pushing her starched petticoats forward. The man says, Are you ready? Here we go!

The blackness is so stunning it takes away whatever breath she has left. She feels Rollo fumble for her hand. She helps him find it. He raises it up—all this felt, not seen—and holds her palm against his cheek. The single minute of utter blackness seems endless. Electric lights buzz on. Around them, startled, their classmates jostle and joke with each other—they weren't afraid, not them!—but Ropes Henley stands silent, holding her hand, gazing into her eyes, and Fran feels the wonder of her life opening out before her, all promise.

A small sound brought her back. She sensed the walled church around her—the sound, not here in the enclosed space, but somewhere near, a sound close and familiar as Rollo's breathing. The sound diminished, then returned. *Yarrow*. Her skin prickled with awareness: the darkness felt looser, the silk of her blouse like bluegreen water.

"Imagine the happiness!" Lucky's voice in the darkness was exultant. What a great tour guide he was! What a grand restorer of old ways! He turned on his tiny light and ran its beam from the horse's face to its rump where a little boy dressed in navy blue pants and a light blue shirt sat, a tiny figure behind the armored, oversized saint. "Imagine the surprise and the happiness in the home of the parents when the little boy walks in!"

The pin-light looped around the blackened edges and faint colors of the rough-plastered wall, and outside the sound of a dinking bell—now close, now far.

Gospel of New Eyes

IT'S THE STILLNESS THAT STRIKES HER, SHE WHO IS ALWAYS IN MOTION. THE May morning seems to be holding its breath, and from the parking lot, the prison looks like a sleepy community college. Emy Lou McCracken thinks, *This isn't so bad.*

The thought is punctured by the electronic whump of the unlocking gate. Her body jerks involuntarily. The door to the psych ward had made this same sound, and in an instant she is there again, in Parkland's halogen glare with Andy's thin cries, *These aren't my real hands, my real hands are smaller.*

Lowering her head, she falls back, lets Bev lead.

An armed guard—male, unsmiling—sticks out an oval basket into which Bev places their drivers' licenses and her car keys. A phone call confirms they're expected. They follow another guard—male, heavy key ring slapping heavy flashlight—toward the cluster of red brick buildings that constitutes the Mountain View Unit of the Texas Department of Corrections.

A mockingbird pours its heart out somewhere close by, the smell of freshly turned earth fills the air.

In a breezeway, at a window labeled INFIRMARY, a line of women in white jumpsuits.

The women eye them. Nothing is spoken directly, but the whispers close in behind. *Check those badass earrings. Dont'cha jes love that belt? Lookit those boots!*

Emy Lou straightens her shoulders, holds her head high. She's followed the warden's directive: "Wear good clothes and jewelry when you come to visit, ladies. The girls love it."

As they walk, gathering whispers, through breezeways, past buildings, she's conscious of offering herself up, a momentary salve against monotony.

The guard opens a door, and they enter a room that could exist in any school: a wall of windows, a big blackboard, rows of laminated desks with writing arms. Bev introduces her to the teacher. Mrs. Betty Keck is short and round and motherly looking. Emy Lou shakes her hand, but she hardly sees her because she's too busy looking at the students, a blur of white jumpsuits with pops of color her mind can't organize. Red, blue, yellow, green—crude kindergarten colors. Then she sees. Tied in bows, folded Brooks Brothers style, thrown casually over a shoulder, *mufflers*. The windows are open, it's spring outside, but inside, every woman is muffled.

Mrs. Keck introduces them: "These visitors are from the Women's Halfway House in Dallas. They're going to tell you why you might want to go there when you get paroled."

Bev, the director, begins the pitch.

Bev's normal navy-blue shirtwaist has been replaced by a peach-colored rayon one; her ripple-soled oxfords by nylon stockings and sandals. A loaded key ring usually jangles at her waist, but today she makes no sound as she walks back and forth in front of the Pre-Release Class. She outlines the support the House provides ex-offenders: drug and alcohol counseling, GED classes. Her voice is flat, factual, filing-cabinet beige. She drones on and on.

Emy Lou's mind wanders. Oversized maps paper the classroom's back wall, and she notices, in front of the large Mercator map of the world, a crocheted cap. There are forty women in the room, women of all shapes and colors, but only one woman on the back row wears a baby-blue cap that matches her muffler. The woman's neck is long and lovely, like those in Byzantine mosaics Emy Lou has seen in her travels. Behind this woman, the world has been broken up and spread flat into loopy oceans and strangely elongated landmasses, and the woman's skull, with its close-cropped hair, looks fine and round, pleasing, against it.

Bev is still droning, and Emy Lou is thinking that if the woman's cap were crimped out of tinfoil, it could be Andy's hat. It fits on her head in the same way. For years Emy Lou chafed against this hat, but now she feels quite tender toward it: it keeps her son safe until he can get well. It blocks the blare of the radios in his head, although it doesn't do much for the invisible helicopters and their chop-chopping sounds. Emy Lou sees Andy as she saw him that morning: a heavy thirty-year-old wearing pajamas covered with tiny brown footballs, and on his head, a tinfoil hat that fits the curve of his head.

It was dawn when she'd opened the door to his room. She had hoped he would still be asleep, because asleep, he borders on beauty. But no, Andy sat slumped in his rocking chair, staring blankly, the only sound, the soft continuous lip-smacking, tongue-thrusting sound he always made. His head with its tinfoil hat jerked slightly but continuously toward his left shoulder, and his right foot circled the worn patch of carpet it always circled. Next to his circling foot, a tin pail decorated with a Dallas Cowboy decal and filled with butt-studded sand.

She'd wrinkled her nose against the cigarette smell of the room—and it wasn't only the nasty brown smell: she worries about cancer. But Dr. Cheney said schizophrenics smoke as a form of self-medication, and Robert, her husband, said to leave it alone, so she does.

Bev's perm has burned her brown hair orange on the ends. But instead of being fashionably frizzy, her hair is a mass of tight sausage curls. They shout "Criminal Justice System." She might as well have her key ring jangling at her waist. The women aren't interested. They are bodies in white jumpsuits with dashes of muffler-color; their task, to endure.

Emy Lou grows impatient on their behalf.

Fifteen deadly minutes later, Bev tries a new lure: she can get them job interviews with companies that know they have prison records; they won't have to lie.

Some bodies sit up, but the woman in the back corner wearing the blue cap doesn't move. Long and lean, masked by sunglasses and slouched against the Mercator map, she is real cool. The pudgy woman next to her has a round face within a big Afro, and around her neck, a bubblegum-pink muffler. Her widely spaced eyes give her the composed look of a friendly porpoise. Bev has hooked her. The woman leans forward, but after glancing sideways at Bluecap, she slumps back.

Bev talks about new opportunities for women to become electricians, plumbers, construction workers. Emy Lou had felt certain this information would elicit interest, but indifference moves up in a slow curl, row by row, from the back. Emy Lou fiddles with her silver bracelets, adjusts her concho belt, crosses and uncrosses her legs beneath her ankle-length white linen skirt. She sees for the first time what a dull piece of business Bev is. No wonder the women aren't interested. She wouldn't be either.

Emy Lou is sitting in a chair next to Mrs. Keck's desk. She is a volunteer, brought along to observe, not to speak. Twice a month she teaches "Creative Problem Solving" at the House, hauling props from the trunk of her car up its warped front steps. Usually four or five women attend the class, gathering after supper in the dining room around the old scarred-with-cigarette-burns table. She listens to their stories, learns their names. Bev has repeatedly told her that she doesn't have to go to so much trouble. She could come and read the phone book to them for all it matters. *They're like plants that need rain. It's the attention that counts.* Emy Lou doesn't believe this. She believes she can teach the women how to be more successful in life.

She carries in armloads of photocopied handouts, an artist's easel to display the illustrations she's drawn and colored, a ping-pong ball in a foot-long copper pipe closed at one end. During her presentation she'll ask, "How do you get a ball out of a pipe you can't get your hand into?" Everyone will be stumped. She'll take a sip of water, stumped with them. She'll gaze at her water glass, then at the pipe. She'll look back and forth between the two. She'll do this—slowly, slowly—several times. She'll make her eyes wide, open her mouth into an O-shape of discovery. She'll pour the water from her glass into the pipe and—ta-daa!—the ping-pong ball will float to the surface.

This is a trick that always delights, as well as teaches. Without skills or money? Addicted to drugs? There is no problem that can't be solved creatively. Emy Lou preaches the gospel of New Eyes. Throw away your old solutions, look from a different angle. The dining room at the House is her venue; this prison classroom is not. She is not scheduled to talk, but finally she can't stand the lack of response in the room.

She jumps up. She interrupts. Mrs. Keck frowns, but Bev gives way and sits down.

Emy Lou is a natural speaker, and she knows it. She believes she will be able to convince where the professional has failed. After introducing herself and her role at the House, her voice becomes emotional, intense, urgent. "Alone in a big city, what chance do you have? We can help you." In her tall brown leather boots, she paces back and forth in front of the teacher's desk. Her long turquoise earrings swing beneath her shoulder-length frosted blonde hair. Her pawn silver, burnished with age, emanates authority. She's speaking to the class as a whole, but mainly she's speaking to Bluecap.

"If you come to the Halfway House, you'll have support. You'll have a whole network of people to help you. Don't you want help?"

She sends her will out, wave after wave, across the room toward the woman slouched against the map, but the woman's thrown muffler flaunts coolness. Below the black glasses, her mouth remains a thin slash.

A bell rings. Emy Lou is still talking as the women push past her out the door.

Betty Keck stabs her pencil through the gray bun of her hair and stands up. She congratulates them on their fine presentation. Bev gathers her purse.

"We can't leave," Emy Lou says.

"We were scheduled for thirty minutes before lunch," Bev says. "It's lunch."

"Does the class come back here after lunch?" Emy Lou says.

"Got to get Amber before dark," Bev says. "Can't be late."

"Neither can I," says Emy Lou, seeing Andy lying alone in his room in the same chunky cowboy-and-lariat twin bed he had as a child. But she says nothing about him, because Bev doesn't know Andy exists. Twelve years ago, after seemingly endless—but, in fact, only three—years of hospitals and doctors and tests, Robert decided that it was pointless to talk to "peripheral acquaintances" about Andy. Such a lawyerly term, *peripheral acquaintances*, perfect for Robert. But Emy Lou had agreed with the plan: explaining the intricacies of their life took too much energy, was too painful. Andy is their invisible star, the black hole that controls them. Are they wobbly? Orbiting nicely? Or are they in free fall, helpless against his gravitational pull? How she and Robert function depends almost entirely on how Andy's voices and meds interact.

"We'll speed. Okay?" Emy Lou says. "It'll be all right."

She had said almost these same words earlier this morning, standing on the front porch with the sky still pink, going over Andy's routine one more time for Robert, who has to fill in as caretaker while she goes to Gainesville to the prison.

"It's the Thorazine plus the Cogentin after breakfast. Just the Thorazine with lunch—and don't forget to check his burger before you give it to him, because even when you tell them, sometimes they still leave the pickles on, and you for sure won't want to deal with that." Robert was watching her, as though memorizing her words.

"He's not going to get well, Emy Lou. It's nobody's fault."

She had felt her neck blotch. The way her husband held his mouth—its guarded slant—told her he was afraid. She put her mouth hard against his, then, pulling away, "It'll be all right! He'll sleep all afternoon. I'll be home in time to give him his pills."

After lunch, the women drift in. Bev sits processing paperwork in a desk with a writing arm by the door. Emy Lou has no paperwork. She sits next to Mrs. Keck on the edge of the big desk, both of them facing Delores, a Hispanic girl on the front row. Delores wears a red muffler tied across her forehead like a bandana. Her black hair is coarse and short-cropped, which makes her features seem delicate. This femininity, however, is belied by her body. She clearly lifts weights. Her shoulders and thighs bulge beneath the white jumpsuit; her neck flares like a cobra's. A tattooed teardrop dangles from the outside corner of her left eye.

Mrs. Keck tells Emy Lou that Delores lives in the Close Security Dorm, the one that houses the tough customers. She teases Delores about spending so much time "downstairs"—in solitary confinement. Delores boasts that she was the one started the fire during the riot last year. "Held off those guards pretty good," she says, and she looks around, smirking, for approval.

As the women drift in, most of them sit close enough to eavesdrop, but Bluecap strolls by and settles herself again in the back right corner.

Delores is telling Emy Lou how everybody comes into this place with their own game. "You can't trust no one," she says, popping her neck to one side, and the other women in white jumpsuits nod *Yeah.* "You can't tell nobody nothin' cause if you do, five minutes later everybody knows your business." She pops her neck to the other side, and the women nod *Yeah.*

"I got two cans Vienna sausages at lunch for describing your boots," Delores says, and the women nod *Yeah.*

Startled, Emy Lou looks up, toward the back corner, and wonders whether Bluecap talked about her at lunch.

Delores, popping her neck, declares that she herself trusts only Mexican girls who have this same teardrop tattooed by their eye. At this admission, two black women poke each other, but only because, at the moment, they are safely behind her well-muscled back.

Emy Lou knows about keeping yourself secret. Haven't she and Robert been doing so for years? In the beginning it was too much to speak: tests, specialists, combinations of anti-psychotic drugs. When the drugs' side effects surfaced, their search for help became more wide-ranging, became *her* search. Dialysis to filter blood toxins at a clinic in Upstate New York; astral body manipulation at an ashram in California; chanting with the Buddhist Center in Dallas in hopes that tonal vibrations might erase Andy's delusional voices. There are things she and Robert tell no one: the experimental drug trials, the consults with medical intuitives and energy healers. Emy Lou knows her friends say she is obsessed, but how can she give up? It's her son.

"Delores," Mrs. Keck says. "Tell Mrs. McCracken what your plans are when you get out." She is smiling and looking at Emy Lou, not at Delores, as she says this, and Emy Lou thinks, *You're going to pop your buttons, Betty.*

Delores launches into a convoluted tale about her friend Alberto who has a car and how the two of them, plus all their friends, are going to California just as soon as she is out. Emy Lou sees an old convertible piled to overflowing, speeding west, and Delores's hair is blowing in the wind—no more red muffler-bandana—and her tattooed teardrop is crinkled with laughter. Emy Lou touches the curved indentation near the outside corner of her left eye. She hadn't known she was cut until after Andy's intake at Parkland when, in a hospital bathroom, washing off what she'd assumed was his blood, saw it was hers also.

In the beginning, she and Robert had attributed Andy's reclusive-ness and mood swings to going-off-to-college jitters. His refusal to eat the food she cooked had been more problematic. It was polluted, he said. He knew this because his hands had grown. Look at them! His real hands were smaller. They told themselves that Andy had always been imaginative and talk of growth hormones in food was rampant. It was a phase, it would pass. No fear. Still, her heart had lifted the afternoon she'd walked in to see him sitting at the kitchen table, head bent over some project. Like old times.

"Hello," she said, trying to banish happiness from her voice, to pretend seeing him like this was a piece of everydayness—the sunlight picking out the weave of the white polo stretched across his back, the prickles of hair on his lovely neck. She closed the back door and the kitchen catch-all drawer that hung open. She had her arms outstretched to enfold him when she saw, over his immaculate shoulder, stipples and blotches of red on the blue and white checked tablecloth—and coming closer: needle-nosed pliers and shredded fingertips, scraps of bloody flesh, extracted nail. She went blind.

A moment later, the room blurred with shouts—her voice?—and struggle, his torso rigid against her franticness, his grip on the pliers unrelenting, and running beneath the blur, a river of silent supplication, *Oh God, Oh God, please, no.*

When he bit her, she must've fallen down—bruises appeared the next day on her flanks—but all she remembers are his unblinking white lashes, his rigid jaw, the strength of his mutilated hands. And the blood. At some point, something—the pliers? a still-intact fingernail?—had sliced out a sliver of flesh near the corner of her eye: a crescent moon, curved to match the bite mark on her arm.

"Do you really think the Parole Board is going to let you drive with Alberto to California?" asks Mrs. Keck, and her gray eyes watch only Emy Lou.

Delores pops her neck. "That's what I put down on the form. That's my plan."

"But don't you have to have three plans?" asks Mrs. Keck.

Delores touches her teardrop, then rubs it. "Yeah, well. Yeah. You gotta have three."

"What're your other two?" asks Mrs. Keck. "You got any family?"

"My mama's waitin' for me," offers a woman in a yellow muffler from a chair near the windows. She has false red lips drawn over her mouth, lavender eye shadow, and on her bleached-white hair, ripples from a hot-curling iron. "She's in Houston. I ain't lived with her in a while, but I put her down and she said it was okay."

"The Parole Board checks out the addresses," says Mrs. Keck quietly. "They won't let these women go back to the environment that landed them here."

"You mean they can't go where they want when they get out?"

Mrs. Keck's smile has the quality of rueful indulgence one shows a child. Emy Lou feels blood rising, suffusing her face.

"My husband's waitin' for me," says a wiry woman with a green muffler tucked inside her jumpsuit's V-neck. She wears heavy black frame glasses that, lacking one earpiece, list on her deeply lined face. "He and the kids been writin' me."

"He's her pimp, not her husband."

Mrs. Keck slants the words softly to Emy Lou, then louder: "Now, Frankie, you know they're not gonna send you back to Miller. You're taking his rap as it is. Where else did you put down? Don't you have an auntie—"

"But my kids," says Frankie, her glasses askew now, so that only one eye looks through a lens. "They're waitin' for me! Miller's been takin care of 'em good. Darnell's gonna be fifteen. He wrote me he's gonna play football."

Emy Lou dreams often about the man Andy could have become: a lawyer like Robert, a doctor, an astrophysicist. Nothing is too good or too much for her son. The reality of his recent descent into madness she refuses a place in her mind.

Fearful voices break through. From all around the room, they come: "I'm going to my auntie when I get out, aren't I, Mrs. Keck?" "I put down my old man's address in Fort Worth. They'll send me there, won't they?" "I got to see Darnell play ball!"

All morning the room has been passive; now all is convulsion, upheaval. Something in Emy Lou vibrates with the fear in the room. She says, "But how can they make plans if they don't know where they're going?"

The teacher's gray eyes are amused. She, Emy Lou McCracken, is *amusing*?

"Not only do they not know where they'll be sent," says Mrs. Keck, "they don't know what day or what time."

"That's right!" says a voice.

"A guard could walk in here right now," says Mrs. Keck, "and tell any of these women they're being released and where they're to go."

"Yeah, that could happen. Easy," says a voice.

Another voice says, "I heard of a woman waked in the middle of the night. They waked her up and walked her to the gate. In the middle of the night."

Everyone is talking at once now. They're sitting up, and several are moving up to the front rows. The single smooth mask of indifference has fallen away to reveal individual faces. They are telling their plans, flooding Mrs. Keck with, *Will I get my first choice? Do you know where I'm going?* Bluecap, alone, on the back row, remains cool.

"What is it you want from us?"

The voice is low, but it carries. The sitting-up bodies slump back. The silence is sudden. The room rings with it.

"What do you want?" repeats Bluecap.

"I want to help you," Emy Lou says.

"We don't need you to save us."

Mrs. Keck heaves herself to her feet, but Emy Lou motions her down with her hand.

"You don't care about us," says Bluecap, and her voice is cultured, smooth and round.

Emy Lou walks through the rows of desks toward her. "You're wrong," she says.

"What could you possibly know about what I might need?" asks the woman. But she's sitting up, and she's taken her sunglasses off.

Gotcha, thinks Emy Lou.

The woman's eyes are almond-shaped and coolly appraising.

Emy Lou is conscious that with frosted hair and pawn jewelry, she resembles no one in this classroom. She might as well be from another planet, one of the aliens whose radio messages Andy's tinfoil deflects. Outwardly, she remains upright, armored in heavy silver, but inside, she wobbles. She looks at the map behind the woman's head and realizes, now that she's close, it is a world she has traveled. Europe is a well-known shape. Her eyes automatically seek out the places she took Andy after alternative medicine failed. She sees her son in his shining hat: in the long, dusty lines at Lourdes; climbing Apparition Hill at Medjugorje; up the steps of a Greek monastery perched so high the birds flew below them. And behind the shuffling Andy, his mother: the not-giving-up, the not-yielding, the Emy-Lou-who-wills.

Standing before Bluecap, she knows who she is. The map has steadied her. "What's your name?" she asks, and immediately hates herself for using her perky creative-problem-solving voice.

The woman settles herself back in her chair, stretches out her long legs, and looks up. "What's *your* name?" She has a dimple at the corner of her mouth that gives her lips an upward tilt of friendliness.

Emy Lou says her name and feels it crumble in her mouth, air-filled and stale.

"Okay, Emy Lou McCracken. I'll ask again. What do you want?"

Emy Lou doesn't hesitate a moment. She talks so fast her words run together. "I'm here to get you to come to the Dallas Halfway House where you can get the help you need."

"I told you before," and the woman's words are round like pearls, "I don't need help." Her black eyes tell Emy Lou that she knows a secret, but she isn't sharing.

"But you're here," says Emy Lou.

"And you're not."

Emy Lou understands the implication. She knows she's blessed in every way this woman isn't. But that's just luck. She could be this woman. She squats down on her heels, white linen settling around her on the scarred linoleum. She's intent on winning, and she has more power, face-to-face.

She asks, in that dreadful Emy-Lou-voice she hates, if the woman has any family.

"Yeah, I got me a boy."

"So do I," says Emy Lou without thought. Behind the woman, pinned to the wall, loops an unrecognizable world.

The woman doesn't seem to have heard her. She's turned to speak to the plump woman on her right, the one with the wide-set eyes and pink muffler. It's as though she's continuing an interrupted conversation.

"After my ex stole my baby. About six years ago—he was two. It's like I went crazy for a while. That's when I started dealing. I felt like a part of my body—an arm or a leg—got cut off."

"Come off it, Cornelia," says Mrs. Keck from her desk behind Emy Lou. "You got used to the fast life and easy money. You like the excitement of dealing."

The woman—Cornelia—smiles easily. "That too, of course. That too."

Everyone laughs except Emy Lou, who's impatient with the interruption.

"Don't you want to see your son when you get out?" she says.

"When I get out . . ."

Cornelia disappears behind a flat gaze.

"My boy's somewhere in Louisiana—Lake Charles probably. When I get out I'll go there and get him. Rent an apartment, be a regular mom again."

Emy Lou sees Cornelia with her long Byzantine neck and perfectly shaped cropped head. With the aid of a road map, she has found her way across the state of Texas and stands now in her baby-blue cap, hugging the rail of a barge, looking out at a watery horizon. She's headed for Lake Charles. She hasn't seen her son in six years. He will have grown, she knows that, but, still, she'll recognize him.

Emy Lou grips the laminated desk and leans in, "My son . . ."

This brings Cornelia back. Her eyes are black fire. "Mine's a fine boy!"

"So is mine," says Emy Lou, and in an instant Andy has pushed through the drawn curtains of her mind. Her son, who for twelve years has alternated between pacing and stupefied staring; her son, who two weeks ago began talking to himself, writing furiously in his notebook, refusing the food she cooked or anything from the refrigerator. Her son. From the neighborhood 7-Eleven, he brought individually wrapped packages of food, but if she or Robert walked in while he was eating, he would push away from the kitchen table and dump the Ding-Dongs, Twinkies, Hostess CupCakes, Cheetos, Fritos in the garbage. He refused to sleep in his bed or sit in his rocking chair, rolled a towel to stuff in the crack at the bottom of his door, and after walking to buy a large sack of supplies at 7-Eleven, refused, finally, to come out of his room.

She and Robert had argued about how long he should be allowed to stay in there. "Give him a few days," Robert said. "He's a grown man. Maybe he needs to pleasure himself. Can't he have any privacy? Do you have to take everything away?"

But Emy Lou can't leave Andy alone. Through the closed door, she shouts, *Are you taking your pills? You can't just eat junk.*

Three days. Four.

Robert is at work when, pushing against the rolled towel, she enters the precious inner sanctum she's been denied. A stench beyond that of stale cigarettes rushes out. Cellophane wrappers overflow the wastebasket, and piled on the desk, the bed, the rocking chair seat, empty cat food cans, their interiors encrusted, dark. Her stomach lurches and comes up; in her mouth, the taste of bile. From his sleeping bag on the floor beside the cowboy-and-lariat bed, Andy raises up on his elbows, *You said I needed more protein.*

"My boy," says Emy Lou in a low, wondering voice.

Cornelia sits up to hear these soft-spoken words, and the jauntiness of her thrown-muffler loosens. Her almond-shaped eyes are confused, uncertain. "I don't know exactly where he is."

From far away, Bev's voice. "*Emy Lou?*"

But already she is reaching out. She touches Cornelia and the blue muffler falls open. Beneath it, in the hollow of her neck, Cornelia's heart is pumping like mad. "Don't know when I'll see my boy again."

Emy Lou doesn't move: she is stone. After a moment she lets go—of the desk, of all striving—and, lowering herself back onto her heels, she bows her head and closes her eyes.

A Method of Reaching Extreme Altitudes

THIS METHOD REQUIRES AN OPEN-ENDED FORMATIVE STAGE WHERE ANYTHING *is possible.*

Seeking a place to live and work, Robert Goddard spends a year studying statistics for the entire country before choosing Roswell, New Mexico. He picks Roswell for its mild weather, its level ground, and scarce population so that his rockets can "rise, or crash, or even explode without wear and tear on neighbors' nerves." At this time—1930—the average projectile is thirteen feet, average flight ten seconds. Liquid-fuel rocketry belongs in the realm of poetry, a flight of Goddard's imagination more than actual, physical flight.

Considered a crackpot, Goddard is shunned by other US scientists. The American military, failing to understand the martial application of rockets, repeatedly rebuff his offers of assistance, but the Germans send a spy to lurk among the sheepherders and cowboys in Roswell's flat, unpopulated landscape.

Nine years after Goddard's move, two young people, white roses still pinned to their wedding clothes, drive west across Texas toward the same destination. It's Christmas Eve day, 1939. The groom, a new graduate of the FBI Academy in Quantico, Virginia, prayed to be assigned to the big time—perhaps Chicago with its precarious hold on law and order. Instead he's been posted to some tiny, nowhere town in New Mexico. Like Goddard, Special Agent Hamm Wilson lives in an imaginative realm. Germany has invaded Poland; Capone is released from Alcatraz; on every horizon, danger looms. Hamm, with his new training, wants only to do good, to save the world and mankind. He is a cliché, but the purity at the heart of his desire is real. Fresh-faced, he doesn't drink or smoke; he believes in God. How else did he win the beautiful Isabelle?

In the late afternoon, the newlyweds drive into the aftermath of a snowstorm. On the Llano Estacado, the "staked plains" of West Texas, there are no landmarks, no stone, nor tree, nor shrub, nor anything to go by. It is an ocean of sky. The Spanish conquistadors and the Comanche stuck yucca stems in the ground to mark their paths through it. For the Wilsons, the highway has disappeared, its only indication tips of distant fence posts on either side of the car. All around them, stretching out to the horizon, a glistening white landscape, unmarked, immaculate, pure.

If anything is possible, the unimaginable can occur.

By 1945 Goddard has launched thirty-one rockets from Roswell—all growing progressively larger and each flying farther—and Hamm has been picked as one of a handful of Special Agents to be informed about an ultra-secret project hidden in the remote Jemez Mountains to the north. The Manhattan Project aims to construct a new type of bomb, which the scientists refer to as "the gadget." Time-pressure is great, activity fevered. When the gadget is ready to test, Hamm is one of three agents invited to the Trinity Site.

On July 16, 1945, Hamm witnesses the atomic age announce itself. The bomb blasts the desert into the sky. The light is greater than any produced before on Earth, great enough to be seen from Mars. It bleaches the land a ghastly white. The sublime terror Hamm feels that morning enters his cells. For the rest of his life, he will never allow his mind to linger on what he saw at White Sands, but that image—the power in a single atom—changes him; and the knowledge that his country controls this power shapes itself around him, bestowing a mantle of personal authority beyond his years.

The two bombs created in the laboratories at Los Alamos end the war. It's a new day. Hamm takes a big breath and looks around. His vision of what might be possible mushrooms. He smokes his first cigarette, drinks his first whiskey. He is twenty-seven years old.

With the world safe and the need for heroes diminished, launcher redesign becomes essential.

When the Wilsons' second daughter is born, Hamm decides to quit strapping on a gun to go to work and takes a job as a landman with Magnolia Oil. A few months after this decision, the *Roswell Record* reports the crash of a mysterious spacecraft outside of town. Hamm reads the headlines, but he's focused on what's below ground, not what's arriving from the stars.

His new office is an oak desk in the middle of a bullpen of oak desks in a building at the Magnolia Refinery. The refinery occupies the acreage across the highway from NMMI, the New Mexico Military Institute. Yellow flares burn atop its tall, foul-smelling stacks; giant storage containers of oil squat amidst the miasmic stink of sulfur. But just as surely as there is luck, Hamm has it: as a landman, he spends his days away from this refinery hell, scouting the territory of Southeastern New Mexico. He drives down dusty, unpaved back roads, stops by ramshackle homesteads. He's always a welcome sight in his '42 Plymouth with the windows rolled down, hair breeze-blown, bright smile. He flashes his old FBI photo ID for assurance of trustworthiness—also for glamour. He's boyish, idealistic, and he sweet-talks a lot of landowners into signing the piece of paper he proffers. He's selling a vision, a dream. Hamm's imagination of what lies trapped beneath the ground where cattle or sheep graze is what seduces. So much possible wealth! The whole Earth a vast promise!

The Wilsons buy their first home, a frame two-bedroom, one bath. The nights are cool in the Roswell desert, and when Hamm stands in his tiny new backyard and looks up at the sky vaulting high and clear above him—the mighty swath of Milky Way so close!—he knows he's a lucky man. When he reaches up to touch the stars, he can feel the spaciousness of his body, his molecules and the vast wheeling sky, a match. For Isabelle, touchable stars do not compensate for windowsills constantly gritted with sand.

That summer of Hamm's new job and the mysterious crash, the Wilsons are awakened in the middle of the night by their older daughter who's run, terrified, from across the hall to tell them Martians are whispering strange words outside her screen window! Hamm and Isabelle are "airing out," which is something they have to do for good health that requires foregoing pajamas, but they take her into their bed. Hamm explains that Mars is unreachable, a pinprick of light in the sky. In the succeeding nights, as the Martians continue to whisper, he sends Georgina back to her room to listen and learn their language.

A steady state requires an explosive booster for higher altitude achievement.
Robert Goddard is the first person in the history of the world to launch a liquid-fueled rocket, but rocketry originated nine hundred years earlier when ancient Chinese alchemists created gunpowder, and the "fire-dragon issuing from water" was born. Fireworks.

In 1950 Hamm brings a grocery sack of Roman candles to the annual Fourth of July party at the Gillespies' house on the NMMI campus. It's a fireworks extravaganza with long pauses where the wives shout, *Is it finished? Are you through?* And from the blackness of the yard that isn't a regular yard but is unfenced, contiguous with the Institute's parade grounds, the fathers call back, *No, we're trying*—and then comes a high-pitched wail followed by a chrysanthemum burst, or a gushing fountain of fire, or a huge pinwheel with colored explosions that go out into the vastness before falling down.

The Gillespies' house is large, all blond brick and square crenellated turrets, and as Hamm walks the line of rockets at the perimeter of its backyard, it shines like a ship in the vast sea of night. Roman candle shafts point toward the empty parade grounds. They are dangerous, forbidden to children, and when Hamm lights their wicks, the rockets whizz up, whistling, one after another, screaming light.

After this finale, children of various ages, in various states of hysteria, chase about in the dark. A warm body hurls itself at Hamm's knees. He reaches down to scoop up his three-year-old baby, but Josie doesn't want to be held. She wiggles free and dashes back into the night, toward Mexican girls lighting sparklers. Georgina squats in a slant of kitchen light, enchanted by the ashy "snake" humped out from a burning flat tablet.

In the kitchen, Hamm fixes a rum and Coke and allows himself to admire the fineness of his fine wife as she stands arranging tomato slices on a white platter. With her dark hair pulled back from her heart-shaped face, her widow's peak is all drama, and it pierces him. Everything about her combines to make his groin ache. Isabelle looks up, reads his mind, and smiles into his eyes. Outside, children run through the dark from one adult to another, holding up firecrackers: *Light mine, light mine.* Multiple sounds of laughter and screams in the cool July night.

Later, after the explosion, after the real screams, Hamm lifts Josie from the patch of blackened grass where tiny flames still burn and carries her in both arms against his chest. He's trotting, and around him a phalanx of men trot with him.

Later, Isabelle sits on the third step of the stairs in the Gillespies' entry hall, sobbing. Georgina's been torn from her and ordered to stay out of the way. She retreats to the bathroom beneath the staircase and peeks out from behind its door to watch women carry cold, wet cloths back and forth from the kitchen to lay across her mother's forehead, her eyes.

Later, in the kitchen with the sliced tomatoes swimming in their juice, the Mexican girls huddle, crying. One of them is inconsolable. It's her fault, she says. She isn't sure, but she thinks she handed the baby a Roman candle. The others say, *It could've fallen over in the grass.* They say, *She could've picked it up herself.*

Later, with a hot bright light pulled down over the examining table on which his daughter lies, Hamm watches Dr. Williams pour water into Josie's eyes. They are wide-opened, huge and black. The doctor hasn't yet touched the bloody mass of her cheek. First, he has to wash out the gunpowder—before it's too late and she's blind. The men hold Josie's plump little arms and legs while Dr. Williams pours seven slow beakers of water. After washing the wound, he says he thinks the rocket imploded—not that it was supposed to be handheld anyway. He sews together the edges of what's left of Josie's cheek with black thread. After each stitch, he cuts the thread so that the ends of it stick out like sharp whiskers from her little face.

For a week, Dr. Williams comes to the house every afternoon. Every afternoon, the gauze pad, held in place by a four-piece grid of tape, is blood soaked, and beneath it, the little cheek gone, as though some creature has taken a bite. Black whisker-stitches follow the red loop of the bite on both sides. Dr. Williams tells Hamm that the rocket missed Josie's temple by a millimeter. She could've been killed; she could've been blinded; it could've been much worse. Hamm should thank his lucky stars.

After the booster, rapid acceleration prevails.

In October 1957 the Soviet Union shocks the world by sending a satellite into space. All over America people gather to listen to the sound of this unimaginable presence. In Roswell, Hamm huddles around a shortwave radio at the FBI office, and in the silence, there's only Sputnik's crackle and hiss, hurtling over the globe. The men do not speak, but what they understand is this: the freedom they fought a war for is threatened.

Hamm goes home early to find his family on the couch staring at a small screen inset in a large cabinet. TV reception is new to Roswell, and there's no programming until late afternoon. Josie's feet rest in Georgina's lap, her head in her mother's. Isabelle is rubbing special "scar cream" into the sunken cheek while they wait for the test pattern to dissolve and Liberace to rise up from the dark surface with his candelabra and white teeth, flinging his cape and playing "Malagueña."

Josie has had two plastic surgery operations and needs more. She and Isabelle have had to travel hundreds of miles to El Paso and spend weeks at a hospital there. Hamm's loneliness in the quiet house during the first surgery and his understanding of the financial commitment ahead combine to push him into "going out on his own." The change in his cells that occurred at the Trinity Site helps him take this risk. It is a leap into the unknown. He leaves the bullpen at Magnolia Refinery and rents a one-room office, touching with awe the black letters stenciled on frosted glass: "Hammond J. Wilson, Independent Oil."

The information he sleuthed for Magnolia, he now uses for himself. Leasing is about oil field intelligence, and Hamm sees patterns others don't, squeezes out information others can't. He knows when a man is keeping something back, listens when an ancient homesteader swears his well water flares in the night. Farmers and ranchers tell their neighbors about the nice young man who's going to drill on their property, and Hamm picks up leases all over Lea and Eddy Counties. He's advanced from gathering signed paper to actually poking holes in the Earth. He loves the hunt, the adventure of being engaged with the planet's mysteries.

The night the radio crackles for the first time from outer space, Hamm drinks three Scotches rather than one. Sputnik circles above, and below, the stitched loop of Josie's scar has tightened into a noose. Isabelle doesn't hear it in his voice and he doesn't tell her: the upheaval, the vibrations of fear he feels in his body. All he wants is to keep his wife and children safe, but how to do this? He wasn't able to protect Josie and now, with Sputnik, the specter of Soviet domination has raised its death's-head. Everything, everywhere: unsafe.

Isabelle has been urging him to accept a job with Sim Davidson in Fort Worth. She aims to escape the dust and grit of this nowhere place. The night Sputnik goes up, Hamm decides to take Davidson's offer. Davidson's one of the big rich, one of the old guys who was around in the beginning. The Allies had floated to victory on a sea of his oil. Working for him will secure Hamm's future—*and* there will be plastic surgeons in Fort Worth. He can be with Josie at the hospital.

He and Isabelle prepare to enter the stratosphere of oil money. He buys a house in Fort Worth that's so large the children get lost in it. If Georgina hears whispering outside her window, she has to run through multiple rooms and climb a long staircase to find her parents. Josie tells everyone that a centipede crawled into her bed one night and burned an image of its body on her cheek—and they believe it. The family's trajectory is on-target, set for stellular success. The landscape of Fort Worth stretches out before them, all promise.

When nothing goes as planned, maintaining control systems is crucial.

Goddard dies believing the Germans stole his work. The V-2 missiles that shelled London bear components he invented in Roswell! Eighteen years later Werner Von Braun confirms these suspicions. The Germans *had* spied out Goddard's experiments. Everything they knew, they'd learned from him.

Von Braun confesses this theft in 1962, the year Sim Davidson dies. Davidson's death is sudden, unexpected, and leaves Hamm once again out on his own—in more ways than one. Isabelle, she of quick wit and bright smile, the reigning beauty of Roswell, is by now reclusive. Sponsored by Davidson, she expected to conquer, but Fort Worth society showed her. At her coming-out party—the first and only large party she would give in her new home—the uniformed help outnumbered the guests. *Just who does this nobody from Roswell think she is?*

After this, she begins to suffer mysterious physical ailments. When Fort Worth's social gynecologist, the smooth Dr. Brown, recommends removal of all female organs, he also prescribes Valium for post-operative care. The prescription is renewable, unlimited, and by 1962, Isabelle rarely ventures outside the big house.

With Mr. Davidson's death, the lawyers and small operators—the satellites who circled his big planet—protect their orbits. Hamm is cut out of promised deals, no longer privy to new leases. He moves his office out of the bustling Davidson empire and down two floors to a quiet corner one-man space: "H. J. Wilson Production Company." His office remains in Fort Worth, but his drilling stays in New Mexico, the old Lea and Eddy County leases. Busy during the day, he returns home every night to a house that is quiet and dark.

Georgina and Josie are teenagers, riding in cars, coming and going, but rarely staying at home. Georgina occasionally succumbs to Isabelle's pleas for a "gown and robe day." Eager for school and friends, on her way out the front door, she'll retrace her steps, put her pajamas back on, and ascend again to the master bedroom where she'll spend the day with her mother in bed. Josie ignores all G&R day enticements.

In late October, Hamm is sitting on a well sixty miles outside of Roswell. With a string of recent dry holes, Hamm's put his faith in this one, has named it "Poker Lake." It's a gamble, a wildcat, a site not adjacent to any other production. Around the rig, the brown land stretches flat and unremarkable all the way to the horizon.

During the day, Hamm and his geologist sit in a temporary hut with seismograph machines, trying to decipher what the Earth is saying. At night, they sit in folding chairs on the gravel outside their motel a few miles from the drilling site, and Hamm smokes and drinks Scotch and grills steaks on the portable grill he keeps in the trunk of his Caddy. The crew has bored to the planned depth of the well without striking oil. Hamm feels as if it's him—not oil or gas, but *him*—trapped down there, seeking a way out. Late one afternoon, catching the sweet hint of gas from chips in the shaker, he orders a core sample taken: an expensive throw of the dice, a long night's wait for lab results.

That evening, he and the geologist listen to the scratchy sounds of the President's address on Hamm's transistor radio. The US bungled the Bay of Pigs invasion, and there's nothing either of them can do about the present crisis. The geologist wanders off to his room; Hamm smokes, looks at the stars.

Early the next morning, they are hurtling down a dirt road on their way to the rig when they see them. On both sides of the road, evenly spaced, miles away but *huge*: glossy white missiles shining in sunlight. They stop the car and get out. Fear, the sick stomach-hollowing that

Hamm learned to strangle as a child, writhes to life and comes up into his throat. The morning is still, and in it, the shining white missiles stand upright. He counts them. Five? Six? As far as the eye can see, they dominate the silent brown land. While he lay sleeping in a ramshackle motel miles from anywhere in a poor, under-populated state, his country went to DEFCON 3. All around him in the night, hidden silos opened, their ghostly ICBMs rising to stand ready.

Two days later, the Cuban Missile Crisis calms and Poker Lake gushes.

Gaining altitude, the atmosphere thins. This may cause shortness of breath.
Early in his career, Goddard publishes a theoretical essay on "a method of reaching extreme altitudes"—or the possible use of rockets not only to reach the upper atmosphere, but to escape Earth's gravitation altogether. Rockets could reach the moon! *The New York Times'* front page ridicules Goddard's ideas, bringing him national scorn. Fifty years later, on July 20, 1969, Neil Armstrong walks on the moon and the nation rejoices.

The next morning, Hamm lights his usual cigarette before he rolls over and sits up to put his feet on the floor. No longer the slim Special Agent, Hamm's handsome head is heavy now with age-accumulated weight, and folds of skin hang beneath his eyebrows, narrowing his eyes. He announces that he wants to celebrate an American walking on the moon. His country has been racing the Soviets for years. The Ruskies have led for too long, but no more!

The country club is closed on Mondays, but the following evening the Wilsons go there as a family, an event so rare it can be counted on the fingers of one hand. The Mixed Grill is crowded, and once they are seated, men stand up from other tables and walk over to speak to Hamm, to shake his hand. Isabelle sparkles at the attention. No longer marked by the drama of a dark widow's peak, she's allowed Fort Worth hairdressers to color and spray her hair into an apricot bouffant like all the other country club matrons. With time, her teeth have shifted so that the small, charming space between her two front teeth has widened. She camouflages this gap by placing her forefinger against her lips when she smiles. Despite these changes, her beauty remains.

The room is lively, the diners celebratory after the moonwalk. Lacking cocktails, the girls finish eating earlier than their parents. They ask to be excused, to go out by the pool. This is not allowed. They're having a family dinner for God's sake, they need to learn to sit still like young ladies, they need to learn patience. Georgina turns sullen; Josie unwraps a piece of bubble gum. Her bubbles are small at first but increase in size. She blows a huge one that Georgina leans over to pop. The sound is audible. Josie rolls her eyes, then peels off the thin layer of pink that covers her nose and face. Beneath the gum, her scar is shiny, the skin stretched tight over bone so that individual stitches show on both sides of the curve. But her lack of two plump rosy cheeks is not so vividly apparent now that she's older and the scar smaller in proportion to the whole.

The girls' suppressed laughter draws Isabelle's attention. She gives them *the look* and shakes her head imperceptibly. Hamm hasn't noticed the gum. He's had his usual Scotches and is concentrating on getting his steak to his mouth. When they exit the Mixed Grill, Isabelle smiles and nods to everyone, Hamm walks, heavy head thrust forward, heavy tread, ignoring all.

He pulls slowly out of the River Crest parking lot. He creeps along Crestline Drive, his right hand on the wheel, while beside him, Isabelle, looking ahead, never turning around, spends two endless blocks scolding Josie for the bubble gum incident. They've passed the rock pillars that mark the entrance to their small, incorporated township when Hamm stops the barely moving car and tells the girls to get out.

What? The females in the car are at a loss. Get out, he repeats. I want you out of the car. You've embarrassed your mother.

The girls sit up in the backseat, talking fast. Josie says, *Has Daddy gone nuts?* Georgina says, *It wasn't me, it was Josie.*

He tells them that they are to run home. Isabelle says how unnecessary this is. He revs the big Cadillac engine. His face is red and hard, his eyes narrow slits. Anger implodes in his chest. *Get out!*

The girls stumble out of the car. They walk down the road toward home. It's dusk, still in the triple-digits. Hamm turns on the car lights and moves up close behind them, one foot on the brake, one on the accelerator, revving the engine. He sticks his big head out the window. *Run!*

The girls begin to trot; he moves the car up closer to them, turns the high beams on. The girls run faster. When Josie loses one of her strappy sandals and bends to pick it up, Hamm almost hits her. Inside the car, Isabelle beats on his arm, screams at him to stop. He allows the girls more distance. Georgina's wearing a girdle; she falls behind her younger sister. The tires scrunch on the gravelly road and the girls run, Josie turning now and then to shout defiant curses. Half a mile? A mile?

As they round the final curve, the house, all lit up, floats at the end of the long drive. Georgina stops on the side of the road and leans over to vomit. Josie runs back, chest heaving, to stand beside her. Hamm speeds up and passes them and goes fast down the drive, down the slanting curve, down to his safe parking spot. First it was the Nazis and the Japanese, then the Communists. Everywhere, enemies. But he's regained control: those two won't misbehave again. The world is dangerous; there must be no deviation from the path.

There's always deviation. It's part of the method.

In April 1970, as Apollo 13 careens through outer space, its control systems lost, Josie tells her parents she's five months pregnant. She's crying, and her body is shaking so hard she can hardly talk. She'd thought she was just gaining weight.

Are you *stupid*? Hamm says. Oh, darling, Isabelle says.

Hamm stands speechless for a moment, then explodes, A stupid *whore.*

Isabelle stands wringing her hands, looking sad, looking sympathetic, but, really, after she couldn't stop Hamm from almost running her down with his car, what did Josie expect?

Abortions are illegal. Isabelle's gynecologist, the socially prominent Dr. Brown, is furtive but experienced. He advises them, in strictest confidence, to send Josie to Cuba where late-term abortions are routinely performed. His right eye twitches as he says he can arrange it.

Yes, it is risky.

At home, Isabelle urges the Cuban solution. She isn't the criminal type—she just wants to get rid of the problem. But Hamm will not risk Josie's life. After sleepless nights and careful phone calls, they send Josie to Isabelle's sister in California. They put out the story that she's contracted hepatitis: she'll have to stay in Encino until she's well. Several months. They swear never to tell anyone about this secret baby—not even Georgina, who's off at college.

The big house resounds in silence. Isabelle tries to cheer up her husband. She says that something happened to Josie's brain in the Roman candle explosion. She says that Josie was altered in the blast, that she's no longer a *real* Wilson.

As with Apollo 13, Josie's chance of re-entry appears nil.

During the months his daughter is living in California, Hamm continues to go to the office, but he can't concentrate. Some scaffolding within him has collapsed. The world is not as he thought. His mind and body wobble, and he feels a nauseating ache, as though a drill bit were doing its business inside his chest. He corrects for this. He contracts; his mantle of surety hardens. Wouldn't he disintegrate otherwise?

Burned-out stages drop off, allowing the final thrust into deep outer space.

Even in childhood, Goddard is fascinated with flight. At age sixteen, he shapes aluminum into a balloon that fails to fly. He's seventeen when he has the inspiration that propels him into his life's work. Having climbed high into a tree to cut limbs, he imagines how wonderful it would be to make a device that could fly to Mars. He comes down from the tree a different boy. Every year for the rest of his life, he celebrates the "Anniversary Day" of this inspiration. Seventy-seven years later, the rocket Goddard imagined finally exists: the giant Vikings 1 and 2 that NASA launches in 1976 to land on Mars.

In Fort Worth, Hamm Wilson has made as much money as *he* can imagine. His goal has never really been money. He's spent his life in pursuit of something harder to find—oil—and has found it. Now what? He continues to go to the office, but it's light work. Using his FBI connections, his savvy insight, he does "favors" for people. Thus begins the final stage of his life.

Did your grown child deliberately disappear? Are his whereabouts unknown? Hamm finds him in a commune in the Arizona desert.

Were you robbed while attending a wedding? Hamm discovers that the thief is your son, a secret drug addict. This news never makes the paper.

Hamm can no longer feel his body's molecules—he could be made of metal so tightly are they pressed together—and his old dream of saving the world has long since died: the world turned out to be irredeemable. Now, instead of wanting to do good, he desires only to hoard goods. A child of the Depression, haunted, he stuffs three huge freezers so their doors barely close, stacks cases of Cutty Sark behind the shower curtain of Georgina's old bathtub, cartons of Winstons in her dresser. He tells Georgina that she's going to end up in a breadline. To Isabelle he says that he doesn't want to live to be old, to be a burden to his children.

What children?

Josie is lost to him, though occasionally she stops by the house to see her mother—the house Hamm bought so Josie wouldn't have to travel to El Paso, so he could be with her after surgery. Georgina, married, lives in Boston, and he calls her every day precisely at noon, and continues to call until she answers. Sometimes the phone sounds through the empty rooms of Georgina's house all afternoon—until she walks in the front door with the baby balanced on one hip and picks it up mid-ring. *Hi, Daddy*, she says.

Hamm's body, through which the vast, star-filled sky above Roswell once streamed, has swollen and clogged until it's become rigid, almost petrified. Sometime during the early morning of March 3, 1976, as he sleeps next to Isabelle and the Viking missiles move silently through space toward their landing on Mars, Hamm's heart explodes. Always on the hunt, he's been seeking death for years. It's Ash Wednesday, a fitting day for a final launch. Fifty-seven years old, Hamm's on his way, headed for the luminous darkness beyond the stars.

I think the poetry of my father's death, though never spoken of by us, then or now, remains a wonder. It's a masterpiece of timing, a mystery, supremely satisfying, that he managed to leave the Earth before becoming truly monstrous. Mother lived for ten years after his death, then she grew bored with Solitaire and TV game shows and quietly expired. Josie lives hostage to prescription drugs and alcohol and a timidity at odds with the brave, rowdy spirit she was as a child. I alone still imagine our adventure.

Impulse

3.

SHE CAN'T FIND IT ON THE KEY RING, CANNOT FIND IT—AND THEN SHE DOES. *Pop/hiss.* The key chatters against the lock. She cannot fit it in, can*not*, but then she does. When the deadbolt clicks and slides back into the body of the door, something slots into place in Annette's brain. What seemed a sudden impulse to come to Helen's house—turning right at the Rosetree Dairy Queen instead of driving straight to the Ranch—wasn't. She has a purpose.

It's the middle of a bright afternoon, but in this house, it's twilight— drapes drawn, shades pulled—the only sound, the short, continuous bursts of her oxygen tank. *Pop/hiss.* She catches a slight, sweetish hint of mouse that says *intruder*. She thinks the odor must be strong—but maybe it's not. Chemo has diminished her capacity to smell. She flicks on the overhead, a frosted, inverted saucer in the center of the ceiling. Upholstered shapes appear to be dissolving, disfigured by the rubbish of tiny creatures, nests of twigs and stuffing. The coffee table is a pelted boney creature on four legs.

Four years since Helen's death, and Lamar has allowed nothing in his mother's home to be touched; no knick-knack sold or even moved. Her husband denies death a place in his mind. Four small stone houses he owns but refuses to enter, their interiors untouched after their occupants—his parents, two uncles, one unmarried aunt—were relocated to the Rosetree Cemetery. She too will be buried there, but as Annette Arvin, not Annette Creases. She has kept her maiden, professional name.

The dust is so thick it's like walking on velvet. *Pop/hiss.*

She'll have to look carefully to find the photo. She can't remember where she last saw it: Ben at age four in his little red cowboy hat. She glances at but dismisses the clouded china cabinet. Tiptoeing to the sideboard, its lion feet declawed by grime, Annette peers at the silver tea service that allowed Helen Creases to rule Rosetree society. She feels the Daughters of the Texas Revolution, ghostly figures clutching pocketbooks, move into the room. Their gathering presence crowds her lungs. Their desire to meet again strikes between her shoulder blades. She gasps with the sharpness of the pain. She knows well the desire for reunion, but she's schooled herself against it. Hadn't she searched frantically when Ben first disappeared? Police, private detectives? And later, diviners, clairvoyants? Caught unaware this afternoon, Annette's longing nauseates her.

Ben had left no note, and he didn't call for two years. Two years! He refused to tell her where he was—somewhere in the California desert. He gave her an answering-service number—for emergencies only. He was fine, she wasn't to worry, his community was godly. She was crying so hard she missed much of what he said.

I'm not supposed to talk to you. Our leader says the dragon has cast his spell on you.

Ben's voice deepened, became a resonant preacherly voice. "*And the dragon stood before the woman so he could devour her child.*" Even in her agony, Annette recognized Revelation 12—but mixed-up, the words skewed. She cried harder. Always the botcher, her Ben.

The oxygen in its sling knocks the sideboard, a hollow note. On the black oval tray of the tea service, four black shapes stand on black curved legs. There's no glimmer of silver—and no picture frame.

In the murky light of Helen's bedroom, Annette sees what she's come for. Dirt-grimed glass obscures the red cowboy hat, but she knows it's Ben at age four. She works consciously to slow her breath. If she starts breathing fast, it jazzes with the oxygen. She lifts the corroded metal frame. The picture resists, as though it were Ben himself pulling back.

Something's wrong with you, Mom. He's a sorcerer, and you're, like, *enchanted*.

The antimacassars Helen crocheted are scalloped crud on the arms of the overstuffed chair; her perfume bottles, dust humps on her dresser. Annette places the image of her only child into the brown paper sack she has brought for this purpose. Ignoring the particles of hair and dust that float free, she steps deliberately, matching her steps to her footprints.

In the hall, she stops at a bookcase shrouded in cobwebs. Should she take the books for the Library? No. They're falling apart. She's almost to the front door when she pauses. *Pop/hiss.* She's promised herself she will not look in the refrigerator. The last time she did, she had to run outside to vomit in the iris.

Short with rounded edges, the Frigidaire opens soundlessly. An interior light comes on, but the inside is not cold. Its contents have desiccated into wild shapes, burst into black flowers. A paper milk carton, collapsed, sucked-in, leans against a mildewed sidewall; the cottage cheese carton that had been swollen and leaking green fluid is twisted flat. Even the vile odor has dissipated—or, at least, she assumes it has. The last time she looked inside, the hum had been loud, if off-key.

Her shoulders sag as she considers how her body is failing her, but then she draws herself upright. Not all has been lost. She can still smell Ben as a baby, fresh from his bath. In her mind she lays him down and opens the towel to admire the perfection of his little body, and when she puts her mouth to the damp folds of his neck, she can hear his baby coos of delight.

The last time she'd heard Ben's adult voice was thirteen months ago after she contacted the answering service, and he called back. He was sorry about her diagnosis, but the leader said he could not see her, no matter what.

Outside Helen's house, purple iris in full bloom flag the front steps, their bed freshly turned. The lawn has been scalped, and in the clipped carpet, tiny glimmering grains. Lamar makes certain the yard is mowed, weeded, fertilized. He likes it to look perfect. Annette has never told him about her afternoons spent unlocking and entering. She had no purpose other than curiosity—really, she had no purpose at all after Ben left.

She's tied a purple silk scarf around her head so that the knot's at the base of her skull. Lamar likes to see her in cowboy hats, and when she ties her scarf this way, he thinks she looks jaunty—sort of Spanish, he says, or Gaucho. The two of them are in his pickup bouncing along a caliche road. Over the sound of the truck, he tells her that he's kept the new cattle separate from the rest of the herd. It hasn't been easy, he shouts. He's been waiting to show her for two months! How can she stay away from the Ranch for so long? Such a beautiful day. Damn shame she didn't want to ride Diablo. He puts an arm around her shoulders and shouts, Next time!

She looks up at him but says nothing. When she told him she was sick, he said he would work hard so he could afford any treatment she desired, but he would not accompany her to medical facilities. He is unable *enter* illness. She knows this.

He pulls her close, and her body loosens and falls into sway against his. The windshield wipers have swept two clean arcs through the dirt on the front window; the oxygen hiss is lost in the truck's rattle and thrum. Staring out at the vast expanse of greening land, the bowl of blue sky, Annette's filled with what might be hope. Time for her has been upended, but the Earth keeps its old rhythms.

Soon Lamar's bumped off the road and headed out across a pasture. The ground is rugged; the bluebonnets straggled. He stops on a rise. Below are limestone bluffs and a long meandering line of cottonwoods that both hides and reveals the presence of water. Little Ben Creek. The land stretches out, rolling hills misted green, punctuated by stands of Spanish oak, clumps of mesquite. A landscape unfolding itself into the horizon. Annette allows her mind to follow it. She'd had no idea how complicated it would be to establish a library in a town that has never had one. Two years of paperwork, and the

Rosetree Public Library won't be in place for another two more. But it will eventually exist.

Lamar honks the horn and she jerks, startled. He grins at her and honks the horn several more times. Like magic, dark spots materialize on the horizon. The spots grow larger, become shapes, sprout legs and heads, become cows. The cows walk, heads down, toward the truck. Lamar puts both arms over the steering wheel and stares out. He says, Lookit those cottonwoods. So green. Ben oughta be here to see them.

Annette is surprised. After Ben and his belongings vanished, Lamar put his grief in a box, shut it tight, and placed it on a high shelf in the back of his mind.

He's your own son, she says. You taught him In nae.

His sudden movement, shoving the steering wheel with the heel of his hand, rocks the cab. I did it for you! There's just some things a mother should not have to see. Her own son. His body defaced. My god! I'll never forget seeing that—that excrement. But I never thought he wouldn't come home. I swear I never— Turning toward her, his eyes glaze with tears.

We've been over this, she says. She doesn't say the word fight or the word yell. She doesn't mention her tears. Her voice is flat.

It was just one tattoo, Lamar. An impulse, an adolescent rebellion.

Lamar flings his door open, steps down, and walks around to open hers. Her long flouncy skirt is a hindrance getting out of the truck, one he doesn't stop for. He clambers up over the tailgate into the flatbed and reaches down, waiting for Annette, who walks slowly, adjusting her oxygen sling. The honking horn promised food and the cattle move toward it. The truck is the center of the cow universe, their distant sun, but they are slow. There is plenty of time. Lamar's arm is outstretched; the cattle are plodding. There is plenty of time. Something about Lamar's excitement, however, translates as hurry, and in her haste, one arm full of skirt, the other gripped by Lamar, Annette trips. Did Lamar release her too soon? Did the weight of the tank throw her off balance? One minute she's climbing over the tailgate, the next she's lurching toward the cab, struggling to stay upright. The oxygen slides out of its sling and rings, metal against metal, when it hits the flatbed. This drags the cannula out of her nostrils, her cowboy hat flies off, her silk scarf slips loose, leaving her head bald. It all happens so quickly.

None of this deters the cattle. They continue; they progress.

Flung down, somehow sitting, onto the tool box, Annette stares up at the wide sky, the blue not stationary but moving. She thinks only that her head is blinding white and that Lamar won't want to see it. She never lets him see it, always keeps it covered with a scarf. She reaches up and covers her head with her hands. Lamar says, Are you okay? She uses one hand to motion him away. Hat, she gasps, keeping one hand on her head. Quick, she gasps, jerking a finger at her hat. Lamar stays where he is.

The cattle converge, their bawling continuous. They crowd close, jostling for space. The air is thick with dust and bits of straw and grass and animal hair. Annette's white head attracts this particulate air, and her baldness is soon spotted. She can't breathe; all she can do is gasp and jab toward her oxygen. Big furry heads with bulging eyes and blubbery muzzles hang over the sides of the flatbed. Again she motions to Lamar. He picks up the oxygen but fumbles and drops it, a loud clang, pure Middle C, amid the phlegmy bellowing. The sound does not startle the cattle. The heads stay where they are; the tank rolls to rest in a metal trough.

Lamar squats and hands it to her. Annette works to untangle the oxygen tube. Her hands are shaky and she is thinking only about getting her bald head covered. Finally, she shoves the cannula into her nose. She looks up, her face close to her husband's.

He grins. What about these cows, huh?

He's called them—the honking horn promised food—but he has nothing to give them. He only wanted to show them off. They're a gamble, a chance throw for a bull calf that can eventually be put out to stud. He bought them, he breeds them, they're branded: his property.

Annette takes a deep, quavery breath. I don't want— She pulls her spine upright. I came out today to talk about the Library.

Lamar cocks his head, his brown eyes uncomprehending.

She feels her life shrink.

After a moment he says, Okay. I get it. The Library.

She gathers herself. *Pop/hiss.* I want you to fund the children's section. I want a plaque that says, *Given by Annette and Lamar Creases in honor of their son, Benjamin Lamar Creases.* I want you to do this for me, not for Ben. For me.

A head pushes itself over Lamar's shoulder. Still squatting, he turns around to scratch the white furry diamond on its flat forehead. He scratches for a long time. He says, Here I thought we were coming out for a nice afternoon.

Perhaps he's talking to the cow.

He turns, and with a vague wave of his arm, indicates their surroundings. It's a beautiful day, I'm with my beautiful wife. I've waited two months! Let's not talk about a *plaque on a wall.*

The cow, given attention, bucks and shoves against the side of the truck. Lamar turns to it. No negativity, he says, petting the horned head. I thought we decided on that.

He turns back. His grin comes to her out of some world of his own she cannot touch. Positive thoughts. That's what I do best for you. As your husband, who loves you.

Her husband, who loves her, never allows negative thoughts into his mind, and he can do this because as a taekwondo champion, he's master of *JahJeh*, self-control.

He leans to finger the metal tag in the cow's ear. How long has it been since he's touched her like this? Her body, for years his obsession, a body he knew as intimately as he knew his own, has become a foreign object, its plastic port implanted for ease of infusion, apparatus from a distant planet—one that has nothing to do with him.

She says, more to herself than to him, I married an alien.

She looks up at the sky, sees herself from its vantage point: bald head, nostrils sprouting green tubes, a body that smells metallic, every cell radiating a chemical-ness no fragrance disguises. She laughs. And look at me, she says to the sky. I'm an alien too.

What? Lamar says.

My hat, she says. I need my hat.

After a moment, he unfolds his long legs. He picks up the hat and starts toward her, but he stops. The cows are moving away from the truck, their cries halfhearted minor chords, and Lamar is studying something tucked inside the crown of her hat. In her mind, Annette sees what he's seeing.

Lamar blows out a huge sigh. He blows out his good health, his strong lungs, his clean breath. He can waste it, she thinks; he has years ahead of him. She squares her shoulders.

He holds the photo out toward her like an accusation: Ben in his little red cowboy hat.

I got it at your mother's, she says, feeling the glaring whiteness of her head.

You *broke in* to Mother's house?

She starts to say, *No, I used a key*, but she stops. She watches the cattle plod—single file, lowered heads gently wagging—toward the empty horizon.

When you see Ben, she says, ask him to forgive me.

2.

Annette sits at a table on the Ranch House patio, studying the minuscule puzzle pieces spread out before her. She bought the puzzle on impulse, for Ben, her precious son. "My little screw-up," she once called him, attempting humor. "My botcher." Ben, the botcher, who's never made a sports team or an honor roll. Lamar doesn't believe in being a botcher. He believes in *Baekjool*, indomitable spirit. *There's nothing you can't do if your Baekjool is great.*

Annette thought the puzzle would be a fun family activity, but so far this weekend, Ben hasn't come out of his room. At least there's none of his music blasting. Lamar will not allow it at the Ranch.

Realizing a thousand tiny pieces is a mistake, Annette retreats into the house to make lunch. When the sharp sound of cowboy boots overrides the Sub-Zero's hum, her stomach tightens, her nerve endings stand alert. Heels snapping against wood report Lamar's progress—down the hall, past the never-used dining room, the sound growing louder on the brick floor—until he appears: slim hips, tiny waist with big oval rodeo buckle, long legs in jeans so tight she doesn't know how he manages to bend his knees.

Where's Ben?

Annette knows that rousting Ben out is not the primary reason Lamar has stabled his horse and come in. I think he's studying, she lies.

Lamar stuffs his work gloves inside the crown of his wide-brimmed hat and throws it onto Annette's piano. An upright, it's become a piece of furniture on which to stack board games, throw magazines, hats. Annette's intentions—strict practice schedule, occasional church or piano bar gigs—evaporated when the baby arrived. And later, at the Ranch, Lamar didn't like it if she stayed inside. *I want you with me, baby. You look so good on a horse.*

Lamar stands with his hands on his no-hips, his long legs spread wide, and bellows for Ben. In Dallas, Lamar works out at the gym for two hours every night. At the end of the month he'll go to Indianapolis for the World Taekwondo Federation Nationals. He believes that his seven straight years as WTF Champion, Seniors Division, are the result of *In nae*. You never give up, you *persevere*. How many years has he preached this? With *Baekjool* and *In nae*, there's nothing Ben can't achieve.

After a while, Ben slouches in and says, Yeah?

He's wearing baggy sweat pants and a long-sleeved tee to hide his tattoo. Annette's seen it. A dragon encircled by roses. Nothing whatsoever unique. She tries not to fool herself about Ben, but he is, after all, only fifteen. She sends him a smile, straightens her shoulders and stands tall. He doesn't take the hint.

Lamar starts in: Does he think Grandma Helen and Papa John ever let *him* lie around? When he was Ben's age, there wasn't any Otto to help *him* mend barbed wire!

Lamar's hair has thinned, and only a few scraps lie sweat-strung across his forehead, but he keeps his old habit of running a hand across his forehead to sweep away any obstruction to seeing *exactly what needs to be done*. His brown eyes are streaked with black, and when he is angry, the jagged streaks flash. On and on he rants.

Shoulders hunched, Ben studies the floor. Looking at him, Annette feels like her heart's being squeezed. She'd step in to defend him, but she's learned not to. Lamar puts no limits on her: she's free to buy whatever she wants, travel wherever. But he thinks she babies Ben, and this he does not allow. It's Ben's body more than any action—or lack thereof—that offends Lamar. Ben shows soft breasts beneath his tee shirt, a pouch for a belly, *white* skin. He has no muscle tone, isn't in any way virile. Allergic to animal dander, he's afraid of horses and detests cows. Annette can imagine many things but not where Ben came from. A boy who spends hours painting plastic fantasy figures?

Having been ordered to saddle his horse and get to the north pasture, Ben slumps out of the room: thick waist, wide hips, flat feet slapping against brick. Lamar's disdain radiates outward, poisoning the air. She opens and closes kitchen cabinets and drawers with furious intensity, grabbing scissors, clippers, a black plastic sheet, white barber's cloth. She snaps the black plastic over the floor, slams a kitchen chair on it; Lamar sits down and hauls off his boots. She whips the white cloth around his neck, pauses to breathe. Lamar allows no one except her to cut his hair and nails, and always at the same time: noon on the last Saturday of the month. It's the reason he came inside.

Entering the well-known routine, Annette's body softens. Lamar's blond hair is fine and she's learned to feather it over his bald spot. As she snips the uneven edges, she suggests that he could be more patient. It's puberty, she says. Don't you remember?

He does not remember.

Taking his hard, calloused hand, she tries again. Don't you remember being confused when you were Ben's age? She works carefully with curved manicure scissors. I really don't know how boys manage their bodies—growing so fast.

Lamar does not remember being unable to manage his body.

Sitting on a stool, she places his bare feet on her knees. Even after twenty years, she's still surprised. Lamar's feet have no crusted edges, no rough spots. They're tender and soft. She strokes them before cutting his toenails with large, parrot-beaked clippers. Your son *is* confused, she says.

Snippets of blond hair, crescent-moons of fingernail, thick chips of toenail—all fall onto the black plastic on the floor. When she's finished, Lamar squats, barefooted. He circles the chair, collecting his scraps, stands, holds out his double-starched shirt pocket and drops them in. When first introduced to this intimate ritual, she'd asked, over and over, Why do you do this? He'd shrugged. He didn't know. She has no idea where he buries his detritus, and if she asks, he's elusive. It's some kind of safeguard, a strange and private bodily voodoo, he shares with her, his partner, his love, and it's bound them in a way their wedding vows never did.

He sits to put on his boots. He has to say that puberty was never a problem for him. Hell, he was driving by the time he was ten. *He* didn't have any bowling alley or movie theater. He made do with the moon and the stars—and the girls on the blankets in the flatbed. He stamps his feet into his boots; his knees creak as he stands.

Speaking of it, he says.

He's standing there, and there is no part of him that does not radiate his intention, the energy of it creating an almost visible aura, like any martial art or negotiation of power. His smile is still fabulous—all those teeth!—and the streaks in his brown eyes are black lasers.

You interested in a little afternoon delight?

It's his usual ploy to avoid any conversation of consequence. She would laugh, but she's learned not to.

I.

At the top of the outside staircase, on the landing, Annette feeling suddenly as if she might fly, swoop out over the driveway's cement apron, then up, into the wide endless blue sky above Dallas, loop-the-loop, light and free. Never again will she have to climb these black metal stairs!

She inserts her key and slips into a shadowy kitchen. The stifling heat sucks the air out of her. Tiny stove, tiny refrigerator with minuscule freezer—a child's kitchen—and always having to cook in her slip because of the heat. How had she stood it? She's come from Lamar's apartment, thrown on jeans and one of his cowboy shirts with pearlized snap buttons, but no panties, no bra. Barefoot. She feels her breasts loose and free beneath Lamar's shirt, her nipples taut, chafed by its double-starched cotton. Tingling with newfound freedom, she opens the kitchen door, strides into the apartment—and there he is, sitting at the white molded-plastic table, his back to her. Her husband.

She shrinks back—can she tiptoe out? But the board that always creaks has already done so, and despite the noise from the window unit grinding away, Howard's turned around. He jumps up from the paper-and-book-strewn table. A university counselor has calmed her with statistics that prove the lack of correlation between Howard's threats of suicide and their fulfillment, but the counselor also told her not to see him.

She stands paralyzed as he walks toward her. You've come home, he says. I knew you would. I've prayed for it. He holds his arms out wide, *Do not be afraid, for I have redeemed you. I have called you by your name, you are mine.*

His voice is loud and resonant in the small attic space, hot as always. Annette recognizes the verse: Isaiah 43. She shakes her cloud of dark hair and pushes past him without speaking.

At the far end of the room, beneath the slant ceiling, miniature marble busts huddle on a bookshelf. Tiny heads: Chopin, Beethoven, Bach. She kneels down to wrap them in newsprint. Howard prowls around behind her, talking about their life together. *Scholars. A life of the mind.*

In her mind, Annette sees triangles of ham alternating with triangles of cheese, stale slices of rye.

She knew the first year of marriage she'd made a mistake. Too proud to admit failure, she'd thought her music would save her, Howard would change, she'd be able to bear it. When he started insisting the non-canonical gospels ought to be included in the New Testament, she realized his mind, the one she'd thought free, was, in fact, caged—circling a wheel of obsession, arguing a moot issue.

Fine particles of marble glimmer in Beethoven's curls.

She wraps the head, stands, picks up her sack, walks toward the bedroom. Howard dogs her, crowding close, his breath raspy and loud. An Apocrypha scholar at Perkins Divinity, he's lost any dignity he ever possessed. That first morning, with her standing barefoot, arms full of clothing, and Lamar gunning his truck down below—and Howard would not believe it. A man she'd met the night before? Someone she didn't know?

Howard, handsome in a regular way, body soft as biscuit dough, on his knees crying, and Annette just standing there, recalling the rough feel of bark as Lamar, the stranger with the fabulous smile, pinned her against a campus live oak. They'd fled the brightly lit fundraiser. Who was that dull event for? Why had she been there?

Annette shakes open a second sack. Meeting Lamar only confirmed what she already knew: she and Howard have nothing; *he's* the stranger. She begins wrapping objects on her bedside table. Her hands are large. They enable her intense playing style where, head lowered, she pulls all of herself inside in order to send it back out into fingers that dominate the keyboard—fingers now busy with newsprint. She has only to wrap these items and she'll be out of here. No more drab parties. No more tedious ecclesiastical hair-splitting.

How many scenes with Howard has she suffered in the past six months? Scenes with tears and recriminations that are actually only one scene repeated: How could she leave him for a *cowboy*? She never mentioned the Dallas real estate company Lamar owns, only the old ranch house in Rosetree. She never mentioned the expansiveness of the land and the sky—the adventure! the freedom! the sex!—because the scene always and only consisted of Howard threatening to kill himself. He had a gun; she mustn't doubt that he would use it if she didn't come back.

Behind her, Howard's hot, ragged breath. He knows she's cutting class because he walked over to the music school to check. He heard she wasn't showing up to practice, although he can hardly believe *that*.

Annette pictures the practice rooms in the basement of the Meadows Building, no windows, airless, dark. She draws a deep breath—against her nipples, the starched cotton of Lamar's shirt; between her legs, a ridge of stiff jean crotch.

All your work! And what about the talent God gave you? Your hands that set pianos on fire? The concert career we've planned?

On and on Howard rants, and Annette thinks only that she won't ever again have to be shut away from life. Don't respond to him, the counselor warned. No matter what.

In the final moment, in the tiny kitchen, she turns around, both arms filled with paper sacks, to tell him how sorry she is, he's a good person, but it just hadn't—

He shoves her out the door into the bright sun and she almost loses her balance. As she steps carefully down the staircase, a little fearful because her arms are full and she can't hold on to the railing, he walks out to stand on the landing. He shouts after her, using the oracular voice he often practices, a big voice meant for a big congregation. *If you bring forth what is within you, what you bring forth will save you. If you do not bring forth what is within you, what you do not bring forth will destroy you.* Words spoken by Jesus in the non-canonical Gospel of Thomas.

Later that afternoon, drinking beer in a bar near the campus, she laughs with Cecelia about how frightened she'd felt. She can hardly believe it, but she was, for a moment, actually scared. Then her laughter fizzes into happiness. She feels giddy, she says. Loopy. She doesn't say every cell in her body feels like it's giving off light.

I was dead, she says, and now I'm alive. I'm alive!

Mehrangarh

ON ACCOUNT OF THE TV CREWS CROWDING ARDITH'S YARD TUESDAY, IT WAS past dark when I headed out to her house and I missed the path we've worn through the pittosporum and got tangled up—that's how come this scratch on my upper lip. It's scabbing now, but I could taste the blood that night! I marched straight back to Ardith's bedroom and told her she's going to have to start coming to *my* house to get unzipped. She didn't hear me, per usual. She was standing in front of the chifforobe unpinning her braid from its white crown. Ardith's tall and large-boned with huge hands and feet. Nothing like me. I didn't mention my lip, and she didn't notice.

I spoke louder. "The years we wasted on that boy. You've got to admit our project's failed."

How could she deny it with reporters knocking at her door all afternoon? I'd sat out on my front stoop, watching. Nobody paid me the least mind. The spring air was fine, with cottonwood fluff from my tree floating through it like tiny lamb fleeces. Next door, the reporters cursed the fibers, swiped their faces, only to turn the next instant toward a TV camera, lethal and composed as any rattler. I might've been entertained if they hadn't interrupted our canasta game. I was not eavesdropping but once I'd adjusted my aids, it was all I could hear: *Chris Murphy, beleaguered oil and gas guru . . . raised by his grandmother here in Roswell, New Mexico . . . ongoing SEC investigation . . .*

The murmurings mingled with the cottonwood floaters and scent of honeysuckle to create a cloud of sweet-smelling nonsense.

Neither Ardith nor I understood what the problem was with Chris's oil business—something about pyramids—but when does Ardith ever admit anything's wrong?

"Who's to say this isn't God's plan?" she mused, placing her hairpins in their saucer on top of the chifforobe. "To bring everyone down, so all can be equal? Isn't that what Jesus preached?"

I wanted to say *God's plan, my fanny*, but I learned long ago you can't argue with Ardith. She's always certain she's right. With her white braid hanging down and her long neck stretched up, she gets *that* look, as though she's seeing something I can't. It's the India Influence. I'm a seeker, she says—all those holy men in loincloths, don't you know? It gives her a sense of superiority.

"We should've sent him to college," I said. This brought her back to Earth.

"How would Freshman Composition help a Maitreya bring world peace?"

The eternal question. I turned around and stood, head bowed, so she could unzip me. *Maitreya, great teacher*—that's the way she talks. She can't help it. When she came home from California in '47 jabbering about "the holy baby," I knew something bad was going to happen. How did I know? My crying hands told me—and this is not a figure of speech. Osteoarthritis is a curse, but it's also an early warning system.

Here comes trouble with a capital T. My daddy used to say this. We might've ridden all day out to some sheep camp the other side of the Apache reservation, but here would come our old dog, Trouble, trotting through the scrub. It's my hands say it now.

When she turned around so I could unzip her—I can only use my thumb and forefinger, but I manage—she said, "For God's sake, Lottie, quit clacking!" I jerked her zipper so hard, she stumbled. I can't help it if my dentures don't fit. I have a narrow jaw. Narrow feet, narrow hands. She's the one built like a peasant.

Never mind. I'm used to her abuse. We've been neighbors forty years and we're more like sisters than friends. She, a child of

Presbyterian missionaries, would have a biblical reference for my position in her life, but *I* don't. I wasn't raised beneath the walls of a miraculous fort in India. I grew up east of Claunch with windmills for water and scrub to every horizon. Sometimes I think that if I have to hear another word about Mehrangarh—built by angels and fairies, she says, rising sheer out of high rock—I'll spit my teeth at her.

We knelt down, per usual, on the floor beside her bed, our dresses sloppy around our shoulders. Ardith clasped her big hands together, I my small claws. But instead of praying, Ardith spoke to God about seeing Chris as a newborn. How many years have I had to listen to this? I'll tell you. Thirty-seven and a half years.

Her voice filled the room. She said she was straight off the train, thirsty as all get-out, drinking a glass of tap water at the kitchen table in Encino, but when she saw him, her thirst disappeared. All sound drained off. Joe looked like a fish, mouth opening and closing. Mary Ruth didn't speak, just laid the baby in her outstretched arms.

Ardith says she is "meant for the stage," which just means her voice is loud. I, on the other hand, have to pull my spine straight to give my lungs space. It's Ardith's script, but I play my part.

"The baby was warm!" I proclaimed.

Again, her meant-for-the-stage voice: she expected her grandson to be a miracle, but a *regular* miracle, like all newborns. There'd been no warning of this. No Gabriel kneeling, lily extended.

I'm not making this up; that's what she said. *No Gabriel kneeling, no lily.* Who is she to expect an Archangel? I never expected a big life and I haven't had it. I'm satisfied with small. But not Ardith. Normal life has never been enough to contain her, and she gets away with a lot. She just does. Her spirit is powerful.

"His eyes smiled *into* me," she said.

"You recognized him," I cried.

"He hadn't wanted to be born."

"He resisted until he had to be cut out!"

"Who wouldn't have lingered in unbornness?"

"Knowing the sacrifice!"

A whisper from Ardith, "Shrinking from grandeur into a tiny newborn."

We always chanted the final words together: "How courageous he was to consent."

It was what Ardith had said in '47—and said and said until even I started thinking that baby in California had courage. I don't know anything about babies. It's a mystery why I never had one, except my body's exceptionally small and I've got this growth, you can see it on my forehead. My mother called it an "angel kiss." Ardith insists there's a third, invisible eye there. I'm a rational person, but I go along.

I know my angel kiss had nothing to do with bearing children, but if I'm marked outwardly, there might be a marker inside, a blister blocking some tube. I know I was lucky to get a husband—my daddy said it at the time, though Mama shushed him—even if it was only a Honeywell boy from the neighboring ranch. The sheep business is precarious. There's always wolves or drought, or in the days before fences, cow patties dirtying the water. Sheep will not drink dirty water. The more land you have the better, so I never fooled myself into thinking Dogie's marriage proposal was anything other than business. I do wish I'd understood that a boy named for the ewe's rejected runt is always going to be hunting teat. Dogie and his women. I'd shut him out of my heart long before I met Ardith.

She doesn't remember how we first met. Me, I remember everything like it just happened. We were standing around a punch bowl at the Commandant's house. It was a party to welcome Major Ephram Ridgeway, transferred from Fort Sam in San Antonio to be second in command on the Hill. (We call the New Mexico Military Institute "the Hill"—don't know why, except Pennsylvania Street does *rise*.) And there was Ardith, Mrs. New Superintendent Ridgeway, tall, with her dark hair braided and coiled on top of her head like a crown, asking me about sheepherding. I couldn't figure it out. Why did this queen want to talk about sheep? Then she said that Jesus was a shepherd, and she was a member of his flock, and I thought, *Oh Lord, a holy roller.* But what I said was—this was the first night we met, mind you, all the men except Dogie standing around in brown uniforms with their brass buttons shining to beat the band—"If you think it's a fine thing to be in a flock of sheep, you're plain loony. Even *if* the shepherd is Jesus."

Ardith and Ephram. Sounds like a magic act. I don't believe in magic, but they were something, those two. Tall and beautiful and so in love. I was halfway in love with both of them myself. Ardith had fallen for Eph the first time she saw him play polo, because as a child in Jodhpur, she *sooo delighted in watching the Maharaja play.* I can still hear her saying it: *I sooo delighted.* I told her I'd been delighted to learn arithmetic sitting in the dirt by a bloody pile of docked lambs' tails. *If you take away three tails, how many are left?*

When Eph fell off his favorite polo pony and cracked his brain, that was trouble with a capital T. This happened three years before Chris arrived on our planet. That's the way Ardith talks: *arrived on our planet.* She believes that if Chris had been here already, he could've saved his grandfather. I keep my dentures clamped tight when she speaks nonsense. I was patient with her Tuesday night, because I knew the trouble with Chris was going to be harder on her than Eph's death ever was. She knew Eph wasn't holy. She's let slip plenty over the years about their *imaginative* sex life. I always just yawn. Does she think there's anything I didn't hear living with cowboys on a sheep ranch?

Our prayers finished, Ardith hauled me standing. Per usual, my joints had rigored and I had to loosen up before I could walk home. I do this by raising one knee after another real high and stomping down hard. I was making my way back through the pittisporum, when a man slipped out of the shadows and said, *Mrs. Honeywell?* The stars swarmed, but I didn't scream. I used up my fear a long time ago watching wolves prowl the edges of campfires. We'd never shoot them, but we'd strychnine a burro and leave it out for them to slink down and eat.

This wolf smelled like garlic, not burro. His bald head glistened, but his face sprouted fur. He stepped up too close and asked could I comment on the accusations made against my neighbor's grandson in the new bestseller, *False Heroes*?

I should've known he was a reporter. "I refuse to dignify that book by talking about it," I said. "Chris was a courageous young man who volunteered—*volunteered*—to go to Vietnam. He won plenty of medals, and nothing written by some ex-soldier can change that." As I swept past him, he said, okay, he was patient, he'd be around. Here was his card.

Normally three raisins plumped in gin works to silence my bones, but I lay in bed and stared at that card, propped against my Apache bowl on the bedside table, and I could not stop thinking about Chris—all our plans for him.

Mary Ruth was Ardith's only child, and when she got sick—I still can't talk about it. Some awful kind of cancer. Long story short: Mary Ruth passed. Ardith quit eating, we couldn't either one of us play canasta, life didn't seem worth dirt. Then Joe called and Ardith went to Encino to help with the baby. He was three, I think. One night, tucking him into bed, Chris told her that his mama had just floated through a corner of the ceiling. "Now she's up by that long crack near the light bulb." Ardith had always felt the presences, but Chris *saw* them. She took this as confirmation of holiness. She blew a kiss in Mary Ruth's direction and turned out the light.

The war had been over for seven years and Joe was making plenty of money at Disney, but he had no time. Ardith said he cared more about his company gods than he did about Jesus—Mickey and Minnie strutting across every coffee mug and ashtray in the house. She wrote that her ancestors were in an uproar: *I have old dead Presbyterians kicking up a ruckus in my bowels.* What does she know about ruckus? What if she'd had my spine that was curving more every year? My hands that were curling into claws? Do I think ancestors inhabit my bones? I doubt they could stand the pain.

The night Chris saw his mother, Ardith determined to get him out of California and home with us. In the mysterious way the world works for her—and I have never understood this but am here to tell it—it was Joe who suggested it. He worked out some financial plan, then lickety-split Ardith and Chris got on the train. How easily that child was orphaned! I could've cried, I know what it's like to feel alone in the world. Ardith told me heroes are often orphans. Something about searching for their heavenly fathers, don't you know?

I could still shift gears and drove my Plymouth to pick them up at the train station they have at the Alvarado in Albuquerque. It was two hundred miles! I know the mileage because Roswell's two hundred flat brown miles from everywhere. I didn't mind doing this. Growing up in India, Ardith never learned how to drive. I was driving by the time I was ten, the old pickup, with a bushel of pinto beans to sit on and a block of wood strapped to the clutch.

Ardith and I always help each other out. I'm her best friend, more like a sister, I think, than a friend.

We moved Chris into Mary Ruth's old room. He fit naturally into the rhythm of our lives. We taught him canasta soon as he could count. He was a natural player. The three of us played every afternoon after naps. The day after Dogie's funeral was the first time Chris beat me. He was eight. I told him I was grieving was the reason he won.

The honeysuckle that edges Ardith's porch and my cottonwood weren't so big back then, but otherwise everything was the same as it is now. Our same two houses, three blocks down from the Institute with the football stadium across the street. Friday nights in the fall, the chain-link fence is draped in canvas so you have to pay to see the game, but you can watch the cadets march down to it for free. We'd stand out on the curb with Chris between us, and here they'd come, flags flying, singing about a girl who wore a yellow ribbon. They'd never break formation, never move their heads, but they'd cut their eyes and see the little blond boy in his PJs, waving and cheering, and oh, they'd grin.

Ardith thinks Chris volunteered for Vietnam because those cadets looked so brave and handsome; I thought he volunteered because he needed a paycheck. We had spent every penny sending him to India after he graduated from high school. When he got home, I said, *What're we gonna do now? Take up a collection for the Church of the Holy Baby?* He got huffy, said he'd never let his granny suffer. It did not escape my attention that he didn't mention me.

Per our plan, Ardith snuck over to my house Wednesday morning. I hadn't slept and after watching the *Today Show*, the world looked grainy and the walls pressed in. That ex-soldier with the bestseller talked to Jane Pauley about the years he'd spent researching *False Heroes* and how he'd investigated Chris precisely because he was different from most Vietnam vets. "An anomaly," he said. "Wealthy and successful." He talked about "all of Mr. Murphy's lies." He talked and talked.

I expected a sorrowful face, but Ardith breezed in, all smiles. "So Chris told us he volunteered for Vietnam when really, he was drafted. What difference does it make?"

I choked and hot tea came out my nose and woke up my wound. I had to hold a napkin to blot the seep; she never noticed. She'd started in on the fiber toast. It's always mesmerizing how she becomes a machine: her hand a steady conveyor of food into a mouth of continuous mastication. It's the India Influence—the starving millions.

"*We* know," she said, "that Chris was in Quang Ngai. We have his letters."

The ex-soldier had told Jane Pauley that Chris was never in the dangerous province of Quang Ngai. He was a typist in Da Nang. "Never in the bush," he said. "Never under fire."

"This is a test," Ardith said, mowing steadily through another piece of toast. "Chris has to be strong to accomplish what he's come for."

Which is, of course, why we'd had to be so careful when he came to live with us. *I feel the responsibility of educating Chris into his destiny as both a privilege and a burden.* Every time Ardith said this, I heard Churchill broadcasting to the people of Britain: *I feel the responsibility . . .*

I'll admit we all perked up when Chris arrived. Even old Dogie, who was reduced by bad lungs to occupying a desk at the Roswell

Wool Warehouse. Was he still hunting teat? Yes. And with Chris, he found new pastures to graze in. There was that divorced preschool teacher and Chris's second grade—

Really, I was too busy to notice. "The boy" became our project. (Ardith dropped the "holy" part after two ministers, one from Grace-Presbyterian, one from First Methodist, came, separately, to see her.) Year after year, Ardith, knees crammed beneath tiny desks, had to listen to Chris's teachers enumerate his failings. They told her she should quiz him before his tests, help him memorize. She'd come home shaking her head. "Lottie," she'd say, "how important is it in the scheme of universal love to know that Bismarck is the capital of North Dakota?"

"My parents were warriors for God," Ardith said this morning, shoveling in a spoon heap of bran cereal. "My husband was a military hero." Another heap. "That's why Chris chose to be born into our family." She waved the spoon around in the air above her head, "Courage and strength in the genes!"

Those were her exact words, accompanied by spit-flakes of bran: *warriors for God, chose to be born.* Could I make this stuff up?

Normally, watching Ardith eat puts me into a hypnotic trance, but this morning it made me nauseous. I started gagging, stomped up and down to release my knees, and left the table. I made sure the screen door slammed behind me. Reporters, those smooth beauties who flick their tongues for the cameras, were lazing on Ardith's front steps, and at the edge of her porch, near the pittosporum, my bald wolf with his furry face. The two of us stared at each other. I'd spent a sleepless night cogitating on Chris's Trouble. The publication of *False Heroes* must've been what sent the government sniffing around his oil business. *If a man lies about one thing, he'll lie about another.* I about-faced.

Inside, Ardith had cleared the dishes, centered the black plastic canasta tray, and was shuffling Bicycle decks. I sat down. She shoved the stack of cards across the table, I cut, she dealt, we fanned our hands. We played quietly for a while. From outside came the low murmur of bored men, and then waves of music, beating louder and louder. We didn't have to look to know the Institute Band was marching down Pennsylvania to practice in the stadium. When the music stopped, there was disharmonious honking, instruments running scales. Silence. John Philip Sousa blared, stopped, blared; and in between the Sousa, shouts of TV crews, clunks of car doors, engines turning over. Not that we paid attention to any of this; we were concentrating on our game.

Several plays later, Ardith said, "What if I showed our Quang Ngai letters to a reporter?"

I tried to lay down my trick discard as if it were of no importance. "Couldn't hurt."

Ardith resembles a polar bear, but I would never have mentioned this if she hadn't pounced on my discard with one of her big paws. She says I play for blood. I say, *It takes one to know one.* It was my turn to win the pot and she knew it, but she scooped up my card, slapped down a meld, and scraped the pennies off the table.

It was the click of her coin purse closing that did it. I told her what a polar bear I considered her. She didn't hear me, per usual.

She shuffled the decks, pushed the stack toward me. I cut, she dealt, we fanned our cards—and all this time I was sizzling.

"There's a bald one with a beard who seems nice," she said as she arranged her hand.

"*He's mine!*" I screamed.

"Yours? What're you talking about? The reporters are here because of Chris."

I threw my cards on the floor. "It's always Chris, Chris, Chris. What about *me*?"

Ardith slung her cards across the room. Every inch of me was quivering. I swept the rest of the game off the table with my arm. The plastic tray made a terrible racket. She wore her holier-than-thou smirk. I glared at her. "Guess you're going to have to play 52 Pickup," I said, indicating the sea of Bicycle cards.

We'd been at her house the last time we played this game. This was at least thirty years ago. For some reason, I don't know why—maybe my bones were talking louder than usual, or maybe it was Chris's prissy attitude. And didn't he come by that naturally? Hah. Anyway, I asked him, Did he want to play 52 Pickup? He had never heard of it, and Ardith didn't say anything to stop me. I raised the deck up high; his little face was shiny, expectant. I squeezed the deck and let the cards fly. He didn't understand. "You have to pick them up now," I said. "That's the game. 52 Pickup."

He crawled around on the carpet on his hands and knees for the longest time. I think he was trying not to cry. I tried not to laugh. "Quit clacking, Lottie," is all Ardith said.

Why did that baby have to be holy? That's what I've never understood. As far as I could tell, the child was normal. Outgrowing shoes and pants, walking the pipe in the vacant lot across the street, tossing rocks into the Rio Hondo. *Come on, come on, hurry up, Lottie.* That was Chris, criticizing me for being too slow to discard and pick up. You try handling cards with arthritic fingers! To get back at him, I started freezing the deck. Every game. I wouldn't have done it if he'd been younger, but he was *eight*. He could beat me. I couldn't slap those black threes down fast enough. His spleen was fiery against me because of 52 Pickup, and when I started freezing the deck, the games got moody.

"I wish you could see yourself," Ardith said. "If you don't look like Amenhotep III, I don't know who does. Saw a picture of his mummy last week in *National Geographic* and I swear I thought it was you."

When she'd quit laughing and could finally talk, she said, "Come on. It's funny!"

She's always encouraging me to be more enthusiastic. *Don't be such an old post, Lottie,* she'll say. I don't know why I'm not good enough like I am. Anyone who's watched sheep on their way to slaughter knows there's not much to be enthusiastic about, and we're all of us in *that* line.

"The reporters are gone; you can go home now," I said.

"Don't pout—it's not attractive."

"I've always been ugly as a piece of soap."

"You're acting like a baby."

"Mind your own beeswax, polar bear."

"I swear, you're enchanted by unhappiness."

The screen had barely slapped her bottom before I'd grabbed the business card propped against my Apache bowl and was dialing the number for that slinking wolf reporter. *Enchanted by unhappiness, my fanny!*

I told the reporter everything. I started with Chris's education, but he wasn't interested in that. He perked up when I told him how we'd managed to send Chris to India. I put in a portion of Dogie's retirement, Ardith contributed part of Eph's life insurance—and off he went. Chris told us later that we showed him how to start Murphy Oil and Gas: "Bits of personal retirement funds, portions of individual pensions. It adds up."

I launched into Ardith's master plan: how Chris was to be "a spot of light in the immensity of India's millions"—which just meant she'd signed him up to be a missionary at Dr. Sommerville's hospital where her parents had evangelized. She told Chris that medical missionaries open highways for Jesus, that the way to change hearts is to heal bodies. The only word Chris seemed to latch onto was *highways*. He stayed long enough in Jodhpur to send a couple of postcards, and then he was off. "Like a real holy man," he said, "wandering the roads from ashram to ashram."

I've never understood about ashrams. I picture sheep camps with temporary shelters thrown up for de-ticking and tagging. All I know is that when Chris came home—this was '68 or '69—he was skinny, his blond hair hung down to his shoulders, and he kept talking about the wonders of *ganga*. Ardith thought he was mispronouncing Ganges. I said he needed shearing. In any case, he wasn't home long, because he volunteered for Vietnam as soon as he got back. At least that's what we've thought these fifteen years.

I wanted to talk more, but the reporter said he'd get back to me. I did not go to Ardith's to get unzipped. I slept in my dress.

I never heard from my reporter, but I believe I had something to do with the headlines of yesterday's *Roswell Record*: JILTED INVESTORS/ NEW EVIDENCE UNCOVERED. All day the TV advertised an upcoming "Peter Jennings Exclusive Interview" with Chris. I sat outside hoping Ardith would open her door, but with all the TV crews crowding her porch, she never did. I kept thinking, *What will our lives be like now? What will we do?*

My phone rang off the wall after the evening news. I picked it up every time, but it was always reporters, never Ardith.

Chris looked used up, I'll say that. But he surely talked fast. As my daddy used to say, *An empty wagon makes a lot of noise.* All his fine talk about oil and gas, how they lie imprisoned in underground pools waiting to be freed, and how money, too, wants to be free to circulate. Oil wells pumping, money flowing. His tongue was flying when Jennings interrupted to ask a question I couldn't make out, but Chris's face got red, and he raised his voice. *Why freeze the deck?* There was no reason for the flow to stop. It could've gone on, one investor giving to the next, to the next. Wasn't that the universal religious ideal? The whole world sharing, everyone's well-being heightened?

It was strange at first having reporters around, and then it was strange not to. And wouldn't you know? Proven to be a major presence in the boy's life—and there wasn't anyone to see me. *If you look around the table and can't tell who the sucker is, it's you.* My daddy used to say this.

All I could get down for supper was a little milk toast, and I wasn't sure I had the strength to get through the pittosporum, or even if I should. Then I saw a fire in Ardith's backyard and, in the interests of neighborhood safety, went to investigate.

The barbeque grill, a charcoal pan on a tripod of tall metal legs, blazed high, and bent over it, close to the flames, Ardith, in her nightgown with her white crown unpinned, her braid hanging long down her back. I went to stand next to her. We didn't speak. In the flickering light, her profile was strong. I've shriveled up, but she's remained straight. She fed white envelopes, one by one, into the heart of the fire. I recognized them of course. We'd haunted the mailbox waiting for them.

The fire ate each envelope—slowly at first, tiny gray bites on the edges—then the paper blackened and curled into gold, and flakes of ash floated up. The greedy fire grew, and if I'd had any letters, I would've gone and gotten them because that fire was so hungry for life. But I didn't and don't. Not a single letter. One postcard from the "Royal Paintings of Jodhpur." It shows two women in harem pants and halter tops breast-stroking through air above a green park. You can feel how light in their bodies these women are. Below them, unaware of them, regular people subject to gravity stroll. I keep this postcard in my Apache bowl. All Chris wrote was "Hi, Lottie! This reminded me of you and Granny."

The sky was jangly with the stars' nightly splash, but my bones kept their silence. When I held out my hands to warm them, Ardith started talking. Chris had called her from "wherever it is they're holding him" and told her to burn his letters from Vietnam. He'd been on a mission so secret he'd had to lie to us about it, and now he needed her to destroy the evidence. The whole time she was telling me this, she was feeding envelopes to the fire. When I asked who "they" were, Ardith waved a letter around in the air above her head. "You know. *They.*"

She turned to look at me, her eyes big and shining in the firelight. "He told me he's innocent, Lottie. He's made some mistakes, but it's not his fault. He talked about sheep and how they won't drink if the stream's dirty."

I said nothing, just stood before the moving light of the fire, wondering why a child puts one thing and not another into memory: the mystery of the individual mind.

"He said Dogie taught him you don't shoot the wolves, but you—"

"*What?* He said Dogie said—*what?*"

"He said Dogie taught him you never shoot the wolves, but you strychnine a burro for bait. He said he's the burro."

This cloud of idiocy affected my eyes. I felt tears pricking. Who drove Chris around all those years? Who read to him every night? *Me*. After everything Dogie took from me, how dare he reach back to steal the boy! I determined at that moment that I would not allow it. I'd block him. I squared my shoulders, made my claws into fists and studied the lies, now flakes of ash, floating away. Everything ash.

After a while, I looked at Ardith—at her face with its lines, its hollows and planes of darkness and light, at her fine figure given over to gravity.

"He's the sacrifice, Lottie, so the sheep can live." Ardith's voice, trembling with wonder, carried through the dark immensity. "I always knew it."

I bowed my head and turned around, and she unzipped me.

She's not so changed from when I first met her at the Commandant's house. Her spirit was huge then and still is; her dream of a better world still lives within her—and she was always meant for the stage.

But loony? No doubt about it. She'll need me now more than ever.

Running

SOON ENOUGH I AM ALMOST THIRTEEN, WAITING, BARELY, TO BECOME A shining new girl, allowed to wear kitten heels and spend the night out. This was in Roswell in the mid-fifties: aliens from outer space were unheard of; TV reception was nascent. It was a mile from North Junior High to my house and every day after school, Rose and I walked it together. Girls from Washington Elementary were "cooler" than we were, more savvy, but they were hostage to mothers in carpools. Rose and I were *free*.

The two of us danced and dawdled our way up Pennsylvania Avenue beneath an always-blue sky. Sometimes it took us two hours. We sang tunes from the Hit Parade, "Don't Be Cruel" or "The Great Pretender," but we made up our own words. We sang Ninth Grade Norm into dedicating his football jacket to us. We stuffed our socks into our bras and sang ourselves into Leanne Dumas, head cheerleader. I was crackerjack at making up lyrics, but Rose carried the tune, her voice lovely and pure.

Every day we passed three massive brick churches before entering a tree-lined neighborhood of old houses. At my house, on the corner of Penn and 13th, Rose turned left. She lived past New Mexico Military Institute, past Mark Howell Elementary and Kling's Drugs, out where the paved roads turned into gravel, then into dirt. Rose's parents didn't have a phone, so on weekends we couldn't talk, but we would scribble with toe-gripped pencils on unlined paper and exchange "footnotes" every Monday morning on the third-floor landing at school.

On this particular May afternoon, I skipped fast past the churches, leaving Rose to catch up. I rarely skipped when I was with her. Rose didn't wear petticoats and I, Georgina, had so many, and when I skipped—my knees coming up high, one after the other—my petticoats flared into glory, the white-starched clouds of them edged with ribbons of various colors. I became dizzy with the magnificence of myself and then everything was sky and clouds—and *me*. Today I didn't care about Rose's lack. It had been the worst day of my life. I skipped.

I had reached Mrs. Ely's honeysuckle hedge before Rose grabbed at my skirt from behind and jerked. I stopped skipping but continued to sing Fats Domino. *"I'm walkin', yes indeed—"*

"Quit it," she said, and I did. We often lingered beneath this hedge so I could spy if Tommy Stapp, Mrs. Ely's other best piano student, was sitting at the baby grand in her bay window. Today I didn't care whether Tommy sat there.

"Why are you acting so weird?" Rose said.

The only sounds were my labored breathing and the bees going about their honeysuckle business. "Not acting weird," I lied.

"You're acting, I don't know. Fake."

The announcement posted in the halls that morning had blind-sided me. I had been so intent on showing myself to be carefree that I hadn't realized it was time for school elections. *Time to run.* My body was porous, taking in the babble in the halls about who was running for what and with whom. No one spoke to me about elections until after lunch in the girls' bathroom on the third floor.

"I am not acting fake. Just feeling, I don't know"—I bobbled my head—"*nonchalant.*"

I watched Rose's mind search. I knew the meaning of the word, but what good was that if I couldn't be nonchalant? I felt the pressure of my waist cincher, its rigid stays. I was certain my pretense had fooled the general audience, but this was *Rose*. I had to act breezier, as though what I needed her to do for me was no big deal, a trifle. I rocked my head and shoulders, *"and I'm talkin' about you and me."*

"Is it because of Caroline?" Rose's eyes were soft; the wind in the cottonwoods and the bee sounds, soft. My heart clenched.

There had been nothing soft about the girls' bathroom on the third floor after lunch. Loud with laughter and prattle, the din shredded into ragged breathing the minute I pushed open the door. Everyone moved back except Caroline Lake. She continued to stand in front of the mirror painting her signature pink lipstick on her perfect lips. Caroline, with her smooth cap of golden hair and fourteen-inch waist, was rumored to wear *seven* petticoats and was a shoo-in for head cheerleader. I hardened my body and uncapped my stick of Coty "Tangerine."

Caroline said, "Heard you're planning to run for student council president. Against *Stephen Wolfe*? Surely not." My face showed not a flicker of interest, and the hand applying Tangerine barely trembled. "You know—of course, you know—that Stephen picked your pal Tommy as his vice president." My lipstick jerked over my upper lip and up, into my nose. Snickers of laughter, quickly stifled. "Whatever you do," Caroline said, leaning forward to look at her lips, not at me, in the mirror, *"everyone* agrees you'll want Rose Garcia as your partner."

And there it was, just as I had suspected. The cloud of hair spray stung my eyes. I wiped my nose and steadied my hand. When I clicked the lipstick shut, I showed my braces. "You're right. Rose and I plan to be partners." A chorus of voices exclaimed how cool that was; the bell rang, and everyone poured out the door.

Alone in the echoing silence, I looked at myself in the mirror. The foul face looking back at me was my own, and I saw for the first time that who was to be my vice president had been vague in my mind. I thought I needed a boy, probably Tommy. I had never seen Rose in this role.

Rose was nothing like my group, which was, in truth, Caroline's group. All of us starched and waist-cinched, with white suede loafers and smiling mouths full of metal. When Caroline had invited me to take afterschool gymnastics with her at the Roswell Youth Center, I told her I wanted to but I couldn't: my mean parents made me practice the piano for two hours every day after school. I did not say I preferred to walk home with Rose, the two of us *free*. Soon, in the halls, conversations among girls who looked like me ceased at my approach, and in assembly where we all sat together, there was no longer room for me. I did not tell my mother the girls at school no longer spoke to me. I said nothing about it to Rose. I played the surface. I cinched my belt tighter, asked for more starch in my petticoats, and at school, I acted so theatrically buoyant I felt I might actually float away.

I glanced at Rose standing beside Mrs. Ely's honeysuckle hedge. She was unstarched, non-metallic, as vibrant with life as the trembling cottonwood leaves above us. Rose wasn't *calculating* like I was. Shame suffused me. "Here's the deal," I said.

"When you start talking deals, I know trouble's coming."

Rose laughed, I didn't.

"Let's walk," I said. Tall cloud castles filled the sky and on the horizon, the eternal blue triangle of Sierra Capitan.

"Do you remember the Brownie troop campout in Louise Kling's backyard? When we lay in our bedrolls and held hands to make ourselves stay awake? We decided to be famous astronomers. Remember? We discovered the Big Dipper and Orion's belt, and you said your prayers on a rosary. I had never heard of a rosary. And then, when we decided to be famous archaeologists? *Remember?* I snuck my mother's *World Book Encyclopedia* out and carried it up the alley—"

"You never *snuck* it," Rose said. "I always knew that was a lie."

How did she know? I had only said that to make myself seem heroic. No one in my house noticed what I did or did not carry up the alley to Mark Howell Elementary. After the Roman candle blew up in Josie's face, my parents' shining selves—the radiance that lit up the world—contracted to concentrate on my little sister. I was obedient, healthy and whole. I followed the rules. Nobody paid me much mind. My father traveled constantly to "sit on wells" (I didn't know what this meant and didn't care), and Mother became a cleaning fanatic. Every morning before breakfast she had to wipe off the windowsills, search for centipedes. But sand on windowsills was a fact of life, and killing one or two centipedes did nothing to deter them. They crawled out of cracks in the foundation and fireplace, up onto the porch or into the living room; crawled across your bare legs if you sat on the floor intent on Monopoly or up your arm if you flung it out of the covers while sleeping. Hurrying to our screams, Mother always brought a butcher knife. Afterward, Josie and I would watch in fascinated horror as the creature's two halves, not dead, not impeded, crawled their separate ways.

"You can't deny we studied Mayans in my *World Book*." In my mind, I saw the two of us huddled on the dirt playground during recess, in secret, in danger, reading.

"Yeah. But you never had to *sneak* it," Rose said. "Your mom's too nice."

"The point I'm trying to make," I said, "is that we were children when we wanted to be astronomers and archaeologists. We're in junior high now, we're almost *thirteen*. Haven't we talked for two years about being popular?"

"*You've* talked, not me."

"Now is the time, Rose."

"Mexicans are never popular," she said.

It was the same thing she'd said last year when I'd urged her to run for cheerleader. Rose had taken my breath away at sixth grade Field Day, scissoring her legs to float over a bar higher than she was tall. When it was my turn, the men with whistles around their necks adjusted the bar. *Lower. No, lower.* I could feel their heavy hearts. I headed out, lumbering through the dirt in my saddle oxfords toward certain humiliation.

I could never be a cheerleader, but I would be a leader, I would be President. For weeks, on our walks home, I had practiced my speech. Loosening my blouse, shrugging a bare shoulder forward, I used my breathiest voice to speak into the microphone of my closed fist.

Student Body, Would you like to see . . . my *student body?* Over and over I breathed out *my student body.* Rose and I laughed until we couldn't walk straight, until our joyfulness staggered us and we bumped against each other, overcome by ourselves.

Now I was serious. "There's never been a girl running for President before. I'm going to be the first, and *you* are going to be my Vice President."

Block after block, I harangued Rose. We had to get organized, we had to make plans! She refused to be infected by my enthusiasm. "Why should I?" she said.

Two blocks from my house, we stepped off the sidewalk, out of the cottonwoods' shade, and onto a concrete bridge. Twenty feet below us lay the Rio Hondo. Depending on rainfall, the river was either swift-flowing or sluggish, but its bed was always rocky. Rose and I had played Mayan princesses beneath this bridge, braving dangerous shallows to gather bitterweed for food, holding each other safe when we spied a snapping turtle (my father said they had beaks that could take a man's thumb); and if the S-shape of a water moccasin flowed by, we screamed and scrambled up the bank. Now we were grown: we walked across the bridge, not under it.

I turned and walked backward in order to throw the full force of my will at her. I accused her of being cruel, of only pretending to be my friend, which I knew wasn't true, but how could I tell her the truth? That Caroline had partnered the two of us out of meanness? That I had no one else? In frustration, I grabbed her forearm. "Come on, Rose!"

She stopped walking and looked at me. I remember the moment: her brown eyes were streaked with black like pecan shells. "I have an idea," she said. Relief flooded my body. I felt I could touch the horizon, hold the blue mountain in my palm. Rose lifted her face, and her eyes shifted sideways. "Why don't *I* run for President and you run as *my* Vice President?"

Shocked, I loosened my hold. Rose jerked her arm free and headed into the vacant lot that ran parallel to the bridge. "Come on!" she hollered. "Let's walk the pipe."

I couldn't move. I was to be *Vice President*?

After a moment, I stomped over the curb. I stepped my way into the weeds, careful of my white loafers, my mind working to find its way back to an earlier time, one with a known future. I had played in the dirt and brambles of this lot for years, had walked across it uncountable times heading for the iron pipe that stretched between dirt embankments high above the river. I have no memory of rain in those years, and the lot, though sparsed with green, gave an overall impression of thirst. The river flavored the air with a hint of decay. Fish? Turtle? Definitely something dead. Did it matter? Glancing at the children gathered around the pipe at the edge of the embankment, I had a vague impression of small boys with buzz-cuts and short shirttails, none of whom I knew or cared to know.

And suddenly: Rose against the sky. She stood barefoot on the pipe, her dress, the blue pinafore with ruffles at the shoulders she had made last year in Home Ec. It was the same blue as the sky's blue, lighter than the mountain. The cottonwoods were shedding and airy fibers drifted, falling on Rose's loose dark hair, the ground, the unseen river below. She looked, with head held high and bare arms stretched out, like an angel lightly landing. On the bank, the little boys danced, arms waving their delight to the sky.

I went blind. My ears roared. I was overcome by Rose's grace, her bravery, her beauty—and then, suddenly, by fury. *She was doing this on purpose.* She knew I was too afraid to walk the pipe. I'd never not been too afraid. Every time a group gathered to walk it, I could only take a few steps before, terrified, I had to sit, straddle the pipe, and scoot backward to safety and shame. My face flamed. I hated myself. I hated Rose.

In my mind I heard *Over the mountain, across the sea, a girl waits for me.* A song from the Hit Parade. Could I sing Rose off the pipe, back to the bridge? *Cross over the river*—

I slammed my zippered notebook to the ground. Dust rolled out around it. My new loafers! I leaned over to wipe them, but hindered by my latex-and-bone waist cincher, I couldn't reach my socks—now constellated with tiny brown sticker-stars. My white socks! I stood up. Taking in as deep a breath as my waist cincher allowed, I leaned over again. A horny toad scuttled away beneath my hand, its barbed body almost invisible against the mottled rocks. I was not afraid of it—horny toads were pets, their flat backs allowing them to be housed in slender match boxes—but I was startled and stepping back, my heel snapped a weed-stalk. Sparrows, hopping unnoticed in the dirt, took off with a ballistic whoosh that sent my heart rocketing. The broken stalk had slung milky juice that stung my skin. I swiped my calf with one of my petticoats, but its heavy starch only smeared the sap. Sticky gunk eating my flesh! I took a big breath and bent until the brass hardware on my belt jabbed my solar plexus.

By the time I'd scrubbed my calf with my skirt and wiped my shoes and stood up, my head pounded with rushed-blood and colored shapes whirled behind my eyelids. When I'd steadied, I looked around. I'd always thought of this vacant lot as empty and flat—*vacant*—but I saw anthills humped here and there and deep-rutted patterns cut by circus wagons. This place-of-the-pipe was its own barbed, bristly kingdom. A cloud passed over the sun, and the earth deepened to black. The cloud-shadow crawled over the hills and gullies, making the ground itself look like it was moving. Never had the lot seemed so strange. Not strange like when the circus camped here: the white horses, the lion in his red cage, the elephant staked out on straw. That was sparkly magic; this was—I didn't know what, but I could feel it.

I caught a glimpse, something crawling out into the sudden shade. The cloud moved swiftly, and sunlight hit the body of the crawling thing: six inches of glistening green carapace moving on multiple orange legs. A centipede, its bite poison, its horrible blunt head pronged, its appearance sucking the warmth from the day.

The creature of my nightmares navigated the rocky ground with ease, and when the sun reappeared, the evil thing flicked itself into a deep crack in the earth. But that didn't change anything. It was there, underground, living its hateful life, hatching hundreds of nightmares just like it. I felt sick to my stomach. Around me, the innocent dirt was littered with rocks and broken glass, and caught in the tumbleweeds, metallic glints of gum wrapper. In a prickle of stubby weed—what?

A single red line of cellophane. Someone had opened a cigarette pack here. I squatted down to pick it out. At my feet, thin weed-lines suckered the ground, making star shapes in the dirt—dirt, which looked at closely, consisted of millions of minuscule grains. Dizzied by the multiplicity, I stood up, head lowered against the sun's dazzle.

After a moment, I saw the anthill. Graveled, cone-shaped, a fortress. Its laboring citizens went in and out of it in a businesslike manner: black legs and red-segmented bodies moving in orderly cooperation. I walked over and kicked the cone flat. Instantly, frenzied ants swarmed my loafer. I stamped madly. I felt as if ants were everywhere on my body: hot bites, thin flames of fire racing over my skin. I stamped and stamped, breathing raggedly, raising dust, dislodging a rock. When my breathing slowed, I saw that the rock had left a shallow grave that bore its exact shape. I was drawn to this indentation. Darker than the surrounding ground, it looked cool and damp. I crouched to touch it. Closing my eyes, I felt calm descend. I picked up the displaced rock, intending to tuck it back into its perfectly shaped home. It was a plain gray stone and fit in the palm of my hand. I stood, hefting it. I wasn't thinking anything. I looked at the blue sky. I looked at Rose against it. The wind had come up. Rose's dress floated, her hair floated, she floated. I couldn't breathe.

I yelled at the dancing boys to "Stop it! Just stop it!" They didn't even turn their heads.

I watched Rose circle toward me on little bare feet that never lost contact with the pipe. Her smile when she saw me was radiant. The little boys, oblivious to my furious shouts, watched Rose with total concentration, mouths open. She turned again, scarcely letting one foot precede the other. Her back with its buttons faced me. Above her, cloud castles to infinity. I wanted her to know how betrayed I felt, how left behind. I had been attacked, poisoned by ant venom! I was probably dying, and no one even noticed. These thoughts charged down out of my head into my arm and fist. The cottonwoods on the embankment flipped their leaves from silver to centipede-green.

I meant to ding the pipe, but the rock hit Rose square in the middle of her back. I screamed. Rose made no sound. The boys were one indrawn breath. In the perfect silence, against the blue sky, Rose wobbled. I watched her feet, saw them lose contact with the pipe and was already running before she fell. I ran up Pennsylvania Street, ran and ran, mind blank. At the corner of Penn and 13th, I slammed into my house and stood panting. All was silent and dim. The venetian blinds were drawn, and Josie lay stretched out on the couch with her head in Mother's lap. Every afternoon they watched the test pattern on TV while Mother massaged "scar cream" into Josie's sunken cheek. Soon, Liberace would materialize with his candelabra and cape. Josie lifted her legs so I could join them. I turned around and slammed out. I had left my notebook in the dirt.

I half-ran, half-walked, gulping air, tripping several times, losing a loafer, putting it back on, mind racing. What if I'd killed her? No, Rose couldn't die. Were those *sirens*? Police? An ambulance? I ran straight through the dirt and weeds to the pipe, heart and mind bursting. But the vacant lot was vacant. I couldn't believe it. I stood bent over, chest heaving. No little boys, no Rose—only my notebook in the dirt and white cotton fibers floating through silence.

I dragged myself home. Without a word, Josie raised her legs. Before I could slide under, Mother suggested I start practicing. It was late, but I could get in at least an hour before supper—and after we'd eaten, I could finish.

I noodled a few scales on the upright in the living room while in the den, Liberace whipped "Malagueña" into foam. I was barely conscious when I tiptoed into Bach's *Fifth French Suite*, my new piece. From the den, Mother said *Wrong*. She had perfect pitch and heard every blunder. I started over, but at the second transition, she said *Wrong*. I slammed my fists down on the keys and yelled at her. How was I supposed to practice when I was covered in ant bites! Mother hurried in, but her sympathetic sounds stopped when she understood ankles were involved. She suggested that if I had been wearing my saddle oxfords instead of—

I ran to my room and banged the door shut. I threw myself on my bed. When Mother knocked on my door, I yelled, I'm not here! She came in anyway.

She didn't want to fight, she said. I said nothing. She was sorry about my bites and was going to Kling's to get calamine lotion. I said nothing.

I lay in bed in my room with the door closed, alternately shivering and rigid with terror. Would Rose's parents call? No, they didn't have a phone. Would they come over, ring the doorbell? What about Rose's brother? Violent images swarmed my mind: dangerous young men in tee-shirts and jeans. Chains, knives, handguns. Blood.

After a while, I got up and undressed. As usual, my waist cincher had bitten bruises. Was Rose bruised? Was she bleeding? *Where was my mother?* To soothe myself I performed my cleansing Noxzema beauty routine, applied my flesh-colored pimple medicine, a color no flesh had ever been. I donned the heavy strap of my headgear, hooking its metal prongs onto my braces. The monster that looked back at me from the mirror was not unknown—I had glimpsed it earlier in the girls' bathroom on the third floor—but never had it stared at me with such awful eyes. There was a terrible person in the mirror.

My mother was gone a long time. The sun died before she returned to my room. She sat on the edge of my bed. I didn't open my eyes. She said she had something important to tell me. My mother had never come into my room in the dark to talk about something important. A great weight came down to rest on my chest. She had found out.

She said, "I saw Mrs. Kling at the drugstore, and she asked if it was really true you were running for President in the school elections?"

School elections? The monster in the pronged headgear flicked its eyes.

She said she and Daddy hadn't wanted to tell me yet, but she had told Mrs. Kling, who would for sure tell Louise, so now she had to tell me. I couldn't run for anything. It wouldn't be fair, I wasn't going to be living in Roswell in the ninth grade. Our family was moving to Texas.

The news spread fast, as news does, and swiftly, magically, I was absorbed back into the social flow. All the waist-cinched girls pretended they loved me, they had always loved me and were so sad I was moving. Only Rose was real. When she appeared with a bandaged left arm, she kept herself surrounded by fierce, sharp-eyed girls, the ones with stiff pomaded hair who wore their collars flicked up. She did not speak to me, she did not look at me. I was not there. I was nowhere.

The weeks passed. I finished learning the *Fifth French Suite*. School ended. Mother was preoccupied with packing, my father with sitting on wells. Nobody paid any attention when I put on my new pedal pusher outfit and white loafers and walked out: past the New Mexico Military Institute, past Mark Howell Elementary and Kling's Drugs, out to where the paved road became gravel, then dirt.

The woman who answered my knock was faded: brown clothes, no-color hair and eyes. She said nothing, just opened the blue door and looked at me through the screen.

"I'm Georgina."

The woman's eyes were shaped like Rose's but blank.

"*Georgina*," I repeated, the name carrying, I imagined, the weight of all the years of my friendship with Rose.

No response. The no-color eyes recollected something. "You the one, parents drive a Cadillac?"

My heart stuttered. I tried to say yes, but my braces had grown larger and sharper and my throat had closed up. Unable to speak, I nodded.

The woman closed the door.

I had used up my courage walking there. I stood staring at the cracks crazing the door's blue paint, trying not to break my heart over something Rose's stupid mother had said.

When Rose appeared, she didn't step outside but stood in the narrow space between the blue door and the screen. She wore red shorts and a sleeveless white blouse. Her arm was no longer bandaged. I couldn't see her feet.

I had prepared a speech but only managed a strangled, "I'm sorry."

She said nothing.

"I never meant to hit you."

Rose's pecan-shell eyes were unfathomable. How was it possible we had nothing to say to each other?

"I'm moving," I said finally.

"I know," Rose said, then she laughed but not really. The sound of it made me turn away.

"Wait," Rose said. "Got something for you." She disappeared.

A child squeezed in front of the blue door and smashed its face against the screen. Rose shoved it back into the darkness when she reappeared. She opened the screen and held out a rectangular piece of cellophane-wrapped cardboard. "So you can think of me sometimes when you're in Texas."

My eyes were busy with Rose's graceful bare feet when she said, "It's only plastic."

I stood on the hard-packed dirt of Rose's yard, clutching the pink rosary, swearing I would be back to see her, nothing would keep me away. But what I didn't understand was that Roswell, New Mexico, was an in-between place, a green spot lost in hundreds of empty brown miles, and that if you were lucky enough to get out, you never went back—at least, that's what my mother said. So when we moved to Texas and got a new life, we never went back to Roswell. My family lived as if we had no past at all, as if we had sprung, fully formed, from Fort Worth's brick boulevards. And it's because of this, I think, that time has not changed Rose and me. It's been a lifetime, but, even now, I can summon our lost world.

The afternoon sky is high above Mark Howell Elementary and on the horizon, a single blue mountain sings. Our ragtag Brownie troop has chanted about the smiles we have in our pockets; we have sucked our popsicle sticks bare. My mother sits on the school steps in her matching sweater set and pearls, and my little sister leans her ruined cheek against her. Mother's nyloned legs are crossed just so and she smokes and nonchalantly dazzles Mrs. Kling. Mrs. Kling's daughter, Louise, hangs with the rest of the troop, screaming in the dust cloud of the moving merry-go-round. Only Rose and I hide behind the bicycle rack. I am resplendently official in a belted brown uniform.

Rose wears her everyday clothes with a glint of golden trefoil stuck to her blouse and a bobby-pinned beanie on her head. We squat on hard-packed dirt, peer out between steel bars. There is the soft feel of Rose's steady breath on my arm. We are Mayan princesses, desperate to escape the evil priest who wants to rip out the bloody jewel of our heart. Sometimes we are racing through a rain forest to elude the evil Mayan king who wants to marry us. But always we are running.

At some shared inner signal, we take off. Rose's sandals only skim the surface. I am heavier, my saddle oxfords clumsy. Rose is ahead, and it looks like I am chasing her.

Camouflage

IN THE LATE AFTERNOON, INSIDE THE SILENCE OF THE FOREST—THE ONLY movement the looping flash of a cardinal's now-here-now-there—a man in jungle camouflage steps out of the wall of woods. He's cradling a shotgun, his face painted to match his coveralls. I look toward Jane's tidy backpack twenty yards ahead. Jane hikes point, the one who leads the way. I hike shepherd. The shepherd brings up the rear, catches strays, makes sure everyone's safe. Gracie hikes between us. Her pack is large, lopsided, wagging from side to side. The three of us have been at it all day. The trail that plunged down in the early morning mist, rocky and steep and ankle-deep in fog-damp leaves, is now sun-dappled and wide, almost a road. Wilderness surrounds us—thousands of acres of pine and hickory and oak—but the trail has been trafficked by a bulldozer, rutted. The man has materialized at the edge of this trail, facing me.

I don't move. I pitch my voice loud, but I don't yell. "*Jane?*"

A silent space, then Jane sings out—"Hello!"—and within half a minute she's sailed in between me and the man. I move to stand beside her. Gracie stays where she is.

The man is as tall as I am with a long, dark-painted face; his eyes, behind the stiff paint, the living blue of a gas flame. I avoid the eyes and concentrate on the camo. My mind moves down and in like a microscope, closer and closer, until the spots on his coveralls transform into single-celled protozoa.

"Hello," Jane repeats, holding her hand out. "My name's Jane Templeton, and this is Alice Straw." She might have been greeting some newcomer at the Opera's Sunday matinee.

I retract the microscope and focus on Jane. I don't let my face show what I feel; I maintain opaqueness. Jane's fifty-one years old, but her fine profile, lifted up with a luminous smile, shows few wrinkles; her silver hair is neat in a girlish headband. Next to the hunter's painted face, she's gracious and civilized, radiating order.

The man lowers his gun and shakes Jane's hand with his dark-painted one. "Claude Alberts."

"We're with a large church group," Jane says, her voice innocent as birdsong. "We got so busy talking we got separated from the men a couple miles back. You haven't seen them, have you?"

I feel my mouth quiver with laughter. But I keep it in a straight line and only slant a quick glance toward Jane. I don't allow my gaze to linger, but I take in her puffed-sleeved shirt with its front darts and how it's tucked into her slim, belted waist.

Claude Alberts shakes his head.

"They must be farther ahead than I thought," Jane says. "What're you hunting?"

The man lays his gun on the ground and unhooks a wooden box from his belt. "Turkey," he says. He hands the contraption to Jane. "First weekend of turkey season."

Jane turns the box over with her graceful hands. "Will you look at this!" After showing me a groove that's been whittled to hold a rubber band, she turns and calls Gracie to join us.

Gracie walks up, noisy with gear: a Nikon on a wide woven strap, steel binoculars around her neck, aluminum canteen at her waist.

"Can you believe this is the first weekend of turkey season, and I didn't know it?" Jane says. "But then, I don't know how we got separated from the rest of our Bible Study. Somehow the men got ahead of us."

"*What?*" Gracie says, shifting the metal load on her chest.

"They just walked off and left us," I say.

Jane holds out the wooden box that is Claude's turkey caller. "Alice, look how it's made to hang from his belt." Her joy in its craftsmanship is genuine. She insists that Claude show her how to work it, and her curiosity—its lightness and warmth—brings the rigid box to life. Together, she and the box make fine-sounding gobbles. Her delight invokes ours. Soon we're all grinning.

When we part, old friends, Claude promises to keep a lookout for the rest of our party. But where should he tell our men we'll be?

Oh, he wouldn't know it, Jane says. It's an obscure campsite, off the trail, where Caney Creek drops and there's a small waterfall.

But what a coincidence. Claude knows exactly where she's talking about. Three months ago a road was cut through from the other side. Blacktopped, too. He and his buddies can drive right up to the river.

Claude melts back into the endless wall of trees, and I turn to Gracie. "Don't worry. He doesn't know. We've camped there a lot and never seen a soul."

"It's hidden," Jane says. "We can bathe nude in the waterfall."

"I'm not worried," Gracie says.

I eye her, standing in the middle of the trail, hands on hips, loaded down. She's a head shorter than I am, but a decade younger. I'm a hushed blonde; Gracie's dark, and her spiky hair glistens with gel. Her olive-green Bermudas, paired with lace-up Vietnam jungle boots, couldn't differ more from my starched safari cloth.

"I coach softball, remember?" Gracie says. "Get me a bat-sized branch and that guy'll be the one with the worry."

"We can't have that kind of talk," Jane says in her elementary-school-teacher voice. Her blue eyes seek mine. She doesn't know Gracie; I'm the one who invited her on this trip. *She has an amazing voice, Janie. We'll put on a show that'll knock your socks off.*

"Is this another rule?" Gracie says. "Like the one about watches?"

Jane and I had been posing in the morning mist by the "Ouachita Wilderness" sign at the trailhead when Jane spied Gracie's chrome watch. "Oh," she'd said. "A watch. We never wear watches when we backpack, do we, Alice?"

Gracie had lowered her Nikon. "I always wear a watch." She'd held out her arm, the arm that she'd called "hirsute" like her Sicilian father's. "I never *don't* wear it." The insistent digital face flashed the passing hour, minute, second.

"The wilderness has its own time," Jane said.

I'd used my harassed, get-this-lab-cleaned-up-now tone. "Just take it off."

Gracie had turned, a fast movement, forcing me to step back in order not to get swiped by her backpack. A dislodged rock clattered down the incline. "Messing up your private party, am I, Al?" Gracie said, emphasizing the shortness of the name, the final consonant.

"There's nothing private about this weekend," Jane said. "I was happy when Alice said a friend of hers wanted to come."

Jane had turned to start down the trail, and after a moment, Gracie had scraped off her expandable wristband and shoved a fistful of chrome into a side pocket. I'd motioned her toward the trail and had watched her climb down, noisy and awkward, her borrowed backpack lurching sideways with every step. I, trusted companion assigned to be rear guard, had also been unsteady, my vision blurry, my boots slipping on wet leaves, sending rocks skittering down toward the shapes who moved below me in the fog.

Jane's husband plays tournament-level tennis, but he doesn't like to hike, so the two of us usually camp alone or with Sierra Club groups—which was where we'd first met three years ago, on a bus headed for Big Bend. Why had I arranged for Gracie to join us on this trip? Among the hundred women in the Dallas Women's Chorus, she had never stood out. I sang alto, she soprano, so we'd never practiced together. We only met five months before when we'd been paired at a tryout for a Mozart duet from *Così fan tutte*. Gracie, I discovered, had an extraordinary gift, and the harmony of our voices had been a thing of wonder. At the September concert, our duet had brought the house down. Was it all vanity, then? My desire to entertain Jane obscuring my usual caution?

Throughout the morning, Jane had stopped often to turn back toward the novice with words of encouragement or warnings of loose rock, and now in the late afternoon, in the middle of the almost-road, she speaks to Gracie in the slow, calm voice she might use with her third graders.

"There'll be no need for a bat—or any kind of weapon. We come to the wilderness for renewal. We'll convert her, won't we, Alice?"

Gracie stands with hands on hips, and what shows clearly in the daylight that was never obvious in the artificial light of the rehearsal hall is her delineated musculature, her manly build. I look to see if Jane has noticed Gracie's lack of feminine attributes, but Jane is already walking point.

"Why're you acting like this?" I say.

She shrugs. "I'm Sicilian." She shifts her stance, adjusts her grip on an imaginary bat and makes a small flick with her wrists. "She has no idea, does she?"

"I won't tolerate any rudeness to Jane," I say.

Gracie's black eyes go flat. She drops her batting stance.

I don't explain that my job is to protect my friend, to keep her safe, that's she's too innocent to be polluted. Jane has twenty years on me, but not only do I look older—I had a hysterectomy six years ago and lack the hormones for youth—I have knowledge of worlds she doesn't know exist.

"I invited you to sing," I say. "We'll have supper, we'll sing our duet. Tomorrow afternoon, we'll be back in Dallas."

By the time the three of us hike off the regular trail and into our idyllic, undiscovered site, we see three pickup trucks and a bullet-shaped silver trailer parked seventy-five yards away, across a flowing cataract of Caney Creek. The vehicles stand on leaf-covered ground, spaced amid tall trees, and behind them, barely visible through the forest, gleams blacktop. The only sound in this remote hollow of the Ouachita Wilderness is the rushing water, but to me, our place feels defiled. It's too late to keep hiking—even if this spot weren't a dead end.

"We've no choice," Jane says.

My job is to gather wood while Jane lets Gracie help her set up camp. I'm an expert wood-gatherer and usually wander far to find deadfall, dragging in huge limbs, like a hunter with his kill, to Jane's shouts of celebration. This afternoon, clumsy with unease, I get tangled in a thick muscadine vine on my first foray. I decide to stay close to the campsite. I gather what's available on the near ground.

Jane, always the teacher, can't get the tents up without showing Gracie the secret life around us: a tiny cricket frog invisible behind a fiddler fern, the poisonous mushroom hidden beneath a greenbrier's tangle; and when she comes across strange scat, she shows the presence they betray. They're owl pellets, powdery pieces of regurgitated fur, which she breaks open to reveal the fragile skeleton of a mouse.

"Remember when we saw the barred owl on the Upper Kiamichi?" I say.

"Oh, yes. Wasn't it thrilling?"

It had been more than thrilling, seeing the owl's round, feathered face, its huge wings working in a steady pumping rhythm as it flew toward us, low, silent and mysterious, out of the foggy twilight. I didn't know what it was, but I could feel its searching intelligence. Beneath the surface of the world I thought I knew: something more. Everything I know about birds Jane taught me.

"Maybe this scat is a barred owl's," she says to Gracie. "*Who cooks for you/who cooks for you*—that's their call. Maybe we'll get to hear it tonight! We'll listen closely, won't we?"

Jane's curiosity and childlike delight in the natural order work to clear away my sense of dread. There's no ambiguity about Jane, no murkiness. When I'm with her, the world is transformed. The light changes; objects—rocks, trees, leaves—shimmer. I'm able to move into this shimmer, wrapped in the musty autumn smell of oak leaf humus, the resinous tang of pine. I stack armloads of dead branches, start the fire with pine straw and broken twigs, and patiently feed it until it's strong—all this before Jane and Gracie get the first tent poles in the ground.

Normally Jane and I would set up our tent on the flat leaf-covered area near the fire ring, but this afternoon we hide it on a slanting hillside in a little thicket of oak and sweet gum. We don't talk about this; we just do it. We are as one in our instinct for caution, but there's no need to worry Gracie, so we say nothing. Like cricket frogs, the hunters are invisible, but their presence is felt. The plan is for Jane and me to share our usual tent, with Gracie in another, borrowed one.

"But we might all sleep in the same tent," Jane says.

"Too crowded," Gracie says.

"No matter what," Jane says, "we better stay dressed."

As we lash aluminum poles together, Jane chatters about the luxuriousness of sleeping naked in a down bag and how she wants Gracie to experience it—but not tonight. I know that she's only trying to convert her to one of the pleasures of backpacking, but my face flames. When I try to make a joke of it, Gracie looks at me with a mixture of disgust and amusement and shakes her head. I put myself behind glass, a tiny insect husk pinned with others of my kind.

When we pitch Gracie's tent, Jane and I work silently, in tandem. Because we're on a slope, we site the entrance so she'll be able to sleep with her head higher than her legs, which means that she'll have to crawl up into the domed space. Our tent is basically flat. This isn't intentional, but I wait for Gracie to complain: *Is this another rule? Make the newcomer suffer?* Instead, as the three of us hook up her fly-cover, she begins humming, an exquisite thread of silver sound.

My body relaxes. I tell Jane how she amazes me: she's so brave—walking up to that painted apparition. "Next to him, you were certain proof of *Homo sapiens'* evolution," I say. I watch her laugh. She always tilts her head back, tosses her silvery hair, and her cheeks lift, curving up to downslant her eyes.

Gracie starts in about the stupid hunter with his painted face and his stupid camouflage and how immoral it is to kill anything, even stupid turkeys, and she's moving on to the stupidity of men in general, when I shoot her a look. She shuts up.

"Wild turkeys are extremely smart and hard to hunt," Jane says. She explains that she told Claude our names because according to a lecture she'd heard, you're supposed to do everything you can to personalize a dangerous situation, to make someone who threatens you know you're human too.

Occasionally, interspersed in the activity of hiding our tents, Jane cups her mouth and pretends she's hollering for her husband: "Ray Templeton. Come help with these tent poles!" Then Gracie, without a husband to call for, joins in, yelling toward the river, "Joey Castellano, bring more wood!" My vocal chords refuse to call out for a nonexistent husband. I am unable to give life to any Bible study kin. Finally, with the tents up, Jane and Gracie are laughing so hard over our church-group masquerade that they collapse on the logs around the fire ring. I watch them, but I'm not laughing. My membership in church groups cannot be shrugged on, a disguise, easily worn then discarded. Born Baptist in Waco—doesn't that say it all?

I pick up my water bottle and leave the campsite to walk down to the river. I wander on the no-path through the timeless evening, and the old flicker-and-cramp in the gut I knew as a child accompanies me. Our church, The True Vine Missionary Baptist Church, was a one-room clapboard building with red double doors on the I-35 access road. In my mind I hear those doors clang shut, I see the lights abruptly extinguished. I am six years old, sandwiched safely between my parents. It is winter: sounds of heavy breathing; acrid smell of close bodies in wool clothing. The blackness in the room spreads, becomes the blackness of my mind. Behind me, from the back of the room, a drum begins to beat. Terrified, I fumble for my father's big, rough hand with its web of skin-fissures, its broken nails. A deep voice cries out, *I am the true vine, you are the branches.* Over and over the drum beats and the voice calls out from the dark, *I am the true vine, you are the branches.* On the altar, candles flicker to life. I scramble out of the pew and run, the first to be saved, toward the light.

It was a scandal. I was too young. But I had run toward the light and after that, what? Growing up, church three times a week until I graduated from Baylor. Sixteen *years* hearing about the sins of the flesh. Even natural flesh—Adam and Eve, the way God intends—sinful. And what about unnatural flesh?

The natural order of things has always comforted me, and now, on the way to the river, I linger—turning to touch a bright leaf, a pincushion of moss, stopping to look up at patches of orange sky.

I feel the wilderness all around me, its secret breathing life, and slowly my insides unclench. The sound of the river is big, and I jump from rock to rock until I am surrounded by the music of its rush. The water is effervescent, bubbling against the rocks. I am squatting, filling up my plastic bottle, enfolded by the joyous, when I look up. Across from me, hunkering at eye level, a turkey hunter—not Claude, but another. I have not heard him, have not seen him approach. He has simply appeared, painted, grinning, snag-toothed.

I bring my fear back to camp with me, but I don't speak it—not even to Jane. The shepherd doesn't scare the flock. As night comes on, the fear comes alive. From the men's camp across the river, music and laughter thread through the trees—gradually dwarfing the water's murmur. The three of us have hiked nine miles into the wilderness bringing only small flashlights, but across the river the curtained windows in the bullet-shaped trailer glow, and a spotlight has been turned on above the barbeque grill. The men seem to be taking turns coming out of the trailer to cook on the grill, and I know that inside the trailer, behind the glowing curtains, a lot of whiskey is being drunk. I know about men and hidden whiskey.

Last spring, Jane and I had shared leisurely cocktails by the fire after a waterfall frolic. But tonight we don't bathe; we start right in on dinner. I pull out the dented and blackened coffee pot that sits in the fire to boil water; Jane produces the torn plastic envelope that contains the collapsible grill. I brought the steak we'll share; Jane, two potatoes wrapped in foil. I brought the butter; Jane, sour cream. I brought a half bottle of wine decanted into a plastic flask; Jane, a tiny cosmetic container of Scotch.

I see Gracie watching us.

We sit on logs around the fire listening to the sounds of men living it up beneath an eye of light that becomes more insistent as the woods darken. My body has grown heavy with dread, but when Gracie pulls out her monster steak and two-liter bottle of red wine, I laugh. For Jane's sake, I attempt lightness. I tell Gracie she'd better get more wood to cook that steak. I say she'll have to hike the bottle out, and if she thought it was bad walking *down* with a heavy pack...

Jane says, "Leave her alone. She'll know better next time."

Gracie and I look at each other across the campfire. She makes a wintery grimace that might pass for a smile in some cold-blooded species. We both know there won't be a next time. In the five months I've known her, practicing twice a week for our duet, we became friends. This has been undone in a single day. How is it possible? We've so much in common: both high school teachers, music for both of us a passion. We'd been companionable, going out after rehearsals for Mexican food. She'd even invited me to her birthday party so we could sing for her parents.

In the waning light, Gracie's spiked hair and black eyes are sharp-edged against the net of branches behind her. There'd been a brown net the night of her party too, a macramé weaving that draped the entrance from ceiling to floor of her tiny dining room, and behind this net, her little white-haired Sicilian parents and her four closest friends. We'd drunk tequila shots and posed for photos. We'd sung Happy Birthday, eaten cake. Did Gracie and I sing our famous, comic duet? We did. It might have been our best rendition, our voices melting together: duped sisters toasting their disguised lovers with Cuervo shots.

After Gracie's parents left, we switched to fifties music. We danced and sang, until birthed into rhythm, inspired, Gracie had shrugged out of her shirt. Then everyone—all women younger than me, none of whom I knew—either shimmied or shrugged her shirt off. Gracie shouted, "For freedom!" and ripped off her bra, and we all shouted, "For freedom!" and did the same. We drank more tequila shots to cement our bond with women around the world, then an elfin child-woman with pixie-cut pink hair touched my breast. And that had been the start.

At rehearsal the next week I'd barely looked at Gracie, but she only asked blandly if I'd had a good time. When I retreated into microscopic remoteness, she never mentioned the party again, and gradually, I grew easy around her. Looking at her now, I see this ease has been an illusion. In the trembling light of the fire, the naked branches behind Gracie morph into a knotted macramé net. Cold slithers through my gut.

We cook and eat our steaks, but as the noise from the men's camp grows louder, we grow more and more quiet. We clean up silently. Their rowdiness gradually subsides, and the single eye of light disappears. When the trailer's generator finally cuts off, no one would know the men's camp is there. All is dark and still. There's only the crackling sound of our fire and, beyond that, in the invisible vastness, the cricket frogs' thin scrape. I had imagined this evening filled with music and laughter—the *Cosi* duo performing beneath the stars and Jane enraptured—instead we huddle silently around a tiny fire. I'd anticipated the Milky Way's bright flow through my veins, but there are no stars, no moon. Blackness rises up around us, only the flames of our campfire lick the face of the night.

"It's been a long day," I say. "I vote for bed."

"Let's not let these guys ruin our trip," Jane says. "You know something unexpected always happens. Snow storms in August, and—remember that flash flood in Big Bend?"

"I agree with Jane," Gracie says. "We can't let men determine what we do. We came to sing, let's sing."

"No," Jane says. "The men have to get up early. We can't disturb them. It's against wilderness etiquette."

"I agree with Jane," I say, putting my arm through hers.

"Of course you agree with Jane," Gracie says.

A silent stutter of time, then, "Do you really think we should let others stop us from singing our song? I mean, come on, Al."

I say nothing, but I realize I'm feeling the wine and curse myself. I take my arm out of Jane's and straighten my spine.

"I do think if you sing softly, it would be all right," Jane says. "We're far enough—"

"Let's sing our song, Al. What do you say?"

"Why do you keep calling her 'Al'?" Jane says.

Gracie stares across the fire at us but says nothing. The flickering light glints off the spikes of her hair. "Good question," she says. She jumps up and slaps at her butt with both hands, shedding dirt and pine needles. "Hold that thought, Jane. I'll be right back."

She walks out of the circle of light and disappears in the darkness. The crunching sound of dry leaves moves in the direction of the tents. Neither Jane nor I stir, then she takes my arm and moves close, the warmth of our bodies a guard against chill.

When I met Jane on the Sierra Club bus to Big Bend, I was a stone. No hormones, drained of juice. A ninth-grade biology teacher for whom all magic had leaked out: a frog merely something to dissect, an object smelling of formaldehyde. I'd adopted protective coloring to ensure survival, but I hadn't been able to protect myself against me. The cancer in my uterus was hate, I think—my own teeth tearing up my guts. Cause and effect, the natural order of things. Three years ago at Easter, the natural order of things had brought spring to Big Bend. The Earth had tilted; tiny wildflowers and flowering cactus had burst forth from Chisos Basin's extrusion of lava and rock. When this beauty struck the tuning fork that is Jane Templeton and she sounded her always-clear note, I'd resounded in sympathetic vibration. I'd come back to life.

"She's surely impulsive," Jane says, leaning into me. "I think you should sing your song. It seems to mean an awful lot to her."

"Yeah," I say, feeling Jane's vest, poufy and soft, against mine.

"Sorry I didn't check about hunting season. It's messed things up, hasn't it?"

I don't say anything. I barely hear her. I've melted into the fire.

Gracie crunches in from the dark to stand across the fire ring from us. I squint up against the smoke. Her Vietnam jungle boots and thick legs in their Bermuda shorts appear in the light, but her upper body is hidden in shadow. "I brought these for you, Al. They're doubles. In the bottom of my pack, so I couldn't get at them last night."

She holds up something. I can't see what—a handful of something against the black night—but in her arm's movement, her chrome watch flashes and my gut cramps.

"Let's go on to bed," I say. "The night's ruined."

"Jane, you know," continues Gracie, "of course you know—*everyone* knows—what it means to be in the Dallas Women's Chorus?"

I go rigid, unbreathing. Gracie's going against all etiquette, breaking every unspoken rule. I feel Jane's mind touch her question. It moves lightly, like a long-legged fly on a stream, leaving no imprint. She slips her arm out from mine and sits up.

"Al, I only want to help you live an authentic—"

"No," I say, and I'm on my feet now. I've realized what the "doubles" are.

Jane stands too. She walks around the fire ring to stand between us, the apex of an equilateral triangle. She looks at me; she looks at Gracie. She examines each of us in turn. So different we are: Gracie, squat, darkly bristled; me, slender, smoothly blonde.

Back and forth, Jane's head moves as she takes us in. Her hair is molten silver, her eyes transparent in the firelight.

"You understand, don't you, Jane?" Gracie says. "I call her 'Al' because that's what everyone in the Chorus calls her."

"Alice?" Jane says. She looks as if she's been thrown a ball she has no idea how to catch.

I squat down off our log: I can't look at her. I'm squatting, looking at the mixture of pine needles and dirt, the blackened stones of the fire ring, while every nerve in my body shouts, *Run.*

"Admit it," Gracie says. "Just say it. Go on."

I shake my head. I don't look up. I feed shredded bark into the fire.

"Quit it," Jane says. "We don't badger people."

Always the teacherly We. But now I am "people," not Alice.

I sink back onto my heels. I scrutinize the fire's interior. It snaps and pops. One of the support limbs burns through, and crashing inward, scatters sparks into the night. I look up. I see Gracie's arm, winking chrome, reach out. I see Jane walk to take what she offers. I want to tackle them both, feed the photos of the birthday party to the flames. I try to go down and in to safety, but putting Jane under the microscope never works. She is irreducible. I go up and out instead. I circle, dangerously high, watching three *Homo sapiens* around a fire—a fire surrounded by a wilderness in the state of Arkansas, which is an arbitrary amount of land surrounded by other United States of America, itself an arbitrary designation for the center of a landmass on a small planet circling an insignificant star. By the time I reach the outer edges of the known universe—all the time watching Jane—she's looked through the photos and her mind no longer seems to be a long-legged fly.

I return from my planetary excursion. High above, an owl sounds its trembling call, but around the campfire: silence. I stand up and leave the light to walk out into the darkness. No one says *Don't go.* I listen for Jane's voice, but I don't hear it. I hear leaves crunch, but I can't see them. The ground slopes upward.

Our tent is a triangular darkness. Near it is Gracie's dark dome. We've hidden them well. I unzip the tent with shaking hands. I manage to tie the flaps back, but when I lean over to untie my boots, my hands won't work. I sit down. My feet seem to have grown, my boots are enormous—huge insensate *things* at the bottom of my legs. I grab at their double-knotted laces, but my eyes are blind. My fingers seek to feel the knots' undoing, but my jerky efforts only strengthen them. I scrabble to get a boot off without loosening its lace. I yank and pull until my ankle is rubbed raw, but the double-stitched, reinforced leather I paid dearly for does its job.

I crawl inside the tent, dragging my huge, heavy feet. I couldn't undress with my boots on, even if I wanted to. I'm not letting myself think or feel. I've put my brain in a specimen jar high on a shelf where it's safe. I stick the clown feet into my sleeping bag and lie down to wiggle in. I sit up, half in, half out of the bag. My body recalls its bedtime routine: put clean clothes inside the tent for morning; cover the backpack with a black leaf bag, otherwise tomorrow morning everything will be wet and—

Tomorrow morning.

I shake myself like a dog shedding water, then jerk into the bag. The tent's darkness holds me close, and in the stillness, as I zip up, fury rips through me. How could I have been so stupid as to bring Gracie! The zipper's sharp teeth chew my down vest. I sit up and tear the vest off, shredding the silence in short, even snaps. I fling it so hard toward the back of the tent that the structure quivers. I don't care. Let it fall down around me. Let the forest burn, fires rage.

What about Jane?

I struggle to hold off the thought of her, to escape the encroaching grief. Given the coffin-shape of the bag, it isn't easy to wrestle myself onto my side, and once there, my nose touches the taut, slanting nylon of the tent wall. I squirm back over through rising waves of panic. I'm alone, encased, mummified. After a moment, when the ocean of my pounding blood calms, I hear low voices coming from the direction of the campfire. I roll onto my stomach and peer out through the mesh opening. My eyes are tired; they see only a hint of firelight in the far darkness. Could I crawl out on my belly to eavesdrop? Creep through the night like some military maniac? But I would have to drag my enormous feet and the leaves would certainly crunch. I would be caught.

The thoughts of crawling and being caught occupy the surface of my mind, but below them, all the time, a deeper mind turns. Over and over I see us, a film strip unspooling in my head. Jane and Alice, Alice and Jane: best friends, snuggling up against each other on Sierra Club buses, massaging tired necks and shoulders, wriggling into sleeping bags at night. *Philia*, not *eros*. When she comes to bed, we'll talk. Without Gracie around to scare her, Jane will understand.

I lie down with this sliver of hope to wait for her.

When Gracie crawls over me into the tent, my face burns with shame. I close my eyes against her flashlight wagging its beam around on the walls. She clanks and grunts; her breath is hard, uneven. I relax my body and my breathing. I go down and in. *Where is Jane?* The immensity of my loss rises up within me. I cover my mouth to muffle my sounds.

When Gracie is a soft-breathing lump of darkness, I rise up onto my elbows and look out. I wait, and the forest waits with me. I have a sense of a sentient wilderness. I hear trees groan, bramble creak, creatures scuttling through underbrush. I feel the whole of it, its thousands of square miles. In the dark, it breathes: remote, unmoved. The night deepens and grows colder. I wait. I look out, but I never see Jane come to bed.

I raise my head, instantly alert. Outside the tent, it's earliest morning, misty, gray. Because the flaps are tied back, I see a turkey hunter walk silently into our campsite. I lower my head, lie flat and still, my eyes level with his boots. The tent's nylon overhang drips moisture, one slow drop, and after a while, another. The camouflaged legs above the boots pause—a drip extends, lengthens, falls; another drip—then the legs move away, up the hill, and the whole hunter comes into view. Now another pair of boots and camouflaged legs appear in the triangular frame. Then another and another. There are more of them than I'd imagined: wraiths with dark-painted faces moving with long guns through our camp into the forest. Their breath smokes in the cold. The early morning surfaces shift; shadows change, become indistinct, undo. No shapes hold. It's a world of apparition and danger. The hunters are almost invisible, mists, ragged fog, nothing but momentary condensations on a rocky terrain that will retain no imprint of their passing. Their boots make no sound on the dew-wet leaves as they walk up, into the unknown day.

Eat You Up

THEY DANCED INTO THE WAITING ROOM LAUGHING—LUCY SKIPPING BACK-
ward, squirting a water gun; Susan trying to catch the squirts in her
mouth. When she saw children in wheelchairs, Susan quit laughing,
and this made Lucy stop too. The room was enormous, green-tiled,
sunlit, and quiet except for the falling-water sound of a central
fountain. Lucy ignored Susan's proffered hand and dropped back
to walk behind her. "Don't turn around, Mom. Don't look at me,"
she said, pretending as always they weren't connected, that she was
an autonomous being.

After Susan signed in, the two of them sat in orange plastic chairs
against a far wall. Rather, Susan sat. Lucy climbed in, then slid out of
her chair. Climb in, slide out. Susan handed Lucy a favorite picture
book, read so often that *I'll eat you up—I love you so* had become a
family saying. Lucy promptly dumped the book on the floor and
began running and sliding—run, run, run, long slide—across the
tile floor. Susan got up, escorted Lucy back to her chair, poked the
picture book at her again, and sat down with her own book, one
from her dissertation bibliography, *Synchronicity: Acausal Patterns in
Time*. When she glanced up, Lucy was across the room using a small
wooden crutch to turn one-armed cartwheels.

Susan had wrestled the crutch away and was handing it to its owner
when Lucy snatched it back. She ran, planted the crutch tip, flipped
her legs—and Susan had her. Lucy went limp. Susan laid her down
on the green tile and walked the crutch back to a small, blond boy in

a full-body cast. After apologizing to the boy's tight-lipped mother, she hauled Lucy standing, gripped her shoulders, and steered her with both hands to her chair. She picked up Lucy's book, then her own; she found her place. Lucy begged to go look at the fountain. Susan said no. Lucy begged. Susan said no. A drop of time.

A voice called out "Lucy Wheeler?" A young man—large and soft—stood at the edge of the room, reading from a clipboard. "Lucy Wheeler?" he called.

In the center of the room, wheelchairs clustered around the fountain, the children in them laughing as they watched Lucy prance around the ledge. Susan walked to fetch her. Before Lucy jumped down, she bent and flicked water at a boy who was all sweet, upward-looking face, no torso, humped back. *Please don't go*, the boy called, as Susan led Lucy away.

The young man with the clipboard wore a white coat and paisley bellbottoms. A cap of brown hair skimmed his eyebrows; his nametag said "Aide." Susan knelt down before Lucy. "I'll be right here," she said. "I'll be waiting for you." Lucy put her hand in the aide's. Down the long hall she skipped beside him, turning backward every few skips to wave at her mother. Skip forward, turn backward. Lucy's scores on the kindergarten readiness test had been surprisingly low. The teachers at the Unitarian Co-op had decided that a hearing loss would explain the scores, but The St. James School refused to admit her without additional testing. Private testing centers had long waitlists, so Susan had brought her to the only place in town available on short notice: Dallas Scottish Rite Hospital for Children.

With Lucy gone, the room settled into itself. The green tile, the falling-water sound, the light quivering on the green walls made it an aquatic world. In these depths, people moved slowly. They seemed heavy, weighted into the orange molded-chairs. Susan experienced a physical change in her body, a lightening of limb, a firming of muscle. She'd danced in here with only a purse and a paperback, but the other mothers carried voluminous bags of magazines, handiwork, food. They were sunk down here. She knew no one, but the other mothers chatted quietly among themselves as they sat knitting or needlepointing. Her daughter had skipped away, but the other children—the ones with lolling heads, twisted limbs—lay passively in strollers and wheelchairs.

Two hours later, Lucy dashed out, scattering the denseness. Susan stood up and Lucy jumped into her arms, wrapping legs around her waist, arms around her neck, pressing against her—so tightly that she could feel Lucy's little heart pounding. "How'd it go, my darling?" she whispered.

"She didn't like me, Mom," Lucy whispered.

"Of course she liked you."

A white-coated woman, redfaced and breathless, arrived. "Told you *not* to run!" she said. She stopped to catch her breath. She could have been a Teutonic opera star, Wagnerian; the nametag going up and down on her impressive bosom said "Psychologist." Beneath her pancake makeup, barely visible, a dim protozoa-shaped stain on her right cheek.

"You understand. The tile is slick. Don't want anybody getting hurt."

Susan ran her hand down the knots of Lucy's perfect little spine.

"I'm Mrs. Witherspoon, the psychologist who saw Lucy," the woman said, still working to breathe. "Will you put her down so we can visit?"

Susan sent Lucy to find a Coke machine and sat in the chair indicated, all the time watching her daughter move. Why had she never noticed how strong and perfect Lucy's legs were? How smoothly her muscles slid beneath her skin?

"Mrs. Wheeler? Did you hear me? I said I couldn't get her to sit still."

"How well I know!" Susan laughed, thinking she would make Mrs. Witherspoon laugh. She was good at making people laugh. But the stain on the psychologist's cheek didn't move and her furry, bleached mustache stayed straight.

"She wasn't able to work any of the puzzles, and her score—"

"What about her hearing? Her teachers thought—"

"Her hearing's perfect. You have puzzles at home, don't you?"

"Sure—Well, to tell the truth, I'm not much on puzzles."

Mrs. Witherspoon's bosom seemed to double in size. She studied her clipboard. "Lucy's score on the Gates-MacGinitie perceptual was in the eighteenth percentile—"

Behind Mrs. Witherspoon, from across the room: Lucy, carrying a Coke. Susan grinned. It was so obviously a mistake they were here. They had wandered in by accident. They were so lucky, so unencumbered. All she carried was her purse. No wheelchair, no bags of knitting. Joy, an actual physical sense, lifted her upright.

"Mrs. Wheeler, did you hear me? Lucy's score on the WISC was an 80."

"Ah," she said. "An 80."

Walking away, holding Lucy's hand, Susan thought, *Not an A, but not a C.*

Two weeks later, on a Friday, mid-morning, George Wheeler's Volkswagen roared up into the drive. Susan was undisturbed by his unexpected appearance. In a neighborhood vacated by men in the morning and reinhabited by them at night, her husband's erratic hours were legend. The back door slammed, the dining room door swung forward. "Dammit, Susan! How many times have I told you not to take the phone off the hook?"

She sat in front of a typewriter at the dining room table, her books and papers spread out. She bent closer to her typewriter. "I can't concentrate with the phone ringing."

"And if there's an emergency?"

"*What?*" Her hand jerked; the typewriter ball clattered crazily across the carriage.

George slammed back through the swinging door, and Susan ran after him. Most kitchens in this neighborhood of young couples redoing old houses sported psychedelic wallpaper, but the Wheelers' was all white tile and stainless steel. The architect of this clean design stood surveying a sink stacked with unwashed breakfast dishes, a trail of Froot Loops, a dried pile of scrambled eggs on the sunlit counter.

"I clean up *after* Lucy gets home," she said. "I have to work while she's at school."

Instead of attacking, George wilted. He looked out the window at the long branches the front yard's red oak sent to shade this side of the house. Above him, suspended over the sink by clear fishing line, was a crudely stuffed paper spider with black pipe-cleaner legs. "Mrs. Reardon called me at the office. You know, St. James? The Headmistress? She's been trying to get you since Wednesday. *Wednesday!*"

Susan hardened herself. "So?"

"*So*, she said there's a problem. Something about some test?"

George's face, knotted up, was exactly why Susan hadn't mentioned the test.

"I didn't tell you," she said, "because it wasn't a big deal. St. James wanted Lucy's hearing checked. We went to Scottish Rite Hospital a couple of weeks—"

"*My child is not a cripple.*"

Susan stared at him hard. "We went to Scottish Rite a couple of weeks ago for testing. There were several. I don't know, but Lucy's hearing was perfect—oh, there *was* one. Some kind of puzzle. Lucy made an 80. Not an A, but not a C."

"The *WISC*—" George said, emphasizing the word, spelling the letters W-I-S-C. "The WISC was why Mrs. Reardon called. She said it showed—" He hesitated. His face drained of color, his gray eyes beseeched her. "She said they couldn't take Lucy for kindergarten. Susan, Mrs. Reardon said she's probably brain damaged."

Susan's mind went blank. Into the blankness jumped a spider with pipe-cleaner legs, and all the pieces that hadn't been fitting fell into place. Over the past two weeks—since Lucy's test—she'd had several phone conversations with Mrs. Reardon, but with each conversation there seemed to be less and less of her there. It was as though the headmistress was gradually disappearing, because every time Susan reached out, she couldn't quite touch her. *Before you send in your tuition deposit . . . I'm not certain St. James is the right school . . .*

In the main room of Lucy's preschool, Susan hit a wall of sustained noise. The din unraveled into rowdy clumps of children moving about the room amoeba-like, forming, sliding to ingest, reforming. One-eyed pirates, firemen in plastic helmets assembled and dispersed around a Lego-littered floor. Clowns, lips overpainted with false grins, clustered at a low table, then side-slipped to envelop the piano. Only Masima, his tiny Japanese face zippered with Frankenstein scars, lay motionless, curled at the threshold, sucking his thumb. Susan stepped over Masima and entered the chaos. Where was *her* precious child? Girls absorbed with scissors surrounded the art table. Their cheeks carried red hearts; long painted lashes encircled their eyes. Scanning the girls, she failed to notice the puddle of red paint.

Her new sandals! She slipped them off and, with every gritting step, grew more annoyed. The place was always so *dirty*. In a bathroom that smelled of old diapers, she stuck a foot in the low sink and turned on the tap. Two years ago, The Unitarian Cooperative Preschool had sounded like the perfect school: progressive and liberal—rare in Dallas in 1975—dedicated to creativity, no rigid patterns. She wanted Lucy to be free, not imprisoned by what it meant to be female. Floating a paper towel down to stand on, she stuck her other foot in the sink. She had learned that in real life, parent-volunteers failed to show, that a three-year-old with a plastic pitcher and semi-frozen can of lemonade was deadly, that children in charge meant tambourines for water bowls in the rabbits' cages, and that Claude, the resident boa constrictor, was often misplaced. The sink gurgled as the pink water swirled away.

She backtracked, swiping at her bloody footprints with a paper towel, and walked outside barefoot, holding her sandals. She stepped off the concrete porch, watching where she put her feet. There was no grass, only sand and, further out, hard ground rubbed shiny with use. A swing set and an iron jungle gym occupied the middle of the playground. Toward the back stood thickets of Spanish oak, and on her right, a dense stand of bamboo.

A rustling in the bamboo caught her attention: bodies belly-crawled through it. Long shadowy gun barrels told her that the bodies belonged to the "big boys" who ruled the playground and never came inside to cut paper or play with Legos. From across the yard came a loud whoop, and a bare-chested boy swung out on a long rope. He held the rope in one hand, a plastic machine gun in the other. Letting go at the top of the arc, he dropped down, landing gracefully on both feet, his little torso bare, muscular, well-shaped. His face was painted red and webbed with black lines. Shocked, she recognized Bobby Morton, a six-year-old from their neighborhood. Other children with red painted faces streamed out from the trees, screaming, waving guns. The boys within the bamboo jumped up with their guns.

Susan was turning away when something familiar caught her eye. Lucy? *Lucy* with a red face? "Kill 'em!" Lucy screamed. When Bobby stopped beneath the dome of the jungle gym, Lucy stopped just behind him, her tiny body on guard, hip cocked, cradling a machine gun. Bobby motioned her forward, the two gangs surged, and Lucy disappeared in the swarming mob.

Susan sat down hard on the concrete. She'd been looking for Raggedy Ann, not this vortex of murder and dirt. Her eyes blurred with tears. Two tiny, scuffed cowboy boots, a hot panting. "Mom?" A drop of red sweat plopped on Susan's foot. "Did you see me, Mom? Did you? Bobby let me be in his gang today."

"Hi, sweetheart," Susan said. She reached to smooth her child's dark curls, but Lucy whirled around to shoot a commando behind her, knocking her hand away. She grabbed Lucy's arm. "*Stop it!*" The teachers had told her that Lucy never played with girls in "housekeeping." Susan had dismissed the information: Why would anyone choose to iron? But *this*?

Lucy jerked loose. "Bobby needs me!" She bounced around in her boots, waving her gun, and her mother sat, looking at the red painted face with its clear rivulets of sweat, and wondered at the strangeness of the world. She, Susan, had been obedient, studious, physically timid. Where had this child come from?

In the bathroom, she scrubbed Lucy's face with a wet paper towel, then, stepping over Masima, curled at the door, thumb in mouth, she hurried her daughter home.

She said nothing, just gathered Lucy in her arms on the couch in the den. "I love you," she whispered.

"Mom? I promise I'll be so quiet if you let me skip my nap and read in here."

Susan grinned and released her. How did she always know when to strike? "Okay, since you asked so nicely." She tried to pull Lucy back into her arms, but Lucy had stiffened her spine. "Can I watch TV then? I'd be lying down."

"You know there's no TV during the week."

Lucy curled in against her and looked up. "Mommy. Just today."

Long silence. Susan sighed. "I guess it doesn't—"

Lucy jumped up. "Since it's such a special day, can I play outside?"

"Who said it was a special day?"

"*Mom.* I get to skip my nap and watch TV."

"You cannot play outside."

"You know it's better to play outside than to lie around watching the tube."

This was a brain-damaged child? "Just today, then, and you have to—" But already the front door had slammed shut.

In her white, stainless-steel kitchen, Susan didn't clean up. She stood at the sink beneath the dangling spider and waited for Lucy's pediatrician to return her frantic phone call. *What did an IQ of 80 mean?* Staring into the green-leaved branches, she waited. When the phone failed to ring, she wandered into the living room and looked out. In the yard, Bobby Morton stood, burr head bowed, palms pressed against the trunk of the Big Tree, and on his shoulders, Lucy, on tiptoe, bare feet straddling his neck, arms stretching upward.

Susan crashed out the front door. "*Lucy!*"

Her shout propelled Lucy up. Bobby sat down from the force of her thrust; Lucy dangled free. She swung her legs up, and hung—arms and legs around the tree's long, lowest branch—then somehow, in one swift movement, she was upright: standing triumphant, feet spread wide on the branch.

"Come down here! You know the rule."

The red oak dominated the Wheelers' house, the entire street. From blocks away, boys rode Hot Wheels to conquer it. The previous year when a pack of boys—some known to Susan, some not—had invaded the front yard, bringing chairs to stack and little brothers and sisters to watch, Susan had issued a rule: If you weren't big enough to get up in the Big Tree without help, you weren't big enough to be there. Everyone obeyed "Mrs. Wheeler's Rule" except Lucy. She couldn't get up without help, but she was always there when others climbed it and she could always entice some boy to boost her.

"You get down here, young lady."

Lucy began climbing up into the tree. In Susan's head, her husband's voice: *Dammit, Susan! What's wrong with you? Good mothers have children who mind.*

"Dammit, Lucy. You mind me!"

The tree was still and then, high up, on a level with the attic window, the green quivered, and Lucy walked out on a limb. "You oughta see our house from up here! It's terrific! Bobby, wanna see?"

Bobby looked at Susan with wild eyes, his Spiderman face a smudged wreck. He shook his head.

"You chicken, Bobby? You are, aren't you?"

"Lucy Wheeler, you get down here right now."

Lucy disappeared within the green. After a moment, her voice, disembodied, floated from the high canopy. "Wow! Now I can see the creek behind Mrs. Spence's house, and there's—"

"Lucy, you're scaring me. Come down. I'm not mad anymore."

There was silence, then scrambling sounds. Susan measured Lucy's downward progress by leaf-movement. Finally, stepping out onto the lowest branch, Lucy walked, tightrope style, to the center and plopped down, legs dangling. The limb quivered slightly.

"Keep coming," Susan said.

"Dammit, Mom."

Susan leaped and grabbed one of Lucy's ankles. She caught her as she fell but got kicked in the chin, and Lucy slipped free. She had streaked the width of the yard before Susan, running full speed, managed a tackle. She tried to carry her toward the house, but Lucy was too strong, too frenzied to be contained, and she ended up having to drag her by one arm, kicking and screaming, through the front door. Bobby watched from under the tree.

She hauled Lucy through the den and down the hall, and dumped her in the middle of her room. She paused to gauge—what? The normalcy of her child? She willed the howling creature on the floor to magically transform, willed Lucy to become a compliant child. When the flailing limbs and screams failed to still, Susan slammed out of the room. Panting, she sat down in the hall, her back against Lucy's door.

The minute the door closed, Lucy stopped kicking and screaming. Her body quivered, various muscles jumped, her throat jerked small sounds, but she made herself lie still. Only her mind moved. It wasn't fair! The Big Tree was *her* tree and she was more sure-footed than any of the big boys! *And her mother knew it.* Her mother knew she was safe in the tree, but she insisted on enforcing the rule. Stupid rule, stupid mother. Round and round Lucy's mind raced, an eternal dark circuit of injustices, of wrongs done to her. Wait—what did she, *Lucy*, want? She wanted to be in the tree. The most important thing was to get back there. She couldn't think about her mother or how unfair the rule was. She couldn't get back to the tree with angry thoughts. It didn't work that way. She willed her mind to empty, her heart to slow. She allowed silence to enter her. She closed her eyes and lay perfectly still. She felt roots striking down the length of her body, tiny feelers like whispers, roots that grew larger as they reached down through the dirt toward the underground stream her father said must run beneath their house. How else could their tree have gotten so big? The stream, a little finger of the big creek behind the houses across the street, and Lucy's roots whispering through darkness, reaching down, searching for it. She felt the earth's power move up through her roots, becoming tree trunk and tree limb, branching, bursting up through the floor. She allowed the walls of her room to sprout tiny leaves that grew and grew until, when she opened her eyes, she looked out through green leaves all around. The Big Tree, Lucy's Tree! She jumped up, triumphant; she spread her arms wide. She was in the tree and she was the tree. Her edges dissolved. The green fizz and force of her body spread out and out. The wind shivered her leaves. She was the wind and the shivering leaves. Standing high up in the tree, she saw her branches wave against a blue sky. Everywhere blue. It filled her. A cloud passed by. She was the sky. Sky, leaves, tree, she. Ruler of the world. All powerful. Queen Lucy. Far, far down below, a little yellow house with an orange door. Poor little girl who had to live in such a tiny house with such tiny parents. Lucky Lucy! Queen of Everything.

A small sound outside the door cracked the edges of the sky. Another sound, and the cracks ran rapidly until the blue was crazed with cracks all over, and the sky fell down. The disturbance was fearful, a noisy crash. The wind stopped, the leaves withered. All around lay scattered blue shards. Lucy's edges clicked into place and she whooshed back into her body. It took a moment to adjust to arms and legs. She tiptoed to the door and lay down on her stomach to listen. She didn't make a sound. On the other side of the door, her mother cried. A pure venomous hate constricted Lucy's heart. Her mother always cried. She hated her mother. It was her self Lucy sought. I want, I want. I want it all. All mine, the world. No boundaries, no limits, no rules. No mother.

Her mother said how much she loved her, but Lucy knew this was a lie. She'd heard the voices. Sometimes she slipped out of her room and quietly belly-crawled, like the big boys in the bamboo, down the hall to lie on her stomach in the dark outside her parents' bedroom. Sometimes she didn't have to leave her room, she could lie in her own bed and hear them. Terrible voices. *A good mother has children who mind. She's a force of nature. Spanking doesn't do any good. When are you going to fix Lucy?* And Lucy got scared then, lying in the hall or in her bed in the dark. Who could protect someone as big as she was? She must stay small. But the next morning the hunger would rise up in her again. She *wanted* to take everything in, to make everything into her *self*.

Lucy kicked the door hard. Her mother was a liar! How could her mother love her? Living in a tiny yellow house beneath the Tree of Lucy? She didn't want her mother's tears, didn't want her love. She kicked the door. Her mother wanted to strip her leaves, cut her branches, chop her down until she was small, so tiny she fit inside the tiny house. She would *not* allow herself to be loved into smallness. Over and over, Lucy kicked and howled.

Susan sat in the hall and listened to Lucy rage. She couldn't understand the words, but she recognized the tune, and her heart answered with a terrible fury. No more tears. She would *win* this time. Soon Lucy's howls became a chant about how much she hated her mother, then came the sounds of books and toys being swept off their shelves. Susan listened to this destruction until she heard a dresser drawer being torn out of its chest.

She jumped up and shoved open the door. "Don't you do it, young lady! Don't you dare!"

Lucy stood across the room, next to a small slipper chair upholstered in a pattern of green leaves. She grabbed the chair. Screaming, tottering under its weight, she raised it over her head and hurled it at her mother. Susan pulled the door shut just before it hit.

Stunned, Susan sank down in the hall, hands shaking. *How had she managed to lift that chair?*

The sounds of Lucy's rage grew smaller and smaller. Stopped.

When all was silent, Susan dragged herself upright. She had to shove hard to open the door against the chaos of hurled books and toys and—Goldy's fish bowl! The bowl lay on its side, unbroken, its interior a jumble of iridescent marbles and plastic palm trees, and near it, on the water-soaked carpet: Goldy. Overfed and adored, talked to, tapped at. *Mom, watch how she swims to the top when she sees me!* Goldy, not gasping, not flipping around, dead.

In the middle of the room, spread-eagled near the overturned chair, Lucy lay on her stomach asleep. Susan knelt beside her. Lucy's breath was shallow, her lashes a shadow on her flushed cheek. Susan petted her, stroking her dark curls, the curve of her ear, her temple with its blue veins and fine flakes of red paint. She was going to be heartbroken about Goldy. Susan lifted Lucy's small hand, kissed it, laid it back on the carpet. She slid down and lay flat and breathed in the breath that Lucy breathed out. Moving to curl her body around the small form, she enveloped her child.

Real Life

Bird Jaguar squats over a bloodletting bowl and pulls a rope through the slit he has cut in his member. Blood pops, round like pearls. The pearls glisten, gather volume, drip down to soak paper strips. Far below, on the main plaza, hundreds of Mayans stand silently, waiting for a column of smoke to signal Bird Jaguar's sacrifice was complete, the realm beyond conjured—Or was the crowd silent? Maybe the scene was a tumult of noise? Drums. Shakers and pipes. Ecstatic dancing. But silent or frenzied, the plaza would have been *hot*. Bogie had just finished breakfast and already he dripped sweat.

A slim young man in tight safari pants and a shirt rakishly unbuttoned, he had imagined this trip to the Yucatan would reveal him as Bogert Lionel Jones, machete-wielding jungle GI. Instead, he stood hunched over the too-short, foldable handle of an Army/Navy Surplus spade in the watery light of a clearing that wasn't really a clearing because there are no natural clearings in rain forests, and there was also no underbrush to slash his way through. Gel, leaking from his molded cockscomb, stung his eyes. He worried he looked like he was crying. *Georgina.* So many aspects of this trip she had failed to mention: the silence, the darkness, the invisible-animal sounds.

Bogie knew about silence, about sitting upstairs during services at the mortuary, forbidden by his father to walk on the creaky floor. *Don't you move, bozo.* And he knew about darkness, his fear of it—but *this place.* Sleeping without walls for protection in nights totally black.

He decided he would not think about this. He would think instead about Bird Jaguar. Georgina had shown him photos of Yaxchilan's famous stone lintels with their hemp ropes and bloodletting bowls, paper strips spotted with the round, crosshatched glyphs that meant "blood." He could see the images clearly, but he could not slip inside them and imagine what Bird Jaguar had felt. After he sliced himself with the stingray spine, he must have been in blinding pain. Did he cry out? Was he drugged? Was he in ecstasy as the paper burned and the Vision Serpent unfurled? Or was it the shock—the massive physical jolt to his system—that carried him through?

Bogie liked to think heroic thoughts, but his genitals shriveled at the thought of a stingray spine. Perforator God, the Mayans called it. *Had Georgina said how much blood was required?*

The trip had been dreamed up in Dallas on a lazy Sunday morning, the two of them snug in her bed. "Aren't we having a lark?" she said. "Or a *cock*-atoo," Bogie said. She laughed and laughed. "How can we not succeed?" she said. "With your expertise in the jungle and my archaeological knowledge?" She fumbled in her bedside drawer. "*And* I have this for luck." Dangling a broken string of pink plastic beads, Georgina chattered about her childhood. Bogie didn't know what a rosary was and he didn't care about her friend. His only focus: her plump belly and the dark triangle below it.

Naked, he had fixed two more Bogie Bartender cocktails, happy concoctions of pink grapefruit juice, vodka, champagne. Again they lifted their glasses. "Here's to our adventure," she said. The crystal sang a clear note. "Our *Mayan* adventure," he said.

And just like that—poof!—*Mayan Adventure Tours* materialized. It was magic.

Bogie had imagined young clients sporting backpacks, mad love among the ruins. Instead, the clients were old, the ruins full of raging insects, and how could anyone fuck in a hammock with the others hanging *right there*? And the birds! Two hundred and twenty-two species, according to Everett Hollewig, Birdwatcher Supremo, all singing their damn hearts out at dawn, flitting their reds and yellows around. A world of birds conspiring to blow his cover—not to mention Philpot.

Cursing, Bogie stepped on the spade with the lug sole of his new boot. Minuscule insects, released from the soil, raced up the short handle toward him. The first few times this had happened, he had thrown the spade down and frantically spanked his body. He knew now to stretch out his arm, shake the tool, continue digging. It was the third day of the inaugural trip. The Mayan adventurers had traveled by dugout canoe to spend three nights in hammocks, hanging beneath a tin roof at Yaxchilan.

In the watery light where Bogie dug, he heard a steady plop of fat raindrops, rustlings of who-knew-what in the canopy above, and intermittent howler monkey screams that his mind easily enlarged to jaguar roars. Beyond and around him, rising up: silent stone monuments of the Mayan dead. Bogie knew about the dead, felt them as light feather-touches all over his body. He knew how they looked "backstage" in the prep room at Jones Funeral Home, the metal gurney and metal sinks, everything done there preparation for what his father called "the performance," the actual funeral service.

"Bogie!"

It was Georgina shouting, unseen. "I'm digging as fast as I can," he yelled. His task was to lengthen the trough that served as the group's latrine. Georgina, in Dallas, had made it sound like a one-time-only job: "You'll dig a trough and put a log in front of it. We'll sit on the log with our bottoms hanging over." In his mind Bogie had seen Technicolor munchkins, shovels on shoulders, singing *And that's how we build latrines in Yaxchilan.*

"Edith's in distress," Georgina called out. "Can we—"

Bogie jabbed the spade in the ground and walked to pull the log along a ditch that he hadn't yet lengthened. "Come on."

Nine hours driving a combé from Villahermosa, two hours motoring upstream on the wide, brown Usumacinta, Georgina bragging the whole time about the fabulous food the "on-site chef" would prepare. On arrival, she was greeted by a uniformed guard, Angel de Jesús Sarabia, a dumpy man with greasy pieces of hair combed across a high forehead. His grin revealed a lack of upper teeth; his strained buttons, a brown belly. The "on-site chef" turned out to be his wife. For two days Bogie had lifted the log and shoveled dirt onto the overflowing ditch behind it. It was Georgina's damn fault. She had seduced him with the reality of Bird Jaguar, "He of Twenty Captives, Lord of the Split Sky Place." This had happened after the first margarita. It was early afternoon, dim in the depths of Hernando's. Bogie had felt both solid and buoyant as he played convivial-bartender, chatting, attending more to Georgina's body than her words. He didn't know what "lintel" or "bas-relief" meant, and he didn't care: he was busy creating *the flow*. Then Georgina placed two large photographs on the zinc bar, and Bogie's throat closed up and the hair on the back of his neck prickled. He had never seen anything like these images, and his awe must have shown. Georgina said, "You're surprising me, Mr. Jones."

In the rain forest, Edith minced toward the log, hanging onto Georgina's arm. A seventy-four-year-old dynamo with pixie-cut pink hair, ravaged, diminished.

"I'm so sorry," she said. "I can't wait."

How quickly six strangers had become accustomed to revealing bodily needs normally hidden! The only good thing about the collective diarrhea was that so far Edith had been unable to give her lecture on Mayan political rights.

A windowless room in the basement of the Villahermosa Hyatt. Six bodies spaced around a banquet table for twenty. If only the group hadn't looked so meager and the lights hadn't been so bright, the ceiling so low, the walls concrete block. If only the mimeographed menus, purple, slightly damp—*Introductory Dinner, June 1980*—hadn't reeked of chemicals like embalming stink, perhaps he wouldn't have been driven to try and kick-start a party by putting on charm. Bogie's looks and social patter—movies, sports trivia, dance clubs—had always allowed him to move smoothly through the world. This ceased when he and Georgina became a couple. In the five months they'd been together, he'd begun to realize how disabling his lack of education was. Georgina could not set up an ironing board, but she could read Mayan hieroglyphics, her mind a vast sea of strange life-forms in which Bogie sank. He learned to listen, to float on currents of conversation without verbalization. He rarely asked questions. But in the uncomfortable brightness of the basement room, trying to get the party started, Bogie Charmer surfaced and asked Edith, because she was old and seemed safe, why *she* was interested in the Mayans.

Her response about the plight of the indigenous Mayans in Guatemala stumped him. He spoke without thinking. "But aren't the Mayans all dead?"

From around the table, a collective stare. Whispers between the prim Hollewigs, a frown on Edith's prune face, barks that might've been laughter from Philpot, and Georgina, standing, laughing, with her hand up. "It's clear Bogie doesn't know about the civil unrest in Guatemala." Bogie felt his neck and face flame.

"Civil *war*," Edith said. "Army death squads, torture, and—"

"*And* he doesn't have a Ph.D. in Mayan Studies," Georgina said. "I do, and one is enough."

Sometimes Bogie liked it when Georgina went into Sherman tank mode, sometimes he didn't. She could roll right over him with young Maize God this, old Paddler Gods that. He turned his attention to Philpot. Unlike everyone else, nervously chatty, he slouched, cool and remote, pouring shots from a bottle he'd brought with him to the table, an expensive tequila Bogie had heard of but never seen. You couldn't buy it at Hernando's.

In Dallas, he and Georgina had laughed at the name. Phillip Philpot? *Really?* But everything about this man signaled he was no one to laugh at. He appeared relaxed—long salt-and-pepper hair licking his shoulders, loose white shirt untucked—but beneath this surface: nerves and watchfulness, finely balanced. *That's a guayabera*, murmured Georgina when Philpot walked in. *A man's wedding shirt. I'll buy you one.* The shirt's embroidered white flowers emphasized rather than diminished Philpot's maleness; the V-neck revealed a salt-and-pepper pelt that turned Bogie's hairless chest radioactive.

Georgina was saying, "I'll manage the educational portion of this Mayan adventure, and Bogie will manage everything else. Your luggage, the driving, setting up camp. He'll be the man in charge." She moved behind him, kneading his shoulders, his knots of tension. She talked about how he was a man of many parts. Not only was he a fabulous bartender, but he'd spent a couple of years in Central America capturing wild birds.

This was a lie Bogie had told Georgina the first afternoon. Her pigtails and the backpack she dropped on the floor at her huarache-clad feet marked her as young, despite the fine lines around her eyes, her throat, the brown spots on the backs of her hands. Bogie knew how to become a mirror reflecting whatever customers needed to see—especially females who came into bars in the afternoon by themselves. Hernando had begged him to work full time, but Bogie didn't like to commit, he liked to "fill in." He liked life in flashes, discontinuous and dizzying, ecstatic dancing beneath strobe lights. He tried to talk up the woman sitting there alone, but she couldn't talk about Dallas clubs because she'd just arrived: she was the new associate curator for pre-Columbian Art at the DMA.

Expert at hiding his ignorance—curator? DMA?—Bogie put on an impressed face, whipped up a margarita, and presented it in a stemmed, salt-rimmed glass. *No, no, it's on the house.* The woman wasn't able to talk about movies or music because she'd spent the last six years in Yucatan measuring an ancient stone city.

He thought later it was the word *stone* that led him to tell her about his past career catching wild birds. The woman drank margaritas in the dimness of the deserted bar and listened to Bogie describe a movie she couldn't have seen: the mountains, the narrow winding roads, his jeep piled with wooden cages, a wreck with a bus, and all his labors—the valuable parrots and plumed birds—lost.

Young girls disintegrated when they had too much to drink; this woman became more beautiful. Her sexiness surfaced. Bogie saw himself as she saw him: a hero with a machete, cutting through jungle. He fell in love with this image of himself, and the love must have been contagious because Georgina took him home with her that night. Her marriage to the orthopedic surgeon had been dull, dull, dull, she said, as she unlocked her door. She'd been working too hard for too long. "A person should strike a balance," she said. "And I can tell you have depths."

In the basement of the Villahermosa Hyatt, under the bright lights, when Georgina related Bogie's bird-catching career, Everett Hollewig, in bowtie and seersucker coat, boomed out that *he* had a life list of one thousand and two birds. He'd packed Howell's *Birds of the Yucatan* and Eisermann's *Annotated Checklist of the Birds of Guatemala*. "Last year a Mexican ornithologist recorded two hundred and twenty-two species of birds at Yaxchilan. He even sighted a Harpy—"

"Haven't been to Yaxchilan," Bogie Birdcatcher said, his smile sticking to his teeth.

Sylvia Hollewig said, "Tell them about its human face, Evie, why it's called a *Harpy* Eagle." Sylvia had fluttery eyes behind black cat-glasses, lips overpainted with red, and a ratted white beehive. "It's from the Greek, don't you know? The Harpies who come—"

A line of white-coated waiters entered the room. Five of them carried plates humped with fish sticks, an entrée the limp purple menu listed as "Angel Fingers." A sixth waiter served Philpot a sizzling slab of meat. Taking a large knife from an unobtrusive leather holder at his side, he cut into it, took a huge bite. "Don't worry," he said, his mouth full. "Told them to put the steak on my tab. And you"—pointing his knife at Bogie. "*Romancing the Stone*, right? And the blonde on the bus that crashed into you? Kathleen Turner."

In the rain forest, Georgina put her hand on Bogie's arm, and they moved away from the ditch. When Edith was invisible, Georgina fingered the knots of his spine as though he were a musical instrument. Bogie allowed Georgina to play him, her pigtails' blunt ends scratching his chest, her nearness resurrecting what he'd imagined sacrificed.

"It's a real hike this morning," she said. "I want you to stay close to Edith."

Bogie reminded himself that this—hammocks and howler monkeys!—was temporary. Temporary was what he did best.

"I know," she said.

"It's stupid, the way she's wearing herself out," he said.

Edith changed clothes *inside* her hammock, presumably so no one would notice. All activity beneath the tin roof stopped while everyone watched her cocoon swing up, down, and sideways. Eventually, corkscrewed inside, Edith would fight her way out—feet kicking, fists punching—until, finally, delivered, she'd appear, panting, eyes glazed, pink hair on end.

"I *know*," Georgina said. "But she might need your help."

Bogie had never hiked, slept outside, used a spade, but he had other skills. He slipped his tongue into Georgina's mouth. She tasted of cinnamon and breakfast buñuelos.

"Tomorrow this will all be worth it," she murmured. "When the sun rises, and you see its rays shoot straight into Structure 33, you won't believe—Mmmm. You are *bad*."

Georgina had scheduled the trip around the summer solstice, when the sun rose in a cleft between two mountains on the eastern horizon: an Earth/sky conjunction that gave Yaxchilan its ancient name, Split Sky Place, and its hieroglyph, two humps with a notch between. She hadn't told the others, only him. *It'll be more stunning if it's a surprise.*

"As a child I wanted to be an archeoastronomer," she'd said their first night. "I'm not. Too much math—and I was thirty when I started graduate school. But in studying the interaction of sunlight with architecture, I did discover a cosmological phenomenon at Yaxchilan."

Bogie had had no idea what she was talking about.

In the rain forest, Georgina put her arms around his neck. "I do believe our enterprise is going to succeed, BJ."

Georgina, with all her degrees, had turned out to be no different from other women: omen-hunters all, believers in magic. When his initials matched her precious Bird Jaguar's, she swore it was a sign they were destined for each other. They both knew she was playacting. Dallas was temporary; she had upcoming interviews at universities all over the country. And what did "destined" mean when there was always and only the drain in the prep room floor?

The farthest Bogie had ever traveled was the beach at Corpus Christi—a surprise that the world was so big. Nine hours from Villahermosa, they parked at the Guatemalan border: monkeys in trees, bare-breasted women wrapped in long skirts, naked babies on hips. Two hours later, Bogie felt they were in a movie, the six of them, sitting in a dugout canoe moving slowly upstream against a strong current, the wide river overhung on both sides with dense foliage, bromeliads, thick whiskery vines. He saw parrots, heard strange animal screams. A man wearing camouflage stepped out of the jungle on the right bank and stood, half-hidden, watching them pass. In his arms, slanted against his body, a machine gun. A while later, Bogie glimpsed another camo-wearing watcher, gun slanted. He didn't ask about these men: after the meet and greet in the bright lights of the basement, he couldn't risk humiliation.

"The Usumacinta divides Mexico and Guatemala," Georgina said. "The trouble at the border was unusual—"

"It was a hassle," Philpot said from his seat in the back, "because two weeks ago an American living in Guatemala was kidnapped. Last week he was found sitting up against the bumper of his Ford Wagon, separated from his head."

In the silence, the sound of the motor.

Edith said, "A month ago the secret police murdered the wife and two-year-old child of a 'disappeared' activist. The *Archivo* tortured them, tore their fingernails out, even the—"

"Haven't heard anything about the American," Georgina said.

"Yeah," Philpot said. "They're keeping it kinda quiet."

Bogie asked if it was so quiet, how come he knew about it?

Philpot said he'd heard it at Retalhuleu. When he changed planes.

Edith said, "Retalhuleu? But that's an *Archivo* air base."

"It was a shortcut," Philpot said, and his grin caused Bogie's leg to jump. "I'm a shortcut kinda guy." His gray-streaked hair hung thick and bristly in the sunlight. His eyes were hidden behind Ray-Bans, but Bogie knew they were yellow, their irises slits.

From across the aisle, Sylvia Hollewig twisted her skirt and made an agitated-wasp sound. Georgina reached to touch her mashed-by-pantyhose knee. "Don't worry," she said. "Yaxchilan's in Chiapas, on Mexican soil."

The Mexican mud on the steep slanted embankment at Yaxchilan would soon suck Sylvia's white pumps off her stocking feet, and with no explanation, her husband, Everett, would lie down on and crawl up, rather than walk. No one except Philpot had obeyed the luggage restriction. Edith and the Hollewigs produced hard-sided suitcases they were unable to carry, and who hauled these suitcases in and out of the combé, the dugout canoe, up the steep bank? The man in charge: Bogie Jones.

The morning's excursion to the South Acropolis, the site's highest spot, had been disastrous: Everett crawled, Edith collapsed. The day was a surprise from the moment they gathered. Everett appeared wearing white plastic leg braces with metal knee-hinges on both legs. The plastic matched Sylvia's Keds and looked startlingly out of place in a rain forest. He said he hadn't listed Parkinson's on the health questionnaire because this was his last chance to see Mayan ruins. There was also the two hundred and twenty-two species of birds. The braces? For inclines, when he had to crawl.

For two days, Bogie had been able to extricate himself from Everett's bird-talk by claiming urgent camp chores, but this morning, Georgina whispered, "I'll look after Edith," and then she was promising Everett that "the man in charge" would stay with him every step (ha, ha) of the way. Watching Everett lie down in the dirt and pull himself up the winding, slanted trail made Bogie sick to his stomach. And when the man wasn't crawling, he talked: *Did you see the Scarlet Macaws? The Green Honeycreeper? Ever seen a Harpy Eagle? Long talons. Can pluck a howler monkey off a branch in midflight.* Bless Edith for forgetting to bring her water bottle.

Bogie the Compassionate walked her back to camp, gentle arm around her waist. He helped her into her hammock, then double-timed it back, carrying water bottles for all. He was the man in charge—not a bozo.

At lunch, Georgina announced an afternoon break. Edith's dehydration had been a sign. A transformative bath was required. No toothless, laughing Paddler Gods canoeing *them* to the underworld! She and Bogie would go first to illustrate the pleasures of bathing in the mighty Usumacinta. "Everyone hold tight to the rope, so you don't get swept away by the current."

Bogie held on with both hands to the rope, a permanent fixture tied around a tall ceiba tree on the bank, and even though he allowed his body to sway with the river's movement so he appeared relaxed, he could feel his shoulders knotted. Behind him, legs wrapped around his waist, rode Georgina, shampooing his hair. Back and forth Bogie's legs waved beneath the brown water; back and forth their torsos moved. Two torsos, four arms, one pair of legs. A mythological river god, Georgina said.

On the bank, three bodies in swimsuits sat lined up next to the ceiba's complicated root system. In his mind Bogie saw three piles of shining white shinbone and clavicle surrounded by rain forest. Then: *That's the damn green room. Right there. The performance is coming.*

A large iguana materialized on one of the tree's horizontal roots, its skin rougher than the smooth bark and darker brown. Bearded, with a tall backcomb that ran the length of its body, the creature stood on squat, thick legs, unmoving. Its hooded slit eyes bulged. Did it see him? Swaying with the current, watching the iguana, Bogie sank into its lizard life: the slowness of blood, the reptile sleepiness. He felt his shoulders relax.

Jones Funeral Home in Ennis, Texas. His home. He had never been able to bring friends there. It smelled. Often, he smelled, no matter that he scrubbed his skin raw with a fingernail brush, splashed on aftershave—so much the other boys called him names. Forced into silence and stillness when young, he had drawn on any paper he could find, usually brown grocery sacks. Horses and dogs, his own hands and feet. No one in Ennis said only sissies and queers draw pictures; they didn't have to. It was the air you breathed. Bogie did not play sports, was not in any way athletic, he had to do something to prove—to himself?—that he was neither sissy nor queer.

In junior high, he started slipping girls through the kitchen into the prep room. The light was always low. Out of reverence for the dead? To simulate a "viewing?" Probably both. One lamp in a far corner, another by the gurney—that was all. In this dimly lit room, Bogie would describe shaving the bodies, massaging them until the skin became pliable and soft. Never pink, that was makeup. Refrigerated corpses remained blue until magicked into cadavers: he always made this point clear. He showed the trocar used to drain hollow organs, the gun that shot a curved needle to sew lips to upper gums, the cotton he inserted beneath eyelids for a rounded, lifelike effect. He never spoke about the cotton packed against leakage into anus and vagina; never told anyone that if the bodies got to the funeral home in the first twenty-four hours or so, you could still feel the livingness. Was it that their souls lingered?

Showing the prep room always created *the flow*. He never understood why. Perhaps it was the girls' intuition of fleeting time, perhaps an appreciation of his body's warmth. Massaging rigor mortis had taught him to value living flesh. His hands became renowned—of this, he was certain.

One May night in the prep room with old Mr. Crook on the gurney, Bogie danced to his transistor radio as he explained—with a pelvic thrust on the downbeat—how he had to drain his blood, *red*, and pump in formaldehyde, *pink*, but when he finished—*Abracadaver!*—Mr. Crook would have a long shelf-life. He could lie at room temp—

He didn't know his father was in the room until he slapped him hard with one of his huge, meaty hands. *You stupid bozo!* Without thinking, Bogie cold-cocked him. *Flash.* His father, in slow-motion, falling. *Flash.* Dark cutout sprawled on white tile.

High school graduation and dancing with old Mr. Crook: Georgina called it "a cosmological conjunction." Bogie blasted his motorcycle straight up I-45 to Dallas, leaving behind the silence, the smell, but never the image of the drain in the floor.

"Will you shampoo *my* hair?"

It was Philpot, standing behind the old people on the bank, coming late to the communal bath, carrying a rolled-up towel. Philpot: broad, hairy chest slimming to a narrow waist, a bulging orange Speedo. Before Bogie could tell him to sit down and wait his turn, Philpot had slipped into the river, sleek and silent as an otter. He hadn't been silent that morning but laconically chatty, the hike uphill no exertion for him, his muscles visible for the first time in clinging tee shirt and shorts—and he'd focused his attention on Georgina. Bogie, stuck at the back with the Crawler, had tried to block out the bird-chatter and listen, but he'd only caught snippets: *What did you do here for six years? Who were your friends?*

In the river, Bogie angled his body to keep Philpot away. The Usumacinta was a heavy river, its currents deep, so although it flowed fast, it appeared sluggish. Philpot grabbed the rope with one huge hand and stayed close. "Was thinking about your lecture last night," Philpot said. "About how the Mayans needed blood sacrifice to keep their little kingdoms running."

Every evening after supper, Georgina lectured in the main plaza. To get there, the group had to troop from the sleeping place through a tunnel that early explorers had labeled the "labyrinth." The passage was narrow, pitch-black, with deceptive dead-end passages. Georgina's instructions regarding it were breezy. "Don't touch the walls—they're crawling with poisonous centipedes—and ignore the bats." Bogie had waited for her to elaborate about her childhood terror of centipedes, but she didn't. Still, every evening the group was shaky and breathless when they burst forth from the labyrinth to gulp the sweet air of a green world.

Georgina had stopped scrubbing his head. "That is *not* what I said. I said the Mayans believed in a universe dependent on humans willing to sustain it with offerings of what is most precious to them—their blood."

"Yeah, that's what I meant," Philpot said. "Offerings. Maybe that's what's going on now. The abductions in Guatemala. The 'disappeared.' Maybe it's not about the actual people but about the blood needed—"

"You're missing the point," Georgina said.

She's so damn smart, Bogie thought, running one hand over the legs that encircled his waist. He was still living his lizard life, moving with the current, but there: a jazz in his groin. Georgina had turned out to be a woman like none he'd ever known. She'd astounded him that first night, lying in the disheveled bed, thighs too big, breasts too small, plump belly. He had never experienced anything like her. Sex for him had been plentiful but driven by constraint—lack of time, threat of discovery—and the girls he'd known had never moved as Georgina did. He might've been wrestling and she, his opponent; her legs nothing like the stick-legs of the girls he usually fucked, her arms as strong as his. Equal in desire, every move countered; the match, a draw—until she took control and it wasn't.

Later, trembling, unable to speak, Bogie lifted up his open hands and spread them wide. Above him, Georgina laughed. "Women don't reach their sexual peak until they're forty-three. Didn't you know that?" He said he knew nothing. She asked how old he was and when he said the highest number he could imagine, she leaned down and bit his nipple. "You're not thirty and I'm a year shy of forty-three, but I've always been advanced for my age."

To Philpot, Georgina said, "The point about blood sacrifice is, the humans have to be *willing*. Only then do the gods manifest. Are the *desaparecidos* willing?"

Bogie's lizard mind thought, *Bird Jaguar was willing every six years of his reign.*

"No," she said, scrubbing harder, the water's invisible particulates rasping Bogie's skull, his head wobbling, shampoo snaking down. "They're forcibly 'disappeared,' tortured and killed. The Guatemalan government is criminal. Why would you think otherwise?"

"He acts like a man from Retalhuleu," Edith said.

Bogie felt Philpot's body pivot.

Edith said, "Tell us about the labor union officials, Phil. Who tortured them?"

"You wouldn't be a pinko now, would you, Edith?"

The danger in Philpot's voice poked Bogie awake. Before he could say how rude it was to tease Edith about her hair, Brenda stood and screamed. She was pointing at the iguana and Philpot was hauling himself to the bank and leaping up, water streaming off his hairy back. He reached for his rolled-up towel. Georgina unwrapped her legs from Bogie's waist and used the rope to pull herself, hand over hand, through the water, shoulders creating a wake, small toes trailing behind. Philpot stepped into the tangle of roots, knife in hand. Below him, Georgina treaded water to keep from being carried downstream. Philpot hesitated. Slightly, almost imperceptibly, Georgina nodded. Philpot didn't move. Screaming, Brenda stamped a foot and threw her head around, beehive be damned. Philpot shot a look at Georgina, flipped the creature with one huge fleshy hand and slit its throat with the other. He held the iguana by its tail upside down over the river as Georgina heaved herself up on the bank.

Bogie hung onto the rope, his eyes stung by shampoo, leaky, red-rimmed.

That evening they sat, as usual, on stools around the wooden table in the Sarabias' hut, a structure with no windows, vertical slats of wood for walls, a dirt floor. They ate here every night, sweating, eyes watery with smoke from the kitchen. Angel de Jesús, that grinning, toothless guard, carried out a large platter. Triumphantly, he placed it in the center of the table. The whole iguana, looking lifelike—lizard skin, open hooded eyes, tongue poking through slack jaws—lay on its belly, clawed feet hanging over the platter's fluted ceramic edges. Only the backcomb was absent—the body having been slit down the middle and stuffed with chunks of flesh mixed with tomatoes, onion, chilies.

"Yum, yum," Philpot said. No one else said a word.

"I think lizards are poisonous," Sylvia said. Her overpainted red lips dominated the haze. From the kitchen doorway, a small boy, naked except for a too-short tee shirt, absently fiddled with himself as he pondered her.

Georgina said, "It tastes like chicken, I promise."

No one moved. Angel de Jesús continued to carry in platters of cooked vegetables, lettuce and tomato salad, fruit. Everyone looked at each other, their smiles knowing, affectionate.

Philpot spooned out a steaming pile from the iguana's back. "Gotta hand it to you, Hollewig. You were a real hero this morning. I couldn't have done it." He passed the platter to Georgina. "Crawling on hands and knees. My god, you deserve a medal."

Bogie was supposed to be the man in charge, but Philpot had usurped his position, his small duffle producing binoculars for Sylvia, Pepto for Edith, white tape to wrap around the metal hinge that had rubbed Everett's knee raw.

"Gonna help you find your Harpy Eagle, bud," Philpot said. "We oughta look for its nest. They're gigantic, right? Mmm-mm, this is good."

"So now you're a *bird finder*," Bogie said.

The room was filled with discrete layers of smoke, but here and there the setting sun shot rays through random chinks in the walls, and one shined on Philpot: his face gleamed.

Sylvia said, "*You're* the one knows about birds, Bogie." She had spent the afternoon pressing her gratitude against him: *Thank you for helping my husband you were so kind how can I ever repay you?*

"Yes," Georgina said, pushing the iguana platter toward him. "Go with them, Bogie."

"Too many camp chores." The response was automatic now.

Philpot said, "As some of you may've guessed this part of the world is sorta my territory. I'm an advisor, you might say—"

"Don't believe it," Edith said. "You're a spy."

"I am an observer, I am not a spy. I pay attention to what's happening on the river is all. I wanted to see Yaxchilan, I heard about this tour. Simple as that. Two birds with one stone."

"A shortcut," Georgina said.

"Exactly," Philpot said, grinning. "I don't believe in ideologies. I observe and report independently. Which is why, although it may come as a surprise—"

Bogie stared at the iguana, its hooded eyes and black tongue hazy in the heavy air. He saw bloody paper burning and within the rising smoke, Bird Jaguar's Vision Serpent uncoiled. It opened wide its jaws and from the other realm, the god leaned out to deliver a message.

"—Bogie's exploits are *legend*."

Bogie jerked alert. Philpot threw an arm over his shoulders. Bogie twitched hard, leaned forward, snatched a chunk of meat from the slit in the iguana's back and stuffed it in his mouth. The powerful arm casually pulled him back and lay slung around his shoulders, the huge palm patting his chest.

"Our Bogie's been much, much too modest. Hasn't even mentioned the giant emerald he found." Philpot's body remained relaxed, his voice amused as his hand moved beneath the wide white lapel of Bogie's *guayabaya*, two straight fingers plunging down hard. Bogie, chewing, felt his body sag. He managed, but, barely, to swallow.

The voice overflowed with laughter; the fingers pressed harder. "El Corazon, wasn't it called?" Bogie could not speak. He felt how skinny he was, how fragile his life. Philpot hadn't wanted to kill the iguana, but he meant to kill him.

Philpot pressed harder. "So imaginative, our Hollywood screenwriters."

"*Stop it*," Georgina said.

Instantly the pressure ceased. Bogie sprang free, sucking for air. He slapped the table hard and the ceramic platter jumped. The iguana's tongue slipped, easy as a little French kiss.

"Whoops," Philpot said.

Bogie felt floaty, lightheaded. He watched his arm reach, watched himself pull the tongue all the way out and wag it at Philpot. "Biggest emerald ever saw," he said. He stuffed the whole tongue into his mouth. "Lost in hoker hame."

"Some game," Philpot said.

"Yeath, Hil, it wath," Bogie said. He continued to work his jaws, but the tongue was unchewable, black rubber. His stomach heaved. Around the table, ghostly faces, shimmery and wet, watching him. He swallowed, gagged, swallowed again—and the tongue slid, whole, down his gullet. Everyone leaned forward.

"In the jungle," Bogie said. He burped, burped again, straightened himself with a sharp downward tug of his shirt. "Everybody sitting around with machine guns. The Colonel definitely cheated. No way he had a full house, but I couldn't call him on it."

"Wise move," Everett said. No one else said a word.

The smoke hung in layers. On the floor, flung out, the little boy continued his small comfort, eyes closed.

Philpot said, "Hollewig! Tomorrow before we take off for Palenque, I swear I'll find you a Harpy nest."

"Tomorrow's going to be a big day," Georgina said. She paused to gather attention. "I've been waiting to tell you because I wanted it to be a surprise. Tomorrow is the *summer solstice*. We're going to witness a cosmological phenomenon that was celebrated here with a bloodletting ceremony for more than a hundred years."

Nauseated, Bogie felt himself retract. The Perforator God.

"We know precisely how the ceremony was performed because the Yaxchilan lintels show us." Georgina's voice deepened as she shifted into her professorial voice. "These lintels are the most beautiful and famous Mayan artifacts in the world. Cut away in 1882 by Alfred Percival Maudslay and floated down the Usumacinta, they're in storage in the basement of the British Museum. I'll lecture about them tonight, but *tomorrow* before dawn I'll lead you through the labyrinth and up the hill to Structure 33. When we enter the chamber—

"Remember how I told you time was circular for the ancient Maya? That it ran in fifty-two-year cycles? *Fifty-two* years, the average Mayan lifespan, and every day with its own unique name. Bird Jaguar performed his final bloodletting ceremony on 3 Imix 17 Mol, a summer solstice more than a thousand years ago. Tomorrow the sun will rise as it did then, and the first ray will shine through the central door of Structure 33 as it did then, but when it strikes the statue inside, *we'll* be there to see it."

The birds weren't yet singing when Bogie's stomach cramps woke him. *That fucking lizard.* He crept out of his hammock, wearing only white boxers. He slipped on his flip-flops. From beneath the hammock, he grabbed a roll of toilet paper and the spade, handle folded. He had no intention of trudging back to the latrine, but headed down toward the river. He could hear the water, but he couldn't see it. The moon was new, the world dark. How could he have forgotten his flashlight? *You stupid bozo.*

The sound of the water grew. He stumbled off the path, felt his way across mossy squish. When the ground hardened, he jerked the spade open and dug. His right shoulder, the deep muscle, tendons and fascia, ached. Was it bruised? Two prints? Or his whole shoulder black and blue? Goddamn Philpot. Squatting over the hole, he evacuated. He continued to squat, despite the powerful odor. That damn black tongue. Why hadn't he spit it out?

He didn't know the time, but the sky had lightened. Soon Georgina would wake everyone, and they'd walk through the labyrinth and climb the hill up to Structure 33. Built to intimidate all who traveled by water below—*I am Bird Jaguar, Look on my greatness*—on land, the building only came into view as one climbed. Every evening, the gradual revelation of its roof comb thrilled Bogie. Then, his mind flashed on Everett crawling up the slope. His stomach turned and his bowels voided a second time.

He was shoveling dirt onto paper, but stopped when he heard the sound of something moving through the dark. It couldn't be a jaguar, you'd never hear a jaguar. He needed to move away from the hole. Its odor might be attracting—what? A ripple of fear crawled his spine: who knew what? *This place.* Too dark and too strange, filled with invisible creatures—not to mention the dead. He felt the familiar light feather-touches all over his body. Moving away through ferny shapes, Bogie stood pressed against a tree trunk, straining to see.

Years of playing "I Spy" by himself as he sat upstairs in the funeral home had sensitized him to minute shadings of shape and form, light and shadow. He knew immediately the shadow was Philpot. He felt a rage he had never known. The shadow crashed down to the river's edge and stood by the dugout canoe and rope-tied ceiba. What the hell was Philpot doing? He held up—what? Binoculars? Philpot was using *binoculars* to scan the river and the bank on the far side. When he turned around, Bogie shrank back. The dark extensions of Philpot's eyes examined the landing, the Sarabias' hut, the canopy of trees. Bogie remained motionless. Everything was silent except for the sound of the river and his pounding heart. Mayan civilization rose, flourished, and fell before Philpot lowered the binocs and headed back toward the sleeping place—making as much noise going up as he had coming down.

All this time the sky continued to lighten. Bogie, in his boxers, bare-chested, felt the chill of earliest morning. He hurried back to his hole. When he finished covering it, he dog-trotted down to the dock, rinsed the shovel, his hands. The sound of the water was big, the river's surface deceptively smooth. The stars had winked out, there were no clouds, only a white mist rising up off the water. A small sound. A plop. A fish jumping? The hair on his arms prickled. Across the river, a silent canoe slid into view, a dark figure paddling. On the left, another canoe with another dark paddler slipped from the wooded bank. Goosebumps covered his body. Philpot had sent some kind of signal. He'd called the evil *Archivo!*

Georgina. He had to warn her. He turned and ran.

When his flip-flops slipped on slick stone, Bogie the Brave stepped out of them and ran barefoot. The sky was graying, and the jungle rose up around him, hungry, alive. Ahead of him, the labyrinth's silhouette bulged. He slowed to gather himself. A thousand years of bats and guano. Giant centipedes. He slowed. On his right, a stone wall loomed. Its three benches, each inset within its own niche, lay in blackest shadow. While he'd been running, his breath, his pounding heart had obliterated all sound, but now he heard scuttles, snaps, creaturely cries. A world pulsing with life—and not just animals. *Dark paddlers.*

Bogie stopped, too terrified to move. His eyes blurred. He willed himself to enter the labyrinth; he had to get through to warn Georgina.

Out of the shadow of the far niche, a white figure rising up, flowing toward him. He went blind. He swung the shovel. Pain shot through his shoulder. He ignored it. He whirled the shovel this way, then that, before him, behind. No sound except that whish, no words, no self. When his arms felt the twang of metal striking stone, his eyes cleared. He struck again and again. The ringing split his brain, but the wall that had stood for more than a thousand years continued to stand. *What'dya think, bozo?*

He threw away the shovel and flung himself against the wall. He fought with his body, stone scraping chest and thighs—until, reduced, he hung, fingers gripping a crack, toes barely brushing the ground. *Please.* Dread encircled his body and squeezed. It was as though a valve opened within him and life drained out. He fell hard.

The taste of dirt in his mouth brought him back. He lay flung out on the trail, his throat jerky with sobs. He rolled his head and saw a white mist floating away from him into the tunnel. Was it Georgina? In a white scarf? The cold shapes that had surfaced to feed on him sank back. He worked to understand what he'd just seen, but he couldn't.

It seemed a long time before he was able to turn over and haul himself to hands and knees. He tried to stand, and when he couldn't, he crawled. Dirt and gravel bit his knees.

The smell of the labyrinth stung his eyes, penetrated his pores. Why hadn't he noticed it before? Because he hadn't been sightless and alone, he'd had Georgina: she'd held his hand, a flashlight. Now, in the absolute darkness, he feared the ammoniac stink might literally knock him out. *Don't touch the walls, bozo, they're crawling with—do not think about centipedes!* After an age, his toes bumped the exit's stone stairs. As he climbed, sliding bare feet in the pitch-black across each encrusted step, the funeral home rose up in his mind: its white tile and clean clinical smell, its scrubbed metal sinks. And then, he was out and running.

He stopped, stunned. The plaza was deserted. Sky and grass, grand staircase, empty, and everything the color of pewter. Nothing was as he expected. He started up. At its edges the ancient stairs lost definition: crumbled stone fragments cut his feet. He moved to the center. The restored steps were shallow, slippery, endless. Up and up he climbed.

The sky grew lighter; Structure 33 materialized above him. When Bird Jaguar reigned, every stone had broadcast rust-red to a green world. Now the roof comb rose up, dirty-white against a no-color sky. Around the structure, the jungle pressed, and within it birds sang, two hundred and twenty-two species, waking up, rejoicing in the new day. *I believe I conjured you.* Georgina's voice. It's what she'd said during one of their afternoons in her bed. *My heart called out across the universe, and you appeared.* Like a fish, his heart flopped in his chest. The glyph for "conjure" and "bloodletting" was a fist closed around a fish. Bogie put a fist around his heart and hurried.

Ascending to the second tier, he stopped. Across the stretch of fresh wet grass, people knelt, heads bowed. Women with shawl-covered heads, old men. In their prayerful hands or on the grass before them, small bowls sent up curls of sweet-smelling smoke. Scattered here and there: young men in camouflage. Men, he realized, who had crossed the river to kneel here, not because Philpot had called them.

Bogie walked with awe through the kneeling groups. No one looked at him, no one spoke. He might have been invisible—a ghost—except his body smelled. In the freshness of the new morning, he became aware of his odor: sour, rank. *Fear.* He smelled like fear. In his fear, he had forgotten the summer solstice, but this was why these people had come. They were waiting for the moment, the crack in the surface of the world, that allowed the other realm to slip through.

Above him, on the stone steps of Structure 33, four figures, the only standing figures at the scene. Amid the muted earth tones, the group radiated white: skin, hair, clothes. The greatest relief of his young life washed over him. He ran to them. Everett wagged a huge feather in his face, "Phil found a Harpy nest!" Sylvia's red lips mouthed *So glad you're here*. "Looking kinda rocky, bud," Philpot said. "Where you been?"

Herded by the others, arms around him, everyone whispering excitedly, Bogie ducked beneath a low stone lintel into an inner space—where the world fell away. He stood quite still.

The bloodletting room.

Edith whispered something, and when he didn't respond, she shook his arm. "*Bogie?* Georgina? Where is she?" He looked at her, uncomprehending. "Didn't you see her? At the labyrinth? She went back to find you."

Before Bogie could make sense of this, Dr. Georgina Wilson stepped into the dimness of the vaulted chamber. Ph.D. in Mayan Studies, Fulbright Scholar, associate curator of pre-Columbian art at the DMA. "It's time," she said. She had unplaited her hair and beneath her loose white scarf, it rippled free. She looked like a bride.

Georgina. Bogie's heart had conjured her; he reached out a hand to claim her. The face she turned to him from within her chiffon cloud was nostalgic, a sorrowing face, the sorrow already slipping away—poof!—already gone.

The sun had appeared in the notch on the eastern horizon and a ray of light shot through the ancient doorway. You could count on the sun. It lit up the headless statue of Bird Jaguar and the bare-chested, barefoot boy standing next to it with arm outstretched.

In later years, when he was interviewed about his development as an artist, Lionel Jones would sometimes unfurl a vast canvas of adventure, sometimes speak only of a fiery motorcycle crash near Palenque and his years of recovery there. He might embroider this well-known tale, tinker with the details of his broken heart, his famous tattooed necklace of flames, but he always said *My real life began in a Mayan ruin the morning the sun split the sky.*

Adventures of
Corn Maiden

A Triptych

Alvarado

INTO THE DINING ROOM OF THE FAMOUS ALVARADO HOTEL, THEY STROLLED, mother and daughter, holding hands. Walls of paned windows welcomed the sun, and in its fullness, their matching white sundresses flashed. The travelers eating, the starched Harvey Girls and brown-skinned busboys—everyone watched! The white accentuated the mother's tan. Peg spent hours lying on a plastic lounger in their graveled backyard, greased-up and naked except for two strategic dishtowels. The daughter couldn't encounter the sun naked. Rhymes had to be slathered with zinc oxide. Her skin was white—a redhead's skin.

The elastic bodice of Peg's dress showed other attributes besides her tan. *Hubba hubba*, a man whispered as they passed his table. Such a strange phrase, its jungle-language so obscure. It entered Rhymes's young mind to stay and would be forever associated with the image of her mother "putting on her face" that morning, leaning into her vanity—a mirror suspended above a jumbled surface of golden jars and golden tubes—and Rhymes sitting cross-legged on the floor, spellbound. The preciseness of the drawn mouth, the plucked brows. The Face. *Hubba hubba.*

Her mother stiffened at the traveler's invocation, but after an infinitesimal pause she smiled and her spirit relaxed so deeply into her body that Rhymes understood she'd been playacting when they first entered the room, and the jungle-words had released her into her beauty. The shock of this beauty never lessened for Rhymes. It was always new. She herself was handmaiden to it. She spent hours brushing her mother's glossy dark hair, massaging cream into her poor feet that ached from dancing in high heels.

Rhymes had never seen her mother look more radiant than she did today. Everything about her gave off light: her gray-green eyes, her sleek chignon, her perfect heart-shaped face. Where did it come from, this mysterious light? Her mother had it and Aunt Carla didn't—never mind they were sisters. Before she could puzzle this, they were seated, and the room lifted up its myriad voices, its musical clash of crystal and silver. Happiness hollowed Rhymes until she felt like she was flying up among the shafts of sunlight. Her mother smiled at her as though to say, *Didn't we two just bring it off?* Then her eyes changed and her mind moved to the approaching Harvey Girl, and Rhymes remembered: it was another one of *those* lunches at the Alvarado. Her body plummeted. Was her father leaving them or coming back? The answer was never one or the other, the discussions about it endless, convoluted. Her father said, "I've only got a small window of time to get my chain started." Her mother said, "Sometimes mommies and daddies have to live apart, even though they love each other very much."

Rhymes knew her parents loved each other. When her mother cried and locked herself in the bathroom and she and her father had to wait for her to come to her senses, he would do magic tricks to pass the time. Aunt Carla's husband had a magic slide rule, but her father could rub a bar of soap into his forearm and make it disappear. Let her mother open the door, even a crack, and he was on his feet, arms around her—never mind if the soap was still inside his arm. He'd whisper to her, rub her bottom with his palm, and her mother would hand her the salt shaker and send her outside. Sometimes Rhymes got the shaker without being told. Either way, her parents were free to "discuss the situation" in their bedroom with the door closed while she chased brown birds around in the yard. Her mother said sprinkling salt on a sparrow's tail would allow her to catch it.

With a rasp of her gold lighter, Peg lit up. She ordered a Manhattan and a Shirley Temple. Rhymes swung her new black patent leather Mary Janes beneath the white tablecloth; her mother tapped her hard red nails on top of it. The ashtray filled with lipsticked butts. Her father, as usual, was late.

Like the hubba hubba man, her father carried a sample case. Her mother said he'd been a hero in the war in Germany, and now he sold German eyeglasses. But he had big plans: "I aim to own a chain of optometry shops along the Rio Grande. Near the pueblos, Albuquerque up to Taos. The government pays for the damn Indians to have whatever they want. The mark-up on lenses? Three hundred percent!"

When her father breezed in, Rhymes jumped to her feet. He swooped her up into his arms, and she flung her legs around his waist. Her mother said, "How many times do I have to tell you, young lady? Comport yourself in public!" But Rhymes didn't care about comporting—only about the feel of her father's strong heart against hers, his smooth, good-smelling face. Uncle Hoyle had a fascinating mustache, but her father was more handsome. He was the most handsome man in the room, her parents the most handsome couple. She had heard many people say this.

She had also overheard her mother on the phone. *I'd like Rusty to worry a little, but that hair. She's so obviously his child.* The connection between her hair and her father worrying was a mystery Rhymes could not unravel. Her mother said her hair was the color of a Manhattan served straight up, but darker—with a wild black cherry, not an ordinary maraschino. She said Manhattans were her favorite cocktail and Rhymes was her favorite daughter.

Her father sat down with her in his lap. "I bought my very own little girl a present."

Rhymes recognized the white paper sack with its stamped "A." It was from the special newsstand in the lobby where she wasn't allowed to touch anything, because the Alvarado was the star hotel in Mr. Harvey's chain. Out of the sack, her father pulled—ta-daa!—*The Kachina Doll Coloring Book*. He'd already given her this book, but she didn't mention this. He'd been so busy starting his chain. His leg went up and down, up and down, as they thumbed through it, but Rhymes felt his body streaming its attention across the white tablecloth, and her mother must have felt it too, because she sat up very straight with her head tilted. They were both playacting.

When the waitress appeared and said she hated to interrupt them, what she interrupted were angry adult voices and a child eating her corn on the cob as fast as she could, so she'd be ready whenever her father needed her to light his cigarette. This was an improbable fancy of his to which Rhymes assumed her mother would object, but she was busy stuffing *The Kachina Doll Coloring Book* into her new purse, bought to match the new shoes her new dress required, and she either didn't hear his desire or didn't care. Peg paid no attention to this act of service that had brought Rhymes close to rapture. Scrambling to her knees, scraping a match: the sudden burst of flame with its accompanying sulfuric smell; the lure of the red glow. Afterward too, placing the thin, burned body with its burned head on the small plate beside her father's hand.

Here at the Alvarado, her parents "discussed the situation" in hushed voices. At home, they shouted and slammed doors and sometimes a highball got smashed in the backyard and Rhymes couldn't go barefoot until her father had picked the broken glass out of the gravel. These Saturday lunches—during which her parents never ate—began with big silences, but after they each had a couple of cocktails, they leaned across the table and slung fast words at each other. Rhymes never paid attention to the words. She counted windowpanes, rode clouds in the golden-framed paintings, but mostly she watched. When her father's neck blotched above the edge of his collar, he would blow smoke out his nostrils. When her mother's beautiful lips turned to chiseled stone, her eyes to ice, she radiated danger. Her parents hid nothing from her. Rhymes had heard everything about the money her father gambled away, the money he loaned people who paid him back with junk. Her mother needed cash, not the paintings and pawn jewelry he hauled home.

"Hate to interrupt, Mr. Nolan, Mrs. Nolan." The primness of the Harvey Girl uniform, the white organza apron with its civilized bow, seemed a rebuke to their sulfurous table. "There's an Indian in the Cantina insisting he has to see you, Mr. Nolan."

Rhymes dropped her corncob and sat up. Lots of Indians sat out on blankets by the railroad tracks and she knew the artisans in the Indian Building, but the only Indian she'd ever seen inside the Alvarado was the little dancer in the main lobby.

Her father took a long swallow of his Scotch and pushed back from the table. Rhymes, who knew how to bring matches to life, ignored her mother's command to sit herself down.

It was dim in the Cantina, all brick and heavy wood. In the dining room, the sounds spread their wings, lifted you up, made you feel you were flying, but in here they knocked you down. Rhymes felt too small for this place. Above her, backs of men standing at a long bar—salesmen with satchels, cowboys in wide-brimmed hats and boots—all of them resting one foot on the brass rail. Her father shook hands and slapped backs and he hadn't noticed she trailed him.

Two men walked up—not to him but to her. Their odd shirts, gauzy with loose-flowing sleeves, were embroidered with flowers. "I kiss your hand," said the rumpled, cozier one of the two. The taller one, whose shirt was tucked in and tightly belted, bowed his silvery head and snapped his heels together. "You have clearly your mother's beauty, Fräulein."

Her father said, "Hey, you two! Stay away from my daughter!" But his voice was happy. "Rhymes, this is Mr. von Winsler and Mr. von Kleist." Their faces sprouted stubble—one dark, one silver—and in the air around them, a subtle odor that made her conscious they had bodies beneath the blousy shirts. "Axel! Karl! I want you to meet my daughter." He pulled her close and she leaned against the solid safety of him.

"Darling, these two bad men are artists. Axel's painting hangs over our couch and Karl's is in the dining room. Or is it vice versa? At any rate, we've got two paintings of the Sandias at sunset. Or is it sunrise?"

She shrank back. Would the men recognize his teasing voice? But they laughed as though he'd made a fine joke. There was some back-and-forth about a whiskey bill her father had paid in exchange for paintings. The men's English was accented and the sound of their words, their strangled endings, reminded Rhymes of Mr. Jaeger. Mr. Jaeger was one of her special friends. He was in charge of the Indian Building and was always kind to her, no matter how many hours she had to spend there when her parents banished her from the table. *Go play. We'll find you when we're ready.*

The man who materialized near the fireplace resembled no one in the Cantina: crimson velvet shirt, silver ear pendant and silver necklaces, red cloth wrapped around his forehead. He wasn't as tall as her father, but in his silence and stillness, he was *bigger*, and his head was huge.

"If you two jokers wouldn't run a tab, I wouldn't have to bail you out. And if you'd repay me in a timely—" The three men saw the man at the same time. "*¿Qué pasó?*" her father said smoothly. He walked to where they stood, and the bar noticeably quieted.

"Darling, Miguelito here is a medicine man." This particularly hearty voice was followed by a particularly soft one. "Who owes me a lot of money."

"Hey, Mr. Miguelito," Rhymes said. "You going to tell a story when the train comes in?"

She felt the big muscle in her father's leg jump. "You know my daughter?"

Miguelito looked down at her. "I know her."

Rhymes burned with embarrassment. Her father's body had knotted, but he smoothed right into, "Fellas, show Rhymes your paints. I need to talk to this big Navajo."

Rhymes wanted to tell him he didn't need to say Miguelito was Navajo. Even if she hadn't known him, the size of his turquoise revealed it: giant pieces, polished and inset into silver squash blossom necklaces, silver bracelets, a massive concho belt. As the Storyteller, Miguelito had the space of honor in the Indian Building. On his left, Sam Joseppa demonstrated how to weave baskets, and on his right, Red Woman sat on the floor before a loom, so tourists could witness an actual Navajo weaving the kind of blanket they would soon have the opportunity to buy. When trains thundered in from Chicago or LA and shuddered to a stop in Albuquerque, disembarking passengers sought the famous Alvarado dining room, but they had to pass through the Indian Building to get there. In staged settings, potters from Acoma fashioned thin black-and-white pots, those from Santa Clara, thick black ones. Rhymes was friends with them all.

She followed Mr. von Winsler and Mr. von Kleist to the near corner where their easels were propped. Von Winsler pulled a thin wooden box from a rucksack on the floor and flicked open its tiny brass fastener to display crumpled paint tubes. She pretended to listen while he explained about the necessity of turpentine, but her attention flowed only toward her father's conversation. Von Kleist made no pretense: he stood, unwrinkled and upright, listening.

Rhymes could barely make out Miguelito's low murmurs—something about trouble with a truck and a hogan needing repair—but her father's voice carried as he spoke at length about his small window of time. The silence that surrounded the big Navajo became visible. Amid the crawling sounds of the bar, he stood there, immovable, remote. Her father kept on about how he had to get his chain started. Miguelito remained silent. Finally her father said something short and pointed at the concho belt. The Navajo stepped back, but her father continued to talk, finger pointing.

Rhymes knew Navajos did not like to be pointed at. Before the artists could react, she was tugging her father's coattail. She wanted to say that Miguelito had to have his big belt—he was the Storyteller! But all she could do was look up and shake her head, *No.*

Von Winsler and von Kleist had followed her. Next to Miguelito, they looked wispy and slight: their long hair not thick, not black, not bound by a bandana; the flowers around their necks not heavy silver, but thread. "Nolan," von Winsler said, "give a break." Von Kleist said,

"The dice game in Gallup, we know you won big. Couple of cowboys in here talking. You're a lucky guy. What harm is—"

Rhymes took her father's hand, smoothed its golden hair, "Daddy, you are so lucky. You have me and Mama. You're going to have a chain. You have to be nice to Mr. Miguelito."

Her father looked down and studied her with thoughtful blue eyes. "You're right, I am lucky." After a moment, he turned to Miguelito. "Okay. One throw. Here, now. I win, I get the belt. You win, your debt disappears."

Miguelito said nothing. He nodded his massive head. Her father moved quickly, calling to the bartender for a pair of dice and a cup. Von Winsler began to clap his hands, and when von Kleist's claps joined his, they sang out in perfect unison, *In München steht ein Hofbräuhaus: Eins, zwei, g'suffa!* Excitement rippled through the Cantina. The clapping spread, and up and down the length of the bar everyone was talking, shouting out, *What? What kind of bet?*

Rhymes and Miguelito regarded each other. She felt very small beside the dark mountain of him. He squatted down on his heels and in the dimness, the small conchos on his ankle-high moccasins winked at her. His head seemed as big as the moon. "Today I will tell the story about Corn Maiden. How she grows tall from rain the clouds bring."

Across Miguelito's chest ran the suede strap of the Storyteller's pouch. He reached into it and pulled out a kachina, which he handed to Rhymes. Carved from cottonwood, the doll was surprisingly light. Corn Maiden. Her body was long and thin, the same width as her head. A knob of dark hair stuck out on each side of her turquoise-painted face, which was featureless except for two thin black slashes for eyes. She was wrapped in a painted green blanket, but there was a space where the edges of the blanket didn't meet, and in that long oval window, rows of painted yellow corn kernels. Her flesh.

In her mind, Rhymes saw the empty corncob on her plate. She looked up. Miguelito didn't smile, but the muscles in his big face loosened. "You keep her for me."

The Cantina's noise level had risen, but Miguelito was dark and silent enough to absorb all the sound. She'd seen it in the Indian Building. The travelers crowding in off the trains, and Miguelito telling his story while they stood talking about him as though he were deaf or didn't speak English. *Lookit! That's a* real *Indian.* Then they would wander away toward the basket or rug weaving, the beading, the pots. Often by the time Miguelito finished his story, Rhymes was the only one standing where there had been a crowd. Oh, she knew all about Miguelito's capacity for silence, and the two of them were surrounded by it now, in another world from the noisy one that frothed around them.

Her father called loudly for Miguelito to join him, and Rhymes followed. She heard someone whisper, *My god, an Indian in the Alvarado bar.* Holding Corn Maiden with one arm, she planted her Mary Janes on the brass rail between the two men and pulled herself up. Her father had a leather cup in his hand, shaking it. He looked down at her and winked. She had never loved him more. His arm stretched out to throw, but he stopped. He turned to Miguelito. "I want my daughter to throw for me."

Miguelito was looking at her father, not at her, his black eyes unreadable. He nodded his big head. Her father picked her up as though she weighed no more than a feather. On top of the bar, she sat with her legs swinging free. Up here the cigarette smoke was thicker, as were the voices, but there was also more light: light glinting off the mirror, the bottles and glasses lined up in front of it, the polished wood.

"I've already shaken them, honey. All you have to do is dump them out—but, first, a cigarette, if you please."

She lay Corn Maiden down and scrambled up onto her knees. She turned her head and saw herself reflected: a child in a white sundress, kneeling, and all around her, reflections of men, bodies pressed forward, faces watchful. There wasn't a sound. The match hissed and flared. Behind the trembling flame, her father's eyes. When she blew out the match, a collective sigh was expelled. It was as though everyone had been holding his breath. Multiple conversations and laughter exploded.

She sank back onto her heels and picked up the cup. Her fingers weren't long enough to reach around it, so she held it with both hands. The leather felt smooth and cold.

Hubba hubba.

She jerked around— Had her mother come into the Cantina? Her movement slanted the cup so the dice tumbled out. Someone muttered *Goddam*, then there was total silence. She turned to look at the two cubes of ivory, quivering, perfectly symmetrical against the dark wood.

She heard Miguelito grunt and felt him turn away, his back broad in its crimson velvet. In the rowdy commotion that followed, her father too walked off. In the mirror, the back of his golden-red head. She grabbed up Corn Maiden, but hesitated before jumping. Von Kleist stood there, tightly belted—perhaps he was trying to breathe. It was cozy von Winsler who lifted her down.

When she climbed up in her chair in the dining room, her father was asking the Harvey Girl for a Scotch, pronto. Above the edge of his collar, his blotched neck. He hadn't waited for her to light his cigarette.

"Almost had you a big old Navajo belt, Peg." He hissed an audible stream of smoke from his nostrils. "I know. You like Zuni needlepoint better, but you could've sold it. Only your daughter here threw snake eyes."

Snake eyes? Was that what they were? She liked the hissing sound of the words, and the two cubes *were* perfect.

Peg wore her dangerous face. "*My* daughter? Why did you allow *your* daughter in the Cantina?"

Rhymes saw the cup tilt and the ivory cubes tumble down. *Miguelito knew what was going to happen.* She didn't question this knowledge, but when she tried to puzzle how he knew, her mind tangled. She looked at the kachina with its tiny head and enigmatic face that was no face. It was an otherworldly being—close to human, but not. The eyes: cold black lines.

The voices—her father's, high-pitched but insistent; her mother's, low and throaty— intermingled, interrupted, overrode each other.

No mouth. No ears. No arms and legs.

A Harvey Girl stopped by the table. Her father dumped burned matchsticks onto her tray and ordered another Scotch; her mother wanted a Manhattan. Rhymes didn't wait for them to tell her to go play. Picking up her kachina, she left the dining room.

She followed a hotel corridor, softly lit and cool. The corridor wound its way into others. She walked past carved wooden chests and benches, beneath barbed-iron light fixtures and wall-sized paintings of armored men in cruel helmets. She had no destination. *We'll find you when we're ready.* She had thought all families were like hers, had never known a home not filled with hard voices until last year when she turned five and received a "big girl present": a train trip to California with her grandmother to visit an aunt and uncle she did not know. In their tranquil apartment, she had never been told to go away, never heard an angry word. Never!

Rhymes wandered through open-air promenades, followed brick paths that wound from shade into sunshine and back into shade, and her mind moved with the winding paths. Images from San Francisco unspooled: tiny paper cartons filled with unthought-of food; her grandmother laughing as she attempted chopsticks. *Chopsticks!* Aunt Carla at her grand piano; Uncle Hoyle dropping lobsters—*lobsters!*—into boiling water. And out every long window, the ocean, stretching away into wonder.

Rhymes walked the meandering paths and her indignation grew, and when grownups in tucked-away patios attempted to engage her, she scowled, wagged Corn Maiden at them, and passed by. Several times she found herself in the same patio with the same geraniums in the same pots, the same trickling wall-spigot. Uncle Hoyle would never have ignored her! He would have pulled her up onto his lap and shown her his magic slide rule. *I can teach you.*

Rhymes walked until her mind calmed, until she didn't know where she was or where she'd been, and it was then she wandered into a space she knew well: the main lobby. The little Indian stood next to the newsstand. Feathers haloed his head and surrounded the sun disk on his back. His chest with its painted red stripes heaved; the sound of the bells on his ankles and wrists hung in the air. He never failed to dazzle her. The adults around this magical boy were ordinary Anglos. Where were his parents? Was he also alone? She started toward him, but he slanted her a brief, haughty glance. Her face flamed; she turned and walked out the front door.

She headed automatically for the Indian Building, but stopped. What if Miguelito wanted his kachina back? And she didn't want to talk to Mr. Jaeger or Sam Joseppa or Red Woman. She was sick of talk, sick from talk. She looked up and saw the giant Indian, eagle wings outspread. If only she had wings, she could fly to San Francisco—but that was silly. She could never *fly*. What if she took the train? Clutching Corn Maiden, her heart soared. It was possible: she and her grandmother had done it last year. She ran toward the platform that fronted the train tracks. In her mind she saw her grandmother's knobby, liver-spotted hand holding out two tickets. The image knocked the breath out of her—as though the conductor had punched her too. It was no use.

She trudged beside the track. She tried to conjure the rocking, swaying rhythm of the train. For two days she had stood in the middle of the aisle, legs spread, feeling the vibration of the moving floor rushing up through the soles of her shoes. She began to trot, then she was running as fast as she could, her Mary Janes slapping concrete, louder and louder. The sun was hidden behind the hotel's gray arches, but its rays poured down on her shoulders and back. She ran until her lunch came up in her throat. She leaned over, dizzy, sweating, gasping for breath.

When she'd gathered herself, she limped back toward the Alvarado. The sky was bright, the air filled with the soft talk of women. She studied pots and jewelry put out for sale, she worked to steady her breath. She could still feel the train's vibration between her legs.

The blankets spread out on the platform were plain, but the ones the women wore were of many colors, and beneath these colors, more color: bright voluminous skirts and velvet blouses. The women paid no attention to her, but the children sitting beside them watched her. None of these children sported feathers like the little showoff in the lobby, nor were they painted. They wore everyday clothes, and their solemn faces were the rich brown of earth. Her dress was too white, she was too white. She stopped at a blanket that displayed the glossy black pots she liked best. Behind the pots, a woman, head bent, beading, and beside her, a small boy. Rhymes squatted down at the edge of their blanket. "Hi. My name's Rhymes Nolan."

The woman looked up: straight black bangs above a face whose roundness resembled Aunt Carla's. Her smile was so kind that Rhymes felt little sparkles of happiness overriding the sun's heat on her shoulders. She thought of her parents and their white tablecloth. "Can't get my dress dirty. May I sit on your blanket?"

The woman smiled and nodded. She was missing some teeth but there still seemed too many. "Severa Tafoya—and Phillip, my son." The boy had his mother's round face. He studied Rhymes with impassive black eyes behind lenses.

"Want to see my kachina?" Rhymes said. "It's Corn Maiden."

"I know her," Phillip said. "We're *Indians*."

Mrs. Tafoya smiled and shook her head, her eyes full of love. The boy laughed so hard he fell backward. He might've lost his glasses had they not been pulled tight to his head by a rubber band. He would probably need new glasses soon. Should she warn Mrs. Tafoya about the mark-up on lenses? She thought about this as she took off her shoes and socks. Would her father want her to tell? She was unsure. She wiggled her toes at Phillip. "Let's play!" she said.

Corn Maiden was forgotten as the two of them chased up and down the platform. A handful of other children joined the running. The concrete was hot and rough, her feet tender. Finally, she tumbled down on the blanket next to her shoes. She was breathing hard; she took a foot into her lap to inspect it. Mrs. Tafoya put down her beading and walked over to squat beside her. She made small crooning sounds from her mouth. She took Rhymes's poor little feet onto her lap and smoothed their soles with a cool palm. She lifted the hem of the white dress. She smiled at Rhymes and reached up to touch the cotton filigree that edged her panties. Her fingertips rubbed the raised stitching—then a flick, a quick pinch, high up inside her thigh. Rhymes jerked away, but already Mrs. Tafoya had pulled out her elastic bodice to peer down. Rhymes peered down too. Her nipples were nothing she'd ever paid attention to. Mrs. Tafoya clucked and let the elastic snap back. She turned away and found a paper sack out of which she pulled—ta-daa!—a small hairbrush. She held up the brush, picked up a strand of Rhymes's hair, and nodded at her. Wary, Rhymes nodded back.

As Mrs. Tafoya brushed her hair, two of her neighbors moved off their blankets to squat near. Phillip and the running children sat down to watch. Mrs. Tafoya lifted and twisted her hair this way and that, a slow dance that moved her head in hypnotic rhythm. The women giggled and talked in a language Rhymes didn't understand. The children kept silent. When shown a hand mirror, Rhymes saw a straight line of pink scalp and dark red hair pulled tight and twisted into sizable knots on either side of her head.

While Mrs. Tafoya and her friends layered silver and turquoise necklaces on Rhymes, covered her wrists with bracelets, slipped multiple rings on her fingers, the children took turns holding the kachina, passing it from one the other. All examined her closely. When the doll was returned to Phillip, he stood and, stalking around, shoved it at each child in turn. Corn Maiden spoke in a high, keening inhuman voice, and one by one the children fell backward. Mrs. Tafoya looked over, her voice sharp in its unknown language. Through her trance, Rhymes watched the children disband.

On the concrete, a shadow: Phillip squatting in front of her. Behind tight-pulled glasses, wondering eyes. He sucked in his breath. Rhymes assumed it was because of her jewelry and hair. She sat up straight and lifted her chin like Peg always did. She waited. But Phillip didn't tell her she looked beautiful, he poked her chest. She looked down: a white fingerprint on her skin.

Mesmerized by the print, she didn't hear the signal, but there must have been one because up and down the platform women bustled back to their blankets. Mrs. Tafoya pulled her standing, guided her to a spot behind the black pots, and sat her down. She draped a brown and green striped blanket over her head, wrapped it under her chin and let it fall over her shoulders. She tucked her shoes and socks under it. Stepping back to admire her work, Mrs. Tafoya showed happy teeth. She squatted and held up her hand mirror again. With glazed eyes, Rhymes saw that she had disappeared. She was a red face in a small window of wool.

The train roared in and heaved to a stop in a merciless screech. Passengers straggled down through its gaseous stink in ones and twos and walked past the women lined up on their blankets. The passengers talked among themselves. Rhymes sat silently, as if she didn't hear their conversations or didn't understand them. *Lookit that one. Never seen an Indian with green eyes.* This comment made her want to laugh, but she didn't. The blanket scratched her sunburned skin, but she didn't move. She squinted her eyes smaller.

The passengers strolled past. They stopped to buy jewelry, baskets, pots. They entered the Indian Building and bought more. They ate at the Alvarado. Time passed. On the tracks, the train panted. The women sat, silent and still—even among the children, there was little movement. The sun sank lower; passengers began to wander out of the hotel, quieter now that they'd eaten. They cast long shadows behind them as they walked down the platform to board the train that would soon depart for LA. Rhymes could barely see them out her slit eyes.

Later, Mr. Jaeger's strangled voice called her name over and over.

Von Kleist marched crisply up and down the platform asking anyone who looked at him if they had seen a young female. Anglo, with red hair?

Through it all, Rhymes sat motionless beneath the burning sky. She didn't wonder where her parents were; they would come for her sooner or later. Her father was busy, he only had a small window of time. Her mother was probably crying. Soon she would come to her senses and hand her daughter the salt shaker. Rhymes could remember that girl, the one who could run with flocks of brown birds, scattering them skyward.

Mezzanine

SHE DIDN'T RING THE BELL. SHE COULD HEAR LAUGHTER AND SOME KIND OF music. She took two deep, shaky breaths, but they did not calm her. There was nothing to do but go in. Cigarette smoke assaulted the fresh, cold air that entered with her. She was late. A storm had delayed her flight from National, and as the cab from Idlewild snaked through Friday evening traffic, her anxiety had grown. But now, finally, engulfed in a din of masculine voices and clink of glasses, she saw him. Her shoulders relaxed. Uncle Hoyle would know what she should do. He would save her.

He had not seen her yet. She stood against the door of the apartment, holding her overnight case, and watched him. He was dressed in black—turtleneck and slacks—with a glint of silver on his belt, and the circle of men around him also wore black. They might have been members of the same monastic order. Did this make her the supplicant? In her head, her mother's voice, *Must you always be melodramatic, Rhymes?* Hoyle's heavy-framed glasses she knew well, but his beard had streaked with silver since she'd last seen him, and this, below the soft brown of his hair and the deeper brown of his mustache, startled her. She felt suddenly, unaccountably shy. She brushed moisture from the front of her Navajo-blanket wrap. Where was the girl who used to fling herself at him, arms and legs atangle, almost knocking him over with joy?

"Rhymes!" Hoyle broke away from his black-clad circle and came toward her with arms outstretched. Even here in this strange apartment so far from home, his smile created the world to which only the two of them belonged.

"I've been worried," he said. But before she could explain why she was late, he had gathered her to him. Beneath the horse-smell-wetness of her wool, there was his smell—as always, fresh, like rain. The cadence of conversation, which had broken momentarily, began again to flow around them.

Stepping back, he lifted her hand to his mouth. "My God, you're gorgeous. A grown woman at seventeen. I can't believe it." He put his other hand on his heart, "'*She walks in beauty, like the night / Of cloudless climes and starry skies*'—That's Shelley for you. Says it better than I ever could."

It was Byron, not Shelley—but she didn't correct him. Nor did she fault him. Hoyle's field was math, not literature.

"I bet every boy on the East Coast is after you. They are, aren't they? Is it possible you still love me best?" His voice was smooth, his tone bantering, but his brown eyes, behind his glasses, were sharp.

"You know I do, Uncle Hoyle."

"Not 'Uncle,'" he said. "Just 'Hoyle.'"

Hoyle had been the only person in her life who shared her interest in Pueblo culture. For her parents, the word "Indian" was an abstraction, a companion word for cowboy. How they managed this, she wasn't sure. In Albuquerque, they lived surrounded by Native Americans, but Peg and Rusty would have never torn themselves away from any party to drive her to some far mud town so she could watch ceremonial dances or wander through ruins. After her train trip to San Francisco, Hoyle came to New Mexico every year, and it suited her parents that he was willing to endure her. It became an accepted ritual for the two of them to visit different pueblos, traveling far distances to flat-topped mesas or touring those closer to home, the ones tucked in among the brown buttes and cones and sparse brush north of Albuquerque.

Home was a noisy maelstrom—her parents constantly separating and coming back together—but with Hoyle, she entered another world. They barely spoke during their excursions. Alone, with only the vibrant, high-keyed quality of the air and the tawny desert stretched tight as a drumskin over the earth, the two of them experienced a presence so vast no sound could express it. Enveloped by this silence, they explored dark kivas whose circular walls were sunk deep into the earth and examined sand paintings—pale geometry—in the brilliant light.

Putting his arm around her shoulders, Hoyle pulled her into the noisy, soft-lit present. "I've got rooms at the Waldorf for the weekend, but I wanted you to meet me here, because—I'll admit it! I want to show you off. You've got to meet Ed—this is his apartment—and let's get you a drink. You allowed to drink Scotch when you come to meet me?"

She'd never tasted Scotch. "Of course."

Hoyle put her poncho and overnight bag in a closet near the front door. Then with his hand pressed low against the small of her back, he guided her into a tremendous rectangular space whose white walls curved up into a ceiling of extraordinary height. The ceiling was covered with squares of white-painted tin, and this gave the voices of the men in the room a strange metallic vibrancy. The men were all math professors, their names—Carl, Frank, Robert—linked in Hoyle's introductions, sine and cosine, to different universities across the country. When her parents had mentioned that Hoyle was planning to attend the American Math Association Winter Conference in New York, she'd insisted that she had to see him. They would both be on the East Coast! She didn't have to plead; they acceded quickly. Anything not to have to listen. Let Uncle Hoyle take care of her.

It was January now. The previous June, her father had sold his string of optometry stores to a national chain. Flush, he'd had an easy time convincing her mother to take him back. He was a bad boy, but he was a rich one. Because her parents, both voluble, were absorbed in the chaos of their marriage, her home had always been a torrent of heated words, but after the sale, their voices joined to become a congenial babbling. In this delirious togetherness, they had decided to ship her off to boarding school.

As they made their way through the crowd, Hoyle introduced her to everyone: "I want you to meet Rhymes Nolan, a student at The Madeira School." Over and over: "This is Rhymes, a student at Madeira." She puzzled over why he didn't say she was his niece, but the introductions flowed too quickly for her to question him.

There were no paintings on the walls in this apartment. No sculptures on the shelves. No images at all. Its stark whiteness, combined with the polished black oak floor and the rich red of the oriental rugs, seemed a perfect setting for men who could understand the signs and symbols of an unseen universe and gesture at infinity during cocktail conversation.

She was openly examined by all the men, but she didn't take offense. She knew her velvet shirt with its stamped-silver buttons and turquoise skirt edged in red rickrack failed to reflect a prep school aesthetic. Her parents had imagined that an Eastern boarding school would shock her out of her obsession with Indians and art—two things her mother declared made her "untenable." (Her mother loved big words; she had been twelve years old when her mother said this and had to look it up: *flawed, defective, unacceptable.*) Her squaw skirts and silver concho belt had rendered her a figure of ridicule at Madeira from the moment she arrived, but the cruelty of the smooth girls in their peter pan collars and brown Weejuns only made her defiant—and social isolation proved a charm. Far from withering, her devotion to her two passions had grown.

Carrying their drinks, Hoyle herded her into a far corner of the room. The two of them stood facing one another, semi-isolated by towering bookshelves. Hoyle leaned against the shelves and traced the rim of his glass with a long finger. "Well. Let's see. How long's it been?"

She bowed her head to sip her drink.

"Why the face?"

She couldn't say it was the Scotch. "You're the professor. You tell me how long."

Hoyle knew. His visits always coincided with her school holidays. It had been August a year ago that he'd driven her to Santo Domingo to see the Corn Dance. She saw a vast sky piled with tall cloud formations. It filled the New York apartment.

The two of them had sat side by side on an adobe wall. Beneath a burning sun, they watched dancers file out of the kiva. Separate lines of men and women stamping the dust to the blood-beat of a drum. The women wore tall cloud symbols on their heads, thin wooden *tablitas* painted turquoise, tied under their chins with rawhide. They shuffled, flatfooted, their bare feet never leaving the earth, while the men, lifting their weight on the upward movement, stamped the downbeat hard enough to rattle the bells and hollow deer hoofs tied to their calves. The plaza teemed with visitors, and everywhere vendors hawked cold drinks and fried bread. She was barely conscious of them. For hours, the men and women danced, and the invisible prayer they wove tied her to Hoyle, to earth and sky. Surrounded by the purity of their intent, she wept. Small, continuous tears.

"Remember how nauseated I was after the Corn Dance? I thought it was because our day together was over. I felt so empty and sick."

"That's the day it was so hot, right?" said Hoyle. "You wouldn't leave until the Indians quit dancing, and they just would not quit. I was sick too—but with boredom."

His smile with the wink said he was teasing. He loved the dances as much as she did. Why else did he go?

She said, "Nausea's a common response when you're subjected to a continuous sound like drumming, and it stops. I read about it this fall in a Psych book."

"Ah, psychology. The layman's panacea. Life's to be lived, Rhymes, not learned from."

She sipped her Scotch, trying not to grimace, and thought about this. Hoyle was a man who spoke wisdom. "I don't know what I'm learning at Madeira except that I don't belong there. I'm just so homesick, Uncle—" He raised a warning finger. "—I mean, Hoyle. I'm homesick. And this sounds weird, but not for people. For the air, the mountains. When it gets really bad, the only thing that helps is thinking about you. Our trips."

And with this admission, it all came rushing out. Rusty had decided that Florida was *the* place to start his new optometry chain. They'd even spent the holidays there—did he know this? In Miami with a silver-tinsel Christmas tree in the hotel lobby and palm trees. It hadn't felt like Christmas at all. No evergreens or snow. No luminarias or bonfires on Christmas Eve. No Indians dancing.

It was such a relief to see Hoyle, she couldn't seem to stop talking. Did he know there'd been a fire at the Alvarado and they were talking about tearing it down? "But it doesn't matter. I think we're moving to Miami, but I don't know if we are—Peg and Rusty won't tell me. I cry and cry, but they say they don't know what we're doing yet."

"Ah, the land of unknowing," said Hoyle, nodding wisely. "The home of all theorems."

He could always make her smile. "Well, it's a bad place to be," she said. "I don't like it."

"It's where we mathematicians live," said Hoyle.

"That's not true," she said, swiping a tear away, laughing. "You live in San Francisco with Aunt Carla." They both spoke at once: "Does she have a concert coming up?"/"She's playing at a little piano bar near our apartment."

They laughed together and then stood silently, regarding each other. She discovered she'd already accepted his silver-streaked beard.

"Remember when you came out with Gran on the train?"

"Of course," she said. She had only ridden a train that once, but she could still conjure its rocking, swaying rhythm. All the way to California, she'd stood in the middle of the aisle, legs spread, eyes closed, the vibrations of the moving floor rushing up through the soles of her shoes.

"What do you remember about it?" he said. He didn't move—his body still leaned against the bookshelves—but something in him shifted, coiled.

She looked at him, puzzled. He'd had to clear his throat to ask this, and he studied his drink rather than looking at her.

She said, "I'd never seen a mustache before the morning I stepped off the train and saw you. It made you so *mysterious.* I'd never heard of Chinese food—much less, eaten it. Never seen a lobster. Or the ocean."

She didn't say how unprepared she'd been for her aunt's round-faced placidity. Because Carla had once been a concert pianist, Rhymes had imagined her wild, almost fierce. But her white hair, spray-netted to immobility, was nothing like the passionate mane Rhymes had expected, and her fingers weren't long, but stubby with bitten nails. Standing now amid the noisy sounds of a New York cocktail party, she saw Carla's short fingers pounding out Chopin, heard the lobster scream as Hoyle plunged it into bubbling water. The scream had thrilled her and she'd eaten it all, even the yellow-green stomach, licking her buttery fingers and wanting more.

"It was some trip," she said, smiling up at Hoyle, remembering that he'd talked to her that summer as if she were an adult, had taken her into his private study to show her his books filled with symbols—magical books whose indecipherable signs she studied. Five years old, sitting on the floor, turning page after page, hypnotized by a world she hadn't known existed. One day he even taught her how to use his slide rule for simple multiplication. He'd sat in his black leather chair with her on his lap and showed how slipping the clear plastic square along the numbered lines could uncover hidden sums. It was a great, mysterious gift.

"Speaking of trips," said Hoyle. "How do you like D.C.? Beats Albuquerque, huh?"

Hadn't he been listening? How could he think she wanted to be anywhere besides New Mexico? But then she smelled it: an acrid scent of nervousness that lay beneath his casually posed exterior. He was talking to cover it.

She touched his arm. "I've got something to show you. I was going to wait till later this weekend but—Is there some place we could go?"

It worked: Hoyle shed his nervousness like a discarded skin. Behind his glasses, his eyes glowed.

The kitchen into which he led her was empty and brightly lit, and when he'd closed the door, the noise of the party sounded far away, muffled vibrations from another world, a variegated world that bore no relation to this white-tiled stillness; the only sound, the refrigerator's hum.

She put her drink down and hopped up onto a white tiled counter. Pulling a folded piece of paper torn from a spiral notebook out of a pocket of her skirt, she opened and smoothed it on her lap. She had read and re-read this paper many times. It was limp, and the creases where it had been folded were gray and worn soft.

"I found this song in a book about the Hopis. You bought it for me. Remember?"

He breathed out the smoky smell of Scotch. "No."

"That afternoon at Walpi? We talked to that old man?"

"I thought you would've quit playing Indian by now, Rhymes. You're almost grown."

"I'm not *playing*," she said, taking another sip of Scotch, surprised to find it less disagreeable. "I found this song a couple of weeks ago in that book, the one you bought me." She looked down. "I've started a sculpture of it back at school. It's the best thing I've ever done, and you're the only one who will understand." She raised her head. "You want to hear it, don't you?"

Hoyle smiled and took her hand in both of his. "Of course I do."

She pulled her hand away. "This is a song the Hopis sing during the Snake Feast. Before they wash the snakes, before they send them off to carry their prayers for rain. I'll read it to you."

She bent forward to read what she had written out, and Hoyle, who had been leaning against her legs, drew back and rested against the counter's edge. He was not touching her as she read—or rather, recited—because after her first, concentrated glance, she hardly looked at the paper. She began softly, but her voice grew. Sitting there, far from school, chanting the words, she felt the flame of the acetylene torch catch light. Usually she worked with clay, but for this piece she had decided to use brass rods. And now she saw the metal burning, felt the white heat, and in her mind she tried to twist the glowing rods correctly:

> Old man, old man, bring the vessel of fluid.
> The snakes are sucking our tongues, for which we are glad.
> Now all the elements are in, stir it well and drink
> The fluid of the spider . . .
>
> . . . The Blind beetle! i-hi-el-o-a
> The Spider Woman! i-ya-a-ha-e
> The Snake-Virgin! o—o-elo-a

The warriors have found her children,
Crawling, crawling, crawling here.
Now we are ready to bathe them.

When she finished, the kitchen gleamed. She watched Hoyle
push forward, knew he'd put his hands on her forearms. They
stared at each other. She didn't move. She felt as though she were
focused with the pure intensity of the acetylene torch into a single
blazing blue point.

Into their stillness, a burst of deep loud laughter. They both jerked
backward. Her head knocked against a cabinet. Hoyle turned his
head toward the closed kitchen door.

She said, "We should go see—"

Hoyle shook his head, but she'd already jumped down. The paper,
blown sideways by her billowing skirt, drifted to the floor. They bent
to retrieve it at the same time.

In the living room, an audience had gathered around the couch—but
all was strangely quiet. Ed, the host, motioned them to join him in the
front ranks. He spoke softly. "Watch the new game Tom's invented."

Two men, both with crew cuts—one blond, one dark—sat side
by side on the edge of a black leather couch, their sleeves rolled up
past their elbows. Another, older man with round granny glasses and
a short gray ponytail stood before them, showing them how to turn
their palms up and place their arms together—the blond's bare right
arm to the other's bare left one—outstretched forearms touching.
The older man with the granny glasses and ponytail—obviously the
Tom who'd invented the game—drew deeply on his cigarette, and
now everyone stilled.

He made a slow dramatic gesture and carefully laid the burning
cigarette into the crease where the men's forearms met. For a moment
nothing happened, then: knees moved, thighs shifted, upper bodies
torqued. The blond grimaced, his mouth contorted. He grunted and

jerked his arm away. The cigarette dropped onto the black leather. Tom grabbed it and beat the couch until red sparks flew.

Now everyone was talking and laughing—except the man who'd quit first. He held his forearm to his mouth and sucked. The dark-haired man who'd won the game ignored his burn and sat accepting congratulations, his grin showcasing small sharp teeth. Tom turned and spoke in a maestro's loud voice. "Who will test his courage against our winner?"

"Come on," the winner said, scanning the crowd. "I dare you."

She looked over at Hoyle. She couldn't see his eyes behind the glint from his glasses. She heard herself speak. "I'll try it."

A part of her watched her body float forward, watched herself sit down on the edge of the black couch, unbutton the stamped-silver disk at her wrist and roll up the dark green velvet to place her arm, fragile and white with blue veins, against a thick, dark-haired arm. She raised her eyes to Hoyle's. He stood at the front edge of the circle of onlookers. She saw a paper cup slip between two metal wings.

Her memory of the cup is clear. She had gone out into the mezzanine to escape the black and white bodies blown up to fill the giant screen. It was the night before she and Grandmother were to fly home from San Francisco. Hoyle and Carla had taken them to see *It Came From Outer Space*, a 3D movie, something unheard of in Albuquerque. At the theater, they were issued cardboard glasses with square corners and red cellophane lenses. In the first row of the first balcony, she sat between her grandmother and aunt, and below the brass railing, on the main floor, hundreds of red seats marched to the screen, and behind and above the first balcony, banks of balconies slanted up into invisibility; and all around, endless sweeping stairways going who-knew-where.

She ducked when the meteor crashed and was just getting used to the sensation of rocks flying at her when the screen turned black. It stayed black despite the whistles and stamping feet. After what seemed a very long time, sound burst from the screen and *Reform School Girls* rolled. She bore it as long as she could—the barrage of bodies being chained and whipped—then she leaned over and told Carla she needed to go to the bathroom. Carla fumbled a dime to her "for the attendant."

But there was no attendant. The mezzanine was deserted, a haven, softly lit and still. She could barely hear the screams. Thousands of red seats, thousands of gray-carpeted steps, and no one, not a single soul, on the mezzanine level. The counter unmanned, sacks of candy stacked behind glass, but no one to sell them. The cavernous restroom deserted. The gray walls were lined with padded gray benches, but no one sat on them. The whole vast enterprise *empty*. She sat down on one of the benches, the dime clenched in her fist. She wasn't aware how long she sat there. Slowly, the quiet dimness of the area filtered through her, erasing with easy sweeping motions the brutal black-and-white images. Slowly the cushioned grayness enveloped her.

She became aware of a Coke machine grinding in its niche.

Its glowing red rushed forth to greet her. In this whole empty universe, she and the Coke machine were the only living things. The dime burned her palm, and for the first time she felt her body, like her fist, clenched. She sat up. On the left, descending carpeted steps; on the right, carpeted steps ascended into darkness. This dim, deserted area was an in-between place. She was solitary, but she was not alone. The machine maintained a vigil here.

Her memory of that evening is blurred and indistinct, like a dream. The horror of the movie she remembers. The safety of the loge. She remembers Hoyle coming out to check on her because she'd been gone a long time. She remembers that he let her keep the dime Carla had given her, and that he fed his own coin into the machine.

She watched the paper cup slip down between two metal wings and after a moment, ice clattered down, and then dark liquid spewed over the ice and foamed, spilling out, running down the sides of the cup. She remembers that she and Hoyle walked back to the padded bench and that they talked while she drank her Coke. She does not remember what they talked about. Heading back toward their seats, they stopped at the entrance of the sloping ramp that led up into darkness. She still held the dime. She could feel the smoothness of it, the heat. She was leaning back—she remembers the rough plaster of the wall snagged her sweater—when Hoyle bent and, lifting her chin with his long fingers, kissed her. Or did he? Was it a dream that his tongue slid between her lips to fill her mouth?

The tender skin of her inner forearm flinched automatically when the burning cigarette touched it, but she never changed expression. She knew this game was inescapable. It was her initiation. She was being tested in front of the one person in her life who could understand. The old Hopi had said it: "If your spirit is pure, the deadly teeth cannot hurt you."

Her spirit was pure; she felt no pain. She was transfixed. She didn't realize the man had dropped his arm. She held her arm outraised and still.

When she came to herself, other men were stepping forward. "Here, let me play." "No, I'm next." The room buzzed. Through all this, she watched Hoyle. His eyes told her how to find her way to him.

She played the game four more times, sitting quietly in the masculine energy that flowed around her, played until long, elliptical burns covered her right forearm. Then someone turned the music up, and the crowd dispersed. Men were getting drinks and some were saying goodbye. She sat in her turquoise skirt, knees together, waiting for Hoyle. He came, took her hands and drew her up, off the couch. He led her down a narrow hallway—past the kitchen, the bathroom, and into the bedroom. Scooping the coats off the bed, he threw them out onto the floor in the hall and shut the door.

The room was in darkness except for one bright spot of red geometry: a perfect circle of light thrown by a goosenecked lamp onto the oriental rug that covered the narrow bed. The bed was pushed beneath a window across the room. Something in her wanted to protest the place, but the click of the lock—the finality of that sound—killed it. Hoyle began whispering her name. As she walked toward the circle of light, his whispers accompanied her, but when she turned, he wasn't there. He had remained by the door, a slim black shadow, almost invisible. She watched herself undress, one silver disk at a time. When she had shed everything except her turquoise jewelry—bracelets and rings, squash blossom necklace—she lay down. In the darkness, the old floor creaked. Now she would understand. This act was the unknown, the quantity "x" in one of Hoyle's equations.

"Turn out the light."

She didn't understand. She had seen men's bodies in life drawing classes, but that was business, all posturing and line, and this was—everything. From the narrow world of the flesh, she was to enter the greater spirit world.

"Turn out the light." Hoyle's voice was urgent, his words incomprehensible.

She raised up on her elbows. She saw his eyes, a pleading stare, as he jerked his empty pants up in front of him. He walked over, holding the pants against him, and clicked off the lamp.

Her eyes struggled to adjust to the new darkness.

He knelt down beside the bed. He took off his glasses, folded them, and placed them on the table. Then he turned to her. His hands and mouth worked slowly. Formless, mumbled words fell from his lips. What was he doing? There was so much between them. This act was too inevitable and too simple to need words. Still he knelt beside the bed. His whisperings rose and fell, covering her body, weighing it down—the heavy syllables piling up, burying her. Why was he doing this?

Against her, his skin was smooth, cold. She arched into him. He moved faster but still coolly, and his words flowed incessantly, soft whisperings, against her. The bristles of his beard scraped her breasts but even in this, it was calculation she felt. Her body lost its tension, died. She turned her head toward the tall window. Snowflakes wheeled and spun in an intricate dance down through the dark. She felt her mind draw back and become interested—impersonally interested—in Hoyle. She watched his body move, and his continuing deliberateness now seemed mannered, a perversion. It made the hot, uneven eagerness of all the boys she had dismissed appear innocent and true.

Her mind drew back further, to the memory of his tenderness she had carried all her life. That tenderness was more real than Hoyle himself. She had forgotten the red cellophane glasses, forgotten the movie and the mezzanine, and, in truth, as she'd stood in front of the Coke machine, Hoyle had hardly impinged on her consciousness. He was a ghost who'd floated in. When he talked, she couldn't hear the words, and when he leaned to kiss her—his mouth so soft, his tongue searching—she accepted it as part of the dream.

The pain brought her rushing back, all body now. It enveloped her. Then it lessened. She was aware of her throbbing arm. With the fingers of her left hand, she touched the burns, felt the ooze.

Hoyle fell back. It was over. She felt nothing. The mystery seeped out of her onto the patterned cover of the narrow bed.

She got up and found her clothes. She could hear Hoyle's ragged breath. The old floor creaked as she walked to unlock the door.

"Rhymes?"

The rough edges of his voice pulled at her. She turned to look back. The room was dark, the only illumination the snow, swirling down outside the window. In front of this maelstrom, a slim pale shape lay curled on the bed. He sat up and groped for his glasses. "Don't leave."

On the mezzanine, she had returned to the bench to drink the Coke he'd bought her. When she finished, Uncle Hoyle crumpled the cup and tossed it at a cigarette stand. It bounced off the metal rim and fell onto the gray carpet, and the two of them headed up toward their seats.

She walked out of the bedroom and down the hall. She gathered her poncho and suitcase from the closet by the front door. No one had seen her enter the apartment; no one saw her leave.

Galisteo

She's standing on top of a toilet lid groping for a light bulb in the frosted half-moon above the sink. She hasn't cut herself in years, has never hidden her arms because no one thinks the scars aren't what she claims: affectionate nips from her parrots. Her fierce need has reduced Nocona's unisex bathroom to a halogen blur, but in her mind, the thought is clear, and it stops her.

A knock on the door, Russell's loud hiss. "Rhymes? You in there?"

"No."

She sounds ridiculous even to herself.

"Rhymes? Maybe I mentioned the commune, I don't know. But I swear I didn't—"

"Go away."

She hates Russell, hates herself. She tries to resurrect the girl she'd been forty years ago. Banished to boarding school on the East Coast, homesick and naïve—but not pure. *Angry.* If she'd been as smart as everyone thought, she would have taken care of the problem. Instead, she'd believed in her heart's purity and had paid no attention to her body, had worn loose sweaters, unbuttoned her uniform skirt—and since all the girls at Madeira were throwing up, *that* hadn't been an issue.

She'd ignored the signs until it was too late. Had there ever been anyone as stupid?

Graduation: four months pregnant, a black cap and blowsy gown, her parents flying in for the day. Peg saying, *Have you put on the fresh-man fifteen already?* Rusty saying, *Don't listen to your mother, darling, you look beautiful.* A lie about postponing college for a backpacking trip to Europe with friends. She had no friends, but with the money Rusty gave her for the trip, she disappeared.

"Rhymes, I'm sorry. Please don't ruin the evening."

How she got to Ray's she isn't sure. Hitchhiking and visibly pregnant, and someone had directed her there. Ray and seven women, five of them pregnant, living in an "earth ship" in the desert outside

Galisteo. An underworld of rooms, one leading into another, circular, convoluted, no windows, no light, mattresses on the floor and pregnant women lying on them, sometimes with Ray, sometimes not. Scattered clothes and naked children, water used only for the kitchen and the marijuana. It was the only green in that brown place, so tall and thick you had to push your way through it. There was an outhouse and, occasionally, when invited, they'd take towels and hike up to the neighbors' to bathe. When Ray appeared the third night after she arrived, a condensation of darkness standing over her mattress, she'd kicked him hard. The next day, he assigned her the hardest chore, hauling water to the marijuana. But he never stopped watching.

"Go away."

Feeling Russell's departure, she jumps down. The room is a box, cold and narrow, its mirror breath-fogged. She swipes a clear space with her fist: burnt eyes, wrecked hair. No one but Russell knows about the baby, and she didn't tell him everything, just the facts: she'd been seventeen, her pregnancy the result of a one-night stand; the delivery inept, leaving scars that caused occasional bouts of uterine pain.

Is she going to cut herself? No. Does she believe giving Hoyle's baby away was a sin? No.

She decides to make her long necklace a choker. The heishe is ancient, its oyster shell beads so finely sized that the strands slip smoothly, serpent-like, through her hands. They make the sound of their name, *hee shee.*

The first wrap, she hears a rattlesnake, upright, alert. *Heishe.* The second wrap, she hears the sonogram sound of amniotic fluid and heartbeat. *Heishe.* The third wrap, and the baby swirls in, bringing with him the earthy smell of that rabbit warren in Galisteo, *his* smell. She feels—foolish woman!—the tingling sensation of milk letting down in her breasts. Even though they'd been bound, when she'd fed him a bottle, he'd rooted.

She splashes water on her face, takes the pine twigs out of her hair and runs her fingers through it. Her hair is obedient and stays where she puts it, the choker glamorous.

Two hours earlier, she'd breezed into Nocona's, carrying the fresh smell of snow and piñon in the folds of her coyote coat, her fiery hair piled up and falling down. The restaurant was packed, extra tables inserted in all the small rooms, fires burning in the fireplaces, the white mantles and horned skulls above them draped in greens, everything smelling of spruce and pine. In the bar, she stepped on plexiglass that had been inset to reveal a seemingly bottomless hole beneath the floor. Some sidled around it. Rhymes usually walked straight across, but tonight she placed her boot there and paused: as far down as she could see, emptiness lined with irregular stones, an absence to witness the ancient people who'd occupied this site long before Time arrived in the form of Spanish conquistadors. She saw them riding up from the destruction of Mexico, appearing out of a fiery horizon in their armor and flying saucer helmets, their cruel beards, the long grass sweeping their horses' bellies, the high desert of Santa Fe only grass then. In this place, on this land, invisible multitudes.

She stepped up onto the barstool Russell had saved for her, her coat so long it swept the floor. She waited for him to turn and smile at her. He didn't. Outside, snow floated; inside was like a railway car, warm, crammed with holiday cheer.

"How was the walk?" she asked herself after a moment. "Magical," she answered.

"Lenore's going to be late," Russell said without turning.

She put on a smooth face. Her marriage might be in trouble, and she needed to take care. Russell talked to Lenore every day, saw her every week. Rhymes hadn't seen her for forty years, but in her mind Lenore remained Head of Judiciary, The Madeira School pronouncements somehow terrifying when made in her high baby-voice.

"You're going to like what she has to say," Russell said, still without turning.

"Farolitos and stars," Rhymes said. "A whole universe of stars. And the Plaza *so* quiet. You should've come with me."

The two of them weren't looking at each other. They might've been strangers exchanging pleasantries in the noisy crush, no one to know they were connected, until their drinks arrived in tandem. Rhymes glanced up at the bartender. A wraith dressed in black: vaporous white face, long hair caught in a ponytail.

"Like your tie, man," he murmured.

Russell said, "Thanks."

Again, Rhymes waited. Now Russell would look over and smile, because his tie—an orange river teeming with eyelashed bodies of green amoebas—was the belt to the paisley dress she'd thought she might wear tonight. Instead, he leaned to sip his overfull Manhattan. Behind him, an arrangement of holly at the end of the bar cast its shadow on the wall: towering, jagged sticks.

She lifted her martini glass. "Happy birthday, darling."

"It's not my birthday yet."

The sharp bite of the Tanqueray, the ragged shadow on the wall, her coat's thick textured hairs—she felt how they fit together. She knew that if she took Russell's hand and smoothed it, it would help him "get back." That's how she always thought of it: *getting him back.* Russell's rage at small frustrations often sent him somewhere out beyond Pluto. Her task: to help him return. It had taken her twenty years to understand this. She let his beautiful hand lie there.

A woman, wrapped in sable, passing through the bar from the bathrooms, stopped. "Russ, you bad boy. You're still in town? Where's Lenore?" The woman had had one facelift too many, but what you noticed was the fur.

Rhymes put her hand on her husband's. Her smile was a boulevard, a Champs-Élysées. "I'm Rhymes Nolan," she said. "The bad boy's wife."

"*Rhymes?* I didn't recognize you. I mean, I wasn't expecting—"

"Lenore's a little late," she said.

"You haven't changed a bit. Your hair. Still gorgeous. How clever to put it up with—what are those?"

"Sticks," Rhymes said. "Twigs. *Pine?*"

The woman's face tried hard but retained its perky incomprehension. Rhymes sat up. Who was this liar? She hadn't changed? And her hair? The bonfire came from a bottle now.

"I'm Babs. Babs Lawrence? You bought textiles from me when you were redoing the Lt. Governor's house before the—" She stopped dead.

Rhymes slid an olive off the toothpick with her teeth and ate it while she watched Babs Lawrence look around wildly for help. The ghost of baby Maren floated in the air between them, and Rhymes let her float: it hurt *and* it felt good. When had she learned to withhold herself, the sweet pain of it? The power.

"I mean, you and Lucien bought a lot of textiles from me."

The doctors had knocked her out when they saw what Maren was, and Lucien, Emperor of the Operating Room, had turned thumbs down. She'd only lived thirty-two minutes. God's payback.

"Did you know he's here? Lucien, I mean. In the back room. I tried to say hello, but they wouldn't let me in. His handlers."

Neither Russell nor Rhymes responded.

"Have to tell you how much I love your work," Babs said.

Rhymes finished her martini and signaled for another while the purveyor of antique textiles went on about how she'd intended for years to buy one of Rhymes's sculptures. "I mean, your shows sell out so quickly." The holly at the end of the bar—its berries juicy, bursting with life—dimmed, grew waxy and died, before Babs wound down with a final question.

"I never know dates," Rhymes said. "Max decides all that."

The truth was she'd had an afternoon meeting with Max—Charlie and Chisos left in the car to shiver and bark, shed hair—and had set the date of her next show for September 2001. The sun had died blazing before she'd walked into the squat adobe duplex behind the Acequía Madre, the dogs bounding in, upsetting Russell's neat piles of paperwork, knocking over his drink with happy tailwags.

"How *could* you?" Russell said. He swatted at the dogs.

"I'm sorry," she said. "I forgot."

Throwing ice into a new glass, he jerked a bottle of Scotch over it. Rhymes counted the painted saints on the bar, a battered wooden altar she'd hauled up from Mexico thirty-five years ago for the Lt. Governor's house.

"You're so wrapped up in your work," he said, "you never think about *me*."

It was true. She never did think about him, and she hadn't wanted to drive down from Taos. Russell had no idea what was required for her to be gone for even one night. Dog paraphernalia to pack, the birds furious about being caged: Pauline ruffling her neck to iridescence, screaming *Another martini, please*; Arthur, pecking at his legs, pulling out feathers.

Russell was used to being away. Tuesday and Thursday, he counseled the crazy children of Los Alamos; Wednesday, troubled adolescents in Santa Fe. She worked at home, and she hadn't wanted to leave the kiln. It had been radiating fire for a week, the corrugated metal walls around it undulating in heat waves, so that she'd had to wear her fiberglass suit and her helmet with its full-face visor. Huge asbestos gloves. Only this morning was the firing-sequence finished, and the kiln turned off—but not opened. The kiln cooling in its railroad container, that monstrous *thing* that squatted in their backyard, and inside the kiln, the three-layered molds, and inside the molds, the beeswax. One egg inside another, inside another, everything safe. Still, she hadn't wanted to leave.

So she was annoyed before she even started driving, and all the way down to Santa Fe, she'd simmered about Lenore—and beneath this, a low flame of worry about how her sculptures would look after she steamed out the wax, divested the layers of plaster and silica. She worked with trash she picked up in the desert, not to make a political statement about materialism or America's throwaway culture, but to save the least-of-things. Everything salvaged, nothing left out, all valuable, useful, part of the whole.

"Russell. I *forgot*. What else can I say?"

"The date's been set for weeks. *You* picked it."

Her voice was cold. "I'm meeting with Lenore because you asked me to—"

"Nocona's requires a coat *and* a tie."

She held up her orange and green belt. "This *will* work."

Maybe it would, he admitted. Okay. But he certainly couldn't walk Las Posadas now. His whole schedule had been disrupted, he had paperwork, he had—

Blah, blah, blah. The nine martyred saints on the bar held up their signature instruments of torture—a barbeque grill, a sword, a stone—any of which she would've gladly used on him. Las Posadas was the real reason she'd driven down from Taos. The procession around the Plaza through the cold starry night, candles and singing, patient donkey. A devil—red face, red horns, red tail—taunting the young, pregnant couple from a white balcony.

"A ghost from the past," Russell said, after Babs Lawrence left to creep around Nocona's plexiglass floor.

"And you, *Russ*, are indeed a bad boy," she said.

He slanted his lazy grin at her and leaned in. Rhymes closed her eyes and savored his kiss, a fine wire within her stretched taunt. For a moment, he was back.

"Lenore says we could buy this restaurant. *Cha-ching.*"

An anger she hadn't allowed herself to feel flashed in her veins.

He took her hands in his. His high, polished forehead and rimless glasses reflected the bar's downlight—and that beautiful mouth. Too full of teeth but defined. All his features, so precise they looked carved; his white hair, layered and sprayed. He was so *clean*. She lived disheveled, covered in plaster and silica, her nails ruined by chemicals; Russell looked scrubbed, ready for any sterile environment.

". . . financial advisor. You refused to be bothered, so I found one. Your father worked hard, and I feel duty-bound . . ."

On her cheek, her father's breath, the whisper of a hissing flame. How *had* his optometry chain turned out to be so valuable?

"Lenore says the S&P and the NASDAQ are going nowhere but up . . ."

Money was all Russell talked about now. Money and the Market and Lenore. What had happened to the young psychiatrist who'd only wanted to save children? Who was this counterfeit spouting acronyms?

"Real estate? It's headed for the stratosphere . . ."

Rhymes envisioned a rocket ship with long fins, Ray's Cadillac, and all of them squeezed in. She saw herself punching in the cigarette lighter, holding it, the coils turning red. A tingling high inside her left thigh: faint burn-image of whorls.

"Lenore says we have a beautiful opportunity here . . ."

Cigarette lighters littered the desert. A handful of them stuck into a beeswax base would create a brutal, bristling form—but if she transformed them into purple glass? She saw an amethyst geode broken open.

"You listening to me? I hate it when you do this."

"What?"

Russell's shoulders sagged with his sigh. "*Why* do you make this so difficult? Why won't you help me? We haven't much time. A consortium's set to buy—"

"You're the one cares about money. I don't."

"You don't care about money because you've always had it. Charge it to daddy."

"I've told you. *Not my daddy.*"

After Lucien, Rusty had refused to help her financially: *We don't get divorced in our family.* How she'd laughed at him.

"After Lucien," she said, "I had nothing. You know that. But I had my work."

She'd moved away—to the edge of the continent—and that's where she'd found Dr. Russell Conner, counselor for the neglected, often drug-addicted, offspring of San Francisco's Flower Children. At the time, she was working with metal.

Hmm, an acetylene torch. You must want to burn.

Twelve years of psychiatric training and that's the best you can do?

They'd married in Vegas at an all-night chapel. After which, she'd enchanted him into moving to Northern New Mexico. It hadn't been difficult: he could save children anywhere. He built his practice, she an adobe house. Not a regular house, a fantasy: curvy walls, fenestrated turrets, a cupola. They huddled over blueprints, pulled square nails from pine planks, laid adobe with the workmen. They made love on or under every piece of furniture, in every room. How she'd loved him! *Taos:* where the vast silence of the Sacred Mountain hummed, and the night sky, a slow-wheeling dome, made you aware of the voyaging planet.

Lenore didn't try to hug Rhymes or pretend they were friends. There was the well-remembered baby-voice. So unfortunate! But if the voice made you discount her, *that* was a mistake. She was tall—taller than Russell, but also bigger. But she had always seemed large to Rhymes, the new girl sitting alone in assembly, looking up toward the stage where the Head of Judiciary reigned. Lenore had been a brunette but was now blonde, the shape of her hair echoed by her giant polymer pearls. She wore heavy, black-rimmed glasses. She told the spectral bartender to put the tab on her bill; she told Rhymes that Melissa would take her coat. Towering over James, the diminutive maître d', she instructed him to seat "her guests at her table in the front room."

James led them into a white room whose windows trickled with water, so it seemed a vessel floating in light: white tablecloths encrusted with glimmering votives, a fire in the fireplace, and above it, a triangular skull dripping strings of tiny white lights. And at the tables, people with pale satisfied faces. In spiked heels and a black sequined sheath, Lenore made her way from table to table, a current of excitement and pleasure, bringing life to the room.

The only dead table was theirs.

"*Look around,*" Russell hissed. "This place is a cash cow."

The tall menu assured Rhymes she could be in New York or LA. There was no menu like this in Taos, no restaurant with this chic, all-white décor. A frisson of superiority traveled her spine. How she despised hypocrisy and posturing. Endless iterations of O'Keeffe had rendered horned skulls cliché—not as bad as coyotes wearing bandanas, but still: commercial. In Taos, no one conformed, you lived an authentic life. It was a hard life, but the easy one was for people like these. She didn't care that they'd stared when she'd walked in wearing jeans and cowboy boots, a plain black shirt. She didn't want to fit in with this Santa Fe glitz. Self-righteous and pure, she was smiling to herself when a small voice in her head whispered, *Who're you trying to fool?*

She felt the blush at the roots of her hair. She looked down, straightened her napkin and made herself admit that everyone had stared, not at her clothes but her jewelry. Money couldn't buy *this* jewelry. Her concho belt, an old pawn piece, huge, museum quality; strands of heishe that hung mid-thigh. She'd draped herself like some tribal bride in order to intimidate Lenore. Wasn't this a normal creaturely response? Marking territory.

The necklace had been a gift from Mr. Jaeger for her sixteenth birthday. Hermann Jaeger, long dead, bones now, small bones, tiny hands and feet. It had come with a note on fine cardstock written in a spidery European hand: *This heishe is from the Chetro Ketl Kiva in Chaco.* (She'd had to explain to her parents that this meant it was ancient—Anasazi.) *The beads were carried up by ants from graves and sieved from anthills. I don't know anyone who would appreciate it more than you, dear child, whom I've had the pleasure of watching grow for these many years. Yours sincerely, Hermann Jaeger, Manager, Indian Building, Alvarado Hotel.*

Shocked, her mother had insisted the necklace be returned; her father argued for locking it away until she was older. They began to look at her suspiciously: all those afternoons she'd spent by herself in the Indian Building? Whispered conversations about sending her away to boarding school.

No one approached them while Lenore made rounds, but the minute she sat down, polymer pearls tunking, activity swamped their table. She scolded James, the maître d'. He gathered their menus, which looked especially large in his small hands. "Forget you ever saw these," he said. "Miss Hensley has pre-ordered everything for her special guests."

Russell gazed at Lenore with happy-eyes. "I can't imagine a better sixtieth birthday."

Rhymes felt breakable, vitric.

"Love your tie," Lenore said. "Is it Hermès?"

The meal was a work of art, a ballet—waiters moving in and out in graceful choreography—exchanging plates, silverware, stemware, a different wine for every course. They ate poached oysters garnished with plump, glistening Osetrea caviar. "So intense and yet so *light*, don't you think?" Lenore said. She hadn't once mentioned Madeira or money, only art—and she'd done her homework. Or had *Russ* told her? She knew about the splash Rhymes had made when she was still in art school. COWBOYS and INDIANS, the two words written separately with neon tubes, one white, one red. Who'd ever heard of making sculpture with light? So daring! Cutting-edge! And the politics of it: subtle, yet pointed.

Rhymes twirled her wrist, wrapping her necklace around it. Of course Lenore was charming. She wanted to manage her money.

The waiters delivered warm quail salads with sautéed artichokes and golden piñons, and they ate in silence for a moment. "So, *that's* when you met Lucien," Lenore said, crunching delicate quail bones. "Now I understand. The most promising young politician in the state and you, the toast of the town."

Rhymes picked threads of meat from the tiny breast with her fingers and thought about how long ago it all was. Neon was old news. She'd gotten waylaid, bogged down, years had passed with small achievement but, finally, she had understood that fake light no longer served.

"We all knew you were destined for *something*. Such a strange bird when you arrived at Madeira. Squaw skirts and conchos. Who'd ever heard of them? I'm afraid we were cruel . . ."

The high desert light—that elixir you feel you can drink, that *substance* you felt in your body—that's what she wanted to capture. She'd taught herself how to cast, the old lost wax method: beeswax, earthly matter, melting away, leaving light-infused glass.

". . . envious of your talent, but you lived in your own world . . ."

She'd finally found a way to redeem the trash she salvaged. Or had she? It seemed transformative, but Max's desire for a splashy mid-September opening meant she'd have to spend most of 2001 in the railroad container. Would that feel like rote work or art-making? Maybe if she—

Lenore had stopped talking. Her attention, the attention of the entire room, was focused on someone passing through. Movie stars often surfaced in Santa Fe; Rhymes didn't turn around. Behind her, the celebrity swept through, everyone watching. The entourage herded past, but the celebrity paused. Black wool flared. The waiters, ready to swoop in with new plates, stepped back. Russell stood up, holding his napkin. Lenore held out her hand. "Lenore Hensley, Senator."

Lucien leaned down, black overcoat thrown over his shoulders. "*Rhymes?* Rhymes. It is you."

Near her cheek, his lean one—and there was his smell, never-forgotten, crisp, with a smoldering hint of piñon. From what underworld had Lucien been conjured? And behind him, a shadow eating her with his eyes. Some gopher with a long ponytail who might've been Ray, skinny, pasty-white, except Ray was long dead, carried away in the first wave of AIDS. Why these apparitions? She fingered her necklace, rare underworld currency rarely worn. Was it the heishe?

"Is there anything you need?" Lucien said. "Anything at all I can do for you? Anything? I'd be pleased."

The room blurred, the walls blushed the soft pink of freshly applied plaster. In the silence, a small sound: trickling water. She and Lucien, standing on a paper-covered floor in the middle of construction after she'd told him she was leaving. Her shoulders burned. The long, almost invisible scars on her arms rippled flame. *Feel* what you felt when he said he'd *never* loved you, had only wanted you because everyone else did; had only married you because the two of you made a good-looking couple and that was good for his career. He'd gone on and on while the fresh plaster dripped and she'd stood, head bowed, tears streaming.

And by the way, I hate your art.

In Nocona's, she raised her head and looked at him. "Nothing," she said. "There's nothing you can do for me."

She saw Lucien consider whether he might get something more out of this. Behind him, the shadow devoured her with his eyes.

Lucien straightened up, nodded his fine Roman head to Russell, then to Lenore. His group folded in to follow him out, and the room shrank back to inconsequence, everyone murmuring, looking their way. Russell took her hand. No one said a word.

"It's *okay*," she said. "It's been thirty-five years."

Russell's grim face relaxed. The waiters moved in to set down what they'd been holding: milk-fed veal chops and a voluptuous, green-tinged tempura zucchini flower. The sommelier revealed the accompanying wine: a 1999 Bodegas Indiano. Rhymes stared at the wall; the skull-eyes stared back. Lucien was nothing; it was the shadow of Ray she needed to shake.

Russell and Lenore talked quietly, not about art, but about what to do with her money. Nocona's: *we have to move quickly.* Stocks: *blue chips? emerging markets?* Rhymes sat silently, moving the food around on her plate. She did not on principle eat veal, but she drank a lot of wine—*Mas blanco? Gracias*—and the waiters swooped in and out.

When Russell offered banks as a safe investment, Lenore argued against safe.

"Such courage," he said, smiling his beautiful smile, touching his wine glass to hers.

Rhymes noted their gestures, but her mind slid off their words: the snake-oil liturgy of easy money. She felt her father's leg going up and down as she sat on his lap and he talked to Peg about his small window of time. He'd worked hard to start his chain, and Russell, doing nothing, was cashing in? Her body felt brittle, pieces stuck together without pattern. She tried to recapture the wholeness she'd felt during Las Posadas: the silence, the stars. They'd let her hold Maren, swaddled to hide the spina bifida, and she'd traced the perfect face with her fingertips, thinking how like her mother's it was. She could see the tiny coffin plainly but could recall nothing of the graveside service except that her breast leaked through the bindings, her black silk wet with milk, the spots when they dried, ghostly, edged with wavy white. Maren would be thirty-four if she had lived.

She felt sick, nauseated by the balletic flow of movement, the perfection of the plates. All those dots of green wasabi and the wavy patterns of sauce. Too *precious*. She concentrated on her found objects, those thrown-away things nobody wanted. If she were lucky, if she could do it, when she got home, she'd find these discarded objects—Dodge Ram hood ornaments with curled horns, Cadillac wreaths—fused with color and light, resurrected as glass. She wanted to go home.

"Rhymes? Your father's stores? Did he own the land? It makes a difference if investment materials are liquid assets or—why are you laughing?"

"I'm sorry," Rhymes said. "I heard 'investment materials' and thought you meant plaster and silica." Behind the black bridge of her glasses, Lenore's forehead furrowed. "The powders I use to make molds?" Rhymes said. "That's what they're called, *investment*—You know, I'm tired and I have to get up early and drive."

"We haven't had dessert yet," Lenore said.

"I don't feel well. I need to go."

"Is it the adhesions?" Lenore said. And at her uncomprehending look, "The scar tissue?"

Rhymes looked at Russell, but he didn't look back.

"I have this wonderful Hungarian healer. I know—Santa Fe's full of them, but she's the real deal. Agni Kodaly. Agni means 'fire.' I send all my clients to her. You have an appointment tomorrow. You can sleep late and—"

Rhymes shoved back from the table and stood, knocking her chair to the floor, a loud clatter that jolted the room's quiet good taste.

By the time Rhymes finishes fixing her necklace and hair in the narrow unisex bathroom and navigates the long bar, the crowd has thinned. The front room still floats in its sea of white light, but it's quiet. She sits down at the table, and Lenore says, "I'm sorry if you misunder—"

Rhymes puts up a hand to stop her, but says nothing. The waiters look wary. She offers them a simulacrum of a smile. They begin to bring out coffee cups, champagne flutes, small plates, silver spoons.

Russell takes her hand and holds it on top of the table. He tells Lenore how hard she works, how she's always striving to create, reaching for something she can't quite grasp. On and on he talks.

"You didn't know my wife was an alchemist, did you?" he says. "You should see her, measuring, mixing potions. And she wears this—I swear it looks like a spacesuit. She would've been burned as a witch in another—"

Lenore claps her hands. "An alchemist! Perfect! I missed the whole counterculture thing. Russ told me you actually lived in a commune. Was it magical?"

Rhymes, who's been hypnotized by the wavering votives, wakes up. She stares at Russell, but he's focused on aligning his spoon and water glass.

"I've always thought I could've been a hippie," Lenore says. "Flower Power. The Summer of Love. All that."

"Oh yes," Rhymes says, seeing the dark underground rabbit warren of bedrooms, one leading into the next. "It was grand."

"I imagine it was like having a family—but without all the problems?"

Rhymes thinks how protected Lenore is in her black-sequined armor. "You're very perceptive," she says. Her life at the commune is like a dream looping back on itself, endlessly repeating. Pregnant, ungainly, lowering herself to a mattress on the floor, desperate to find comfort and sleep, only to wake with the shadowy figure of Ray standing over her—not every night, you couldn't be sure when he would appear—but night after night, waking her with his stillness, his watching, and she exhausted because she'd spent the day hauling water to the marijuana. There was only one way to get kitchen duty, and really, finally, what difference did it make? The baby was already coming.

"How'd you get here?" Rhymes says. "Aren't you from Philadelphia—the Main Line, or something?"

"Asthma," Lenore says. "Doctors recommended this climate."

"Never told me that," Russell says.

Lenore looks at him, touches her pearls. "That's what I tell everyone. The truth is my second husband strangled me—I have trouble breathing. I can't wear anything around my neck. Not scarves or turtlenecks. I could never wear your necklace, Rhymes. I thought my third husband would—well, it's not worth talking about. *Function in disaster, finish in style.* Miss Madeira's motto."

A circle of waiters, some walking backward, all taking small steps. "And asthma's not exactly a lie. I did move here for the air."

Ta-daa! Sparklers on a bombe, champagne popping.

In the commotion—sparkles, refractions, multiples of tiny lights, everything fizzy—Rhymes gauges Lenore, she of the ping-pong-ball pearls, the relentless enthusiasm and good cheer. Her sequins faceted. Not invincible, perhaps courageous.

The waiters begin to sing, and Rhymes thinks Russell will be embarrassed, but the candlelight shines off his happy high forehead. It's a ceremony of chocolate, meringue, and Dom Perignon. With a sweeping gesture, Lenore orders champagne for the whole room. Granted, there aren't many people left in the room and she's ordered a local label, but Rhymes wonders if perhaps Rusty had made more money than she realized. Then she remembers: the Market's headed for the stratosphere.

Around the room, people lift their champagne flutes toward Russell. Rhymes looks at him and raises her glass. He's smiling and nodding to everyone, his beautiful face, its fine structure, shining. He turns to say something to her, but he stops. With an infinitesimal jerk, he sits upright, moves his head a fraction, and a startled look comes into his eyes.

Rhymes is suddenly and completely sober.

Lenore continues toasting the room, too busy to understand something has happened, but for Rhymes the room and everything in it have fallen away. There is only Russell's face that has softened to become a child's face. There's an odd look in his eyes, a little-boy look of such surprise and wonder, and a slight smile as though what he sees is round and full. *Sufficient.* His face softens again, and she sees how he must have looked as a small child, the purity, and her heart reconfigures itself and grows large and moves out to enfold him, all the years of contention and strife wiped away.

This vision lasts only a minute, probably not a full minute. A blank space cut out of time, a hitch in the ongoing pattern. The silence of deep outer space surrounds them, and then sound, like an old record beginning again, trailing an echo, begins to roll, and the busyness and commotion start back up.

Rhymes reaches out for his hand. "Are you all right?"

Lenore says, "All right, what?"

Russell sits back and shakes his head, as though to clear it. "Don't know what happened," he says. He shakes his head again. His hand lies boney and limp in hers. He sits still, his face chalk, beads of moisture on his forehead. "Don't know," he says.

No one speaks.

After a moment, he takes his hand away from Rhymes, picks up a spoon, and leans forward to scoop a bite of chocolate bombe. Another moment, and Lenore picks up a spoon and leans to scoop a bite too.

They are making small ecstatic sounds when Rhymes picks up her spoon. In the tranquil tail end of the evening, the three of them eat and drink and talk of inconsequential matters, as though the blank space hadn't opened, as though Rhymes hadn't seen within it her husband's death.

A Method
of Reaching
Extreme
Altitudes

Acknowledgments

It is commonly assumed that stories spring fully formed from the mind of their creator, like Athena from the head of Zeus. But if you are eighty years old and lucky enough to be publishing your first book, you know what a myth this is. It took a lifetime of friends.

Thanks to Lynn C. Miller for soliciting this manuscript for the great University of New Mexico Press.

Toni Nelson, thank you for that long-ago afternoon in Taos at the bar of the Sagebrush when you suggested graduate school and said you would write me a recommendation. I had never heard of Warren Wilson, had no idea I could go to graduate school for *writing*. I was sixty-five years old. I went.

I won the jackpot there and was privileged to study with Jane Hamilton, David Haynes, Dominic Smith, and Kevin McIlvoy, stardust now. Could I have made it through that rigorous program without my Wild Bloomers? I doubt it. We were older women—well, *I* was older—among young hotshots. We loved each other in Swannanoa and have loved each other ever since.

Thanks to Kalita's mom for hosting the Five & Dime until we all finally ran out of change.

To the Fabulous Fountaineers, thank you. Who knew the magic of Aspen Summer Words could continue?

Special thanks to the greatest book club ever—still meeting monthly after fifty-three years! You are my foundation. What we have been through together no one will ever know.

And, finally, those whose names must be spoken individually here: my beloved baby sister, Jamie Jennings, Lynette D'Amico, Jane Saginaw, Lee Prusik, William Hawkins, Diane DeSanders, Barbara Corn Patterson, Jaina Sanga, Mary Jane Kinnebrew, and Peg Cronin. This book would not exist without you.

Thanks also to the following publications in which the following stories first appeared:

"Stolen Boy": winner of 2017 Short Story America Fiction Prize, published in *Short Story America Anthology*, Sixth Edition, September 2018; nominated for Pushcart Prize.

"The Gospel of New Eyes": Finalist, 2017 New Millennium Fiction Award.

"A Method of Reaching Extreme Altitudes": winner of 2013 *bosque* Fiction Award; published in *bosque (the magazine)*; November 2013; nominated for Pushcart Prize.

"Camouflage": shortlisted for 2009 David Nathan Meyerson Fiction Prize; published in *Shadowgraph Magazine*, Winter 2015; nominated for Pushcart Prize.

"Eat You Up": published in 2016 Best Short Stories from the Saturday Evening Post's Great American Fiction Contest.

"Mezzanine": a version published as "Calculation" in *Southwest Review*, Volume, 93, Number 2, 2008.

"Galisteo": Finalist, StoryQuarterly's Fiction Contest, a version published as "Heishe" in *StoryQuarterly* 49, February 2016.